CREATURES OF HORROR

They await, at the turn of a page, to terrify, to mystify, to haunt the reader with their sinister evil. Here are nine harrowing tales from the great horror-masters:

D. SCOTT-MONCRIEFF's *Count Szolnok's Robots*—a spine-chilling masterpiece about a newspaper reporter who follows the trail of a legend far up the Amazon—and finds himself in a vast uninhabited mansion in which a fatal secret lurks.

AMBROSE BIERCE's *The Man and the Snake*—a harrowing confrontation between the logical, reasoning mind of man and the core of primordial terror which surfaces in every human being when aroused by visions of hideous dread.

IRVIN ASHKENAZY's *The Headless Miller of Kobold's Keep*—a dealer in antiques discovers a strange mountain community older than memory—and a race of nightmarish beings more horrifying than the human mind can imagine.

FREDERICK MARRYAT's *The White Wolf of the Hartz Mountains*—the timeless story of a woodland hunter on the trail of a rare white wolf . . . and how the animal drew him slowly, inexorably into a living hell.

Plus five more vintage tales of animal terror . . .

A Walk With the Beast

EDITED BY CHARLES M. COLLINS

AN AVON BOOK

ACKNOWLEDGEMENTS

Note: The editor has made every effort to trace the ownership of all copyrighted material. In the event of any questions arising as to the use of any selections appearing herein, the editor, while expressing regret for any error he may have made, will be pleased to make the necessary correction in future editions of this book.

"Prince Alberic and the Snake Lady" by Vernon Lee, published by Peter Owen Limited. By permission of Peter Owen Limited. "One of the Dead" by William Wood, copyright 1964 by William Wood. By permission of The Author and the Author's agent, James Brown Associates, Inc. "Count Szolnok's Robots" by D. Scott-Moncrieff, from *Not for the Squeamish* by D. Scott-Moncrieff; Background Books Ltd., London, 1948. "The Headless Miller of Kobold's Keep" by Irvin Ashkenazy, copyright by Irvin Ashkenazy. Reprinted by permission of the author. "Curious Adventure of Mr. Bond" by Nugent Barker, from *Written with My Left Hand* by Nugent Barker, copyright 1951 by Percival Marshall & Co. Ltd., London. "Tiger Cat" by David H. Keller, copyright 1938, by Popular Fiction Publishing Company; copyright 1952, by David H. Keller. By permission of Arkham House. "The Elephant Man" by Sir Frederick Treves, from *The Elephant Man and Other Stories* by Sir Frederick Treves. Reprinted by permission of Cassell & Co. Ltd., London.

This is the first publication of
A Walk with the Beast in volume form.

AVON BOOKS
A division of
The Hearst Corporation
959 Eighth Avenue
New York, New York 10019

First Avon Printing, June, 1969
Third Printing

ISBN: 0-380-00506-9

AVON TRADEMARK REG. U.S. PAT. OFF. AND FOREIGN COUNTRIES, REGISTERED TRADEMARK— MARCA REGISTRADA, HECHO EN CHICAGO, U.S.A.

Printed in Canada

A WALK WITH THE BEAST is dedicated
to Mel Wiener and Walt Tkazcyk.

*From Ghoulies and Ghosties; and long-
Legitty Beasties; and things that go bump
in the night—Good Lord deliver us.*
Old Cornish Litany.

CONTENTS

A Walk
With the Beast

INTRODUCTION

THE NATURE OF THE BEAST
Charles M. Collins

FROM EARLIEST times the beast has stalked through legend and literature, evoking terror and dread, awe and wonderment, love and challenge. The most cursory survey cannot circumvent the salient paradox: The beast has been damned, hunted, and killed for sport, and yet, through the centuries, man has also feared, deified, and venerated this very same species. Curiously enough, despite complex philosophic systems to prove otherwise, man has rendered unto the beast the kind of anthropomorphic attributes generally reserved for his gods.

The myths evolve—from the tombs of Thebes to the temples in Chichen Itza; a body of literature exists—from the Old Testament to Franz Kafka. The mind of man is not so dissimilar that we are unable to find universal motifs reflected in the tales and folklore indigenous to the remotest areas of this planet.

The beasts of ancient times were grotesque and terrible. They were depicted as such in the crude wall paintings dating back to neolithic times, and later in the bas-reliefs and artifacts of a more sophisticated antiquity. Graeco-Roman myth and legend would add a new dimension of color and animation to the chimeras populating the ancient world. Nearly all twelve labors of Hercules pit him against some beast; Perseus slays the snake-haired Medusa whose very look is certain death; Theseus single-handedly destroys the Minotaur inhabiting Daedalus' virtually inescapable labyrinth. The stories are endless, and their heroes return to mind with God-like splendor. Their counterparts exist in the myths and epic poems of most nations. The striking point, however, is revealed in the prevailing image of the beast. They were creatures of awesome and supernatural power, and only a superhuman being could defeat them.

Notwithstanding all the physically repellent characteristics, there remains a strange attraction to the beast. Primitive man donned the skins of animals during ritualistic communal ceremonies, while a more advanced people gave their dead lycanthropic powers. From medieval superstition the tales developed: vampires, werewolves, and all manner of weird transformations. And from the legends emerged new images of the beast—images that would fire the imagination of artists, writers, poets, and musicians. The beasts were dreadful and benign, tragic and malevolent, powerful and sadly innocuous. But, like George Orwell's backyard animals, the beasts were becoming more recognizably human—though not for the purpose of satire.

A child can experience empathy for the enchanted prince in the story of beauty and the beast. Yet the theme of this childhood fable has fascinated and intrigued countless adults of even this enlightened century. The film KING KONG has enjoyed frequent theatrical revival, and influenced hundreds of imitations. Jean Cocteau brought a visual artistry to his BEAUTY AND THE BEAST, which evokes a genuinely eerie feeling and captures a remarkable degree of sensitivity. The beast in popular culture is examined at length in Jean Boullet's LA BELLE ET LA BÊTE (Le Terrain Vague, 1958).

The beast was taking on a more ambiguous and terrifying character as far back as Herman Melville's MOBY DICK. Unlike the heros of ancient mythology, Ahab fails to conquer the sea beast, and is ultimately destroyed by his indomitable foe. Melville imbues Moby Dick with a power and fury akin to the Old Testament Jehovah. The surprise Edgar Allan Poe reserves for us in MURDERS IN THE RUE MORGUE is that the murderer, whom everyone assumes is a man, turns out to be an orangutan. The ambitious Dr. Moreau of H. G. Wells' classic, THE ISLAND OF DR. MOREAU, attempts to transform beasts into humans. The question Vercors explores in his weird novel, YOU SHALL KNOW THEM, is at what stage does the human transcend his animal ancestry.

The myths and tales of childhood take on more subtle implications in the wake of Darwin, Freud, and Jung. The nature of the beast becomes more ominous when related to concepts of the id, racial memory, and the collective unconscious. It was Robert Louis Stevenson who would fuse the then contemporary theories of evolution and modern psychology into a story which was destined to become a horror classic, DR. JEKYLL AND MR. HYDE. JEKYLL AND HYDE is more than a study of the schizophrenic personality. It is the nature of the beast lurking in the dark side of the psyche that gives the tale its horrific power as well as its universality. This concept inspired many imitation works in the weird genre, the best of which is probably Leonard Cline's novel, THE DARK CHAMBER. Written in 1927, this book explicitly depicts the nature of the beast in man. Its hero, through drugs and bizarre stimuli, attempts to preserve every moment of his past. His mania carries him beyond his own life, and atavistic manifestations soon become apparent. Beast-like at the end, he roams the countryside until he is finally destroyed by his own dog.

Modern psychology affords us some understanding of the human beasts who have populated literature and history. Gilles de Rais allegedly sacrificed hundreds of children, dismembered them and drank their blood to the glory of Satan, while his one-time companion in arms, Joan of Arc, was burned at the stake for the glory of God. Marquis de Sade wrote enormous volumes of sadistic fantasy during a period in French history seething with lust, debauchery, and social unrest. England's Saucy Jack, or Jack the Ripper, has fascinated three generations, and has been the subject of novels, films, plays, as well as numerous studies researched by professional and amateur criminologists. Pétrus Borel, who penned a number of *contes cruels*, affected an ogre's beard, had distinctly feline teeth, and was known among his coterie of friends as the lycanthrope. Our last great black magician, Aleister Crowley, poet, writer, world traveler, drug addict, and modern day diabolist (among other things), called himself The Great Beast, after The Great Beast in Revelations.

Historical evidence of the beast within has been recorded in thousands of volumes of fact and fancy; nor will we begin to dwell on the wars, religious persecutions, and attempted genocides man has perpetrated on his fellow man to buttress the arguments herein.

The aim of this anthology is to present a cross section of stories about the beast. It has been divided into two parts— the supernatural and the human—and attempts to show the image of the beast in its literary variegations.

The first beast we encounter in Vernon Lee's charming and at the same time sardonic tale, PRINCE ALBERIC AND THE SNAKE LADY, is quite benevolent and endearing. It is the effete and devious Duke Balthasar, who, from the start, we realize will precipitate the tragedy. Vernon Lee (Violet Paget) has written some of the finest supernatural tales of an era when supernatural fiction had transcended the melodrama of the 'Gothics' and had evolved into a distinct art form. Her fiction generally evokes the age of the Italian Renaissance with its baroque palaces and ghostly canals. But PRINCE ALBERIC's roots extend further back into the past. Vernon Lee's Snake Lady is related to the Eastern legends of benign dragons, which were brought into southern Europe by the Crusaders.

Far more terrible and traditional is the werewolf in Fred-

15

erick Marryat's THE WHITE WOLF OF THE HARTZ MOUNTAINS. The tale, complete in itself, is actually extracted from Marryat's lusty recounting of The Flying Dutchman legend entitled THE PHANTOM SHIP. Here is the beast in perhaps its most primitive and fearsome image— savage, a killer, the lycanthrope who battens on the flesh and blood of others. Marryat vividly reproduces the stark, bleak countryside of the Hartz Mountain region, and gives his beast all the characteristics of medieval legend.

William Wood's ONE OF THE DEAD is a combination of tradition and present day reality. His horror emanates from a very urban and civilized social strata, and exists on several levels. It is one of those rare and remarkable tales which become more frightening in retrospect because the ultimate shock is reserved until the very last line. The image of the beast is somewhat less distinct, for, as Mr. Wood writes: "It is a story peopled almost exclusively by ghosts: it just happens that one of them is dead." William Wood has published two novels, and a book of poems. His main body of work has been in the film industry, and, more recently, in the theater.

D. Scott-Moncrieff's COUNT SZOLNOK'S ROBOTS is included as it rather represents a science fictional metamorphosis of the beast. There are, of course, thousands of tales about extra-terrestrial creatures, but the robot has been selected since it is in the tradition of the golem, and reflects still another interesting image: Though man attempts to create human life, his results inevitably fall short for they lack the essential essence which separates man from the beast. Neither Count Szolnok nor Dr. Moreau were successful with their respective experiments on animals and machines. After all, there is something special and ineffable in the human psyche . . . Or is there?

Part two, the human, is composed of tales wherein the human barriers are exceedingly tenuous. Ambrose Bierce, in a sardonic gem, pits man against the beast—or so it seems at the start. In the end, however, we are left with the feeling that Bierce has pit man against himself. The Minotaur of antiquity now resides in the labyrinth of the human mind.

Irvin Ashkenazy's THE HEADLESS MILLER OF KOBOLD'S KEEP is more in the tradition of pure fantasy, though it depicts the results of centuries of inbreeding in a remote village virtually inaccessible to the rest of the world. It might take an Aquinas to determine whether or not the creatures in Kobold's Keep possess a soul. I think Mr. Ashkenazy would rather leave it up to the reader, who, I'm certain, will have a hard time forgetting the "tainted humanity" of Kobold's Keep. Irvin Ashkenazy has scripted over

2,000 radio plays (including THE SAINT, COUNT OF MONTE CRISTO, GANGBUSTERS, and THE THIRD MAN—a series produced in England by Orson Welles). He has motion picture (THE BLOODSUCKERS and THE MASK OF THE VULTURE, among others) and television credits, and has written numerous short stories and magazine articles.

There are many who contend that the female of the species is deadlier than the male. The image of the fatal woman has fascinated and inspired any number of writers and artists. She is often envisioned as cat-like, or feline. Dr. David H. Keller, who was a practicing psychiatrist, combines a subtle blend of psychology and horror in delineating her sadistic strain in TIGER CAT.

The diversions of the Sasserach clan in Nugent Barker's CURIOUS ADVENTURE OF MR. BOND are decidedly inhuman. The shock effect is heightened by the casual and almost pastoral manner in which the horrors are disclosed. To say any more would lessen the impact of discovering the horrors along with the itinerant Mr. Bond.

Not all human beasts are as terrible as the Sasserach family. In THE ELEPHANT MAN, Sir Frederick Treves presents a poignant and tragic picture of a man rejected from every strata of society because of physical defects which render him more beast than human. Merrick, the elephant man, is shunned, mocked, exploited, and in the end one must consider whether Merrick is really any more beast than those who taunt, deride, and use him. Does the elephant man represent something we dimly recognize and fear in ourselves? Despite all the inhumanity contained in THE ELEPHANT MAN, Sir Frederick Treves has also written a story of hope, compassion, and empathy. It is a story of human communication and understanding—values which most contemporary existential literature tends to deny. It leaves one with the vision of the inherent nobility of man; a nobility which ultimately disjoins man from the lower animals, and which can triumph over the beast that lurks within.

Charles M. Collins
New York
Jan., 1969

PART 1

THE SUPERNATURAL

PRINCE ALBERIC AND THE SNAKE LADY

Vernon Lee

IN THE year 1701, the Duchy of Luna became united to the Italian dominions of the Holy Roman Empire, in consequence of the extinction of its famous ducal house in the persons of Duke Balthasar Maria and of his grandson Alberic, who should have been third of the name. Under this dry historical fact lies hidden the strange story of Prince Alberic and the Snake Lady.

I

The first act of hostility of old Duke Balthasar towards the Snake Lady, in whose existence he did not, of course, believe, was connected with the arrival at Luna of certain tapestries after the designs of the famous Monsieur Le Brun, a present from his Most Christian Majesty King Lewis the XIV. These Gobelins, which represented the marriage of Alexander and Roxana, were placed in the throne-room, and in the most gallant suite of chambers overlooking the great rockery garden, all of which had been completed by Duke Balthasar Maria in 1680; and, as a consequence, the already existing tapestries, silk hangings, and mirrors painted by Marius of the Flowers, were transferred into other apartments, thus occasioning a general re-hanging of the Red Palace at Luna. These magnificent operations, in which, as the court poets sang, Apollo and the Graces lent their services to their beloved patron, aroused in Duke Balthasar's mind a sudden curiosity to see what might be made of the rooms occupied by his grandson and heir, and which he had not entered since Prince Alberic's christening. He found the apartments in a shocking state of neglect, and the youthful prince unspeakably shy and rustic; and he determined to give him at once an establishment befitting his age, to look out presently for a princess worthy to be his wife, and, somewhat earlier, for a less illustrious but more agreeable lady to fashion his manners. Meanwhile, Duke Balthasar Maria gave orders to change the tapestry in Prince Alberic's chamber. This tapestry was of old and Gothic taste, extremely worn, and represented Alberic the Blond and the Snake Lady Oriana, as described in the Chronicles of Archbishop Turpin and the poems of Boiardo. Duke Balthasar Maria was a prince of enlightened mind and delicate taste; the literature as well as the art of the dark ages found no grace in his sight; he reproved the folly of feeding the thoughts of youth on improbable events; besides, he disliked snakes and was afraid of the devil. So he ordered the tapestry to be removed and another, representing Susanna and the Elders, to be put in its stead. But when Prince Alberic discovered the change, he cut Susanna and the Elders into strips with a knife he had stolen out of the ducal kitchens (no dangerous instruments being allowed to young princes before they were of an age to learn to fence) and refused to touch his food for three days.

The tapestry over which little Prince Alberic mourned so deeply had indeed been both tattered and Gothic. But for the boy it possessed an inexhaustible charm. It was quite full of things, and they were all delightful. The sorely-frayed borders consisted of wonderful garlands of leaves and fruits and flowers, tied at intervals with ribbons, although they seemed all to grow like tall narrow bushes, each from a big vase in the bottom corner, and made of all manner of different plants. There were bunches of spiky bays, and of acorned oak leaves; sheaves of lilies and heads of poppies, gourds, and apples and pears, and hazelnuts and mulberries, wheat ears, and beans, and pine tufts. And in each of these plants, of which those above named are only a very few, there were curious live creatures of some sort—various birds, big and little, butterflies on the lilies, snails, squirrels, mice, and rabbits, and even a hare, with such pointed ears, darting among the spruce fir. Alberic learned the names of most of these plants and creatures from his nurse, who had been a peasant, and he spent much ingenuity seeking for them in the palace gardens and terraces; but there were no live creatures there, except snails and toads, which the gardeners killed, and carp swimming about in the big tank, whom Alberic did not like, and who were not in the tapestry; and he had to supplement his nurse's information by that of the grooms and scullions, when he could visit them secretly. He was even promised a sight, one day, of a dead rabbit—the rabbit was the most fascinating of the inhabitants of the tapestry border—but he came to the kitchen too late, and saw it with its pretty fur pulled off, and looking so sad and naked that it made him cry. But Alberic had grown so accustomed to never quitting the Red Palace and its gardens, that he was usually satisfied with seeing the plants and animals in the tapestry, and looked forward to seeing the real things only when he should be grown up. "When I am a man," he would say to himself—for his nurse scolded him for saying it to her—"I will have a live rabbit of my own."

The border of the tapestry interested Prince Alberic most when he was very little—indeed, his remembrance of it was older than that of the Red Palace, its terraces and gardens—but gradually he began to care more and more for the picture in the middle.

There were mountains, and the sea with ships; and these first made him care to go on to the topmost palace terrace and look at the real mountains and the sea beyond the roofs and gardens; and there were woods of all manner of tall trees, with clover and wild strawberries growing beneath them; and roads, and paths, and rivers, in and out; these were rather confused with the places where the tapestry was worn out, and with the patches and mendings thereof, but Alberic, in the course of time, contrived to make them all out, and knew exactly whence the river came which turned the big mill-wheel, and how many bends it made before coming to the fishing-nets; and how the horsemen must cross over the bridge, then wind behind the cliff with the chapel, and pass through the wood of pines in order to get from the castle in the left-hand corner nearest the bottom to the town, over which the sun was shining with all its beams, and a wind blowing with inflated cheeks on the right hand close to the top.

The center of the tapestry was the most worn and discolored; and it was for this reason perhaps that little Alberic scarcely noticed it for some years, his eye and mind led away by the bright red and yellow of the border of fruit and flowers, and the still vivid green and orange of the background landscape. Red, yellow, and orange, even green had grown an odd dusty tint; and the figures seemed like ghosts, sometimes emerging and then receding again into vagueness. Indeed, it was only as he grew bigger that Alberic began to see any figures at all; and then, for a long time he would lose sight of them. But little by little, when the light was strong, he could see them always; and even in the dark make them out with a little attention. Among the spruce firs and pines, and against a hedge of roses, on which there still lingered a remnant of redness, a knight had reined in his big white horse, and was putting one arm round the shoulder of a lady, who was leaning against the horse's flank. The knight was all dressed in armor—not at all like that of the equestrian statue of Duke Balthasar Maria in the square, but all made of plates, with plates also on the legs, instead of having them bare like Duke Balthasar's statue; and on the head he had no

23

wig, but a helmet with big plumes. It seemed a more reasonable dress than the other, but probably Duke Balthasar was right to go to battle with bare legs and a kilt and a wig, since he did so. The lady who was looking up into his face was dressed with a high collar and long sleeves, and on her head she wore a thick circular garland, from under which the hair fell about her shoulders. She was very lovely, Alberic got to think, particularly when, having climbed upon a chest of drawers, he saw that her hair was still full of threads of gold, some of them quite loose because the tapestry was so rubbed. The knight and his horse were of course very beautiful, and he liked the way in which the knight reined in the horse with one hand, and embraced the lady with the other arm. But Alberic got to love the lady most, although she was so very pale and faded, and almost the color of the moonbeams through the palace windows in summer. Her dress also was so beautiful and unlike those of the ladies who got out of the coaches in the Court of Honor, and who had on hoops and no clothes at all on their upper part. This lady, on the contrary, had that collar like a lily, and a beautiful gold chain, and patterns in gold (Alberic made them out little by little) all over her bodice. He got to want so much to see her skirt; it was probably very beautiful too, but it so happened that the inlaid chest of drawers before mentioned stood against the wall in that place, and on it a large ebony and ivory crucifix, which covered the lower part of the lady's body. Alberic often tried to lift off the crucifix, but it was a great deal too heavy, and there was not room on the chest of drawers to push it aside, so the lady's skirt and feet were invisible. But one day, when Alberic was eleven, his nurse suddenly took a fancy to having all the furniture shifted. It was time that the child should cease to sleep in her room, and plague her with his loud talking in his dreams. And she might as well have the handsome inlaid chest of drawers, and that nice pious crucifix for herself next door, in place of Alberic's little bed. So one morning there was a great shifting and dusting, and when Alberic came in from his walk on the terrace, there hung the tapestry entirely uncovered. He stood for a few minutes before it, riveted to the ground. Then he ran to his nurse, exclaiming: "O, nurse, dear nurse, look—the lady—!"

For where the big crucifix had stood, the lower part of the beautiful pale lady with the gold-thread hair was now exposed. But instead of a skirt, she ended off in a big snake's tail, with scales of still most vivid (the tapestry not having faded there) green and gold.

The nurse turned round.

"Holy Virgin," she cried, "why, she's a serpent!" Then, noticing the boy's violent excitement, she added, "You little ninny, it's only Duke Alberic the Blond, who was your ancestor, and the Snake Lady."

Little Prince Alberic asked no questions, feeling that he must not. Very strange it was, but he loved the beautiful lady with the thread of gold hair only the more because she ended off in the long twisting body of a snake. And that, no doubt, was why the knight was so very good to her.

II

For want of that tapestry, poor Alberic, having cut its successor to pieces, began to pine away. It had been his whole world; and now it was gone he discovered that he had no other. No one had ever cared for him except his nurse, who was very cross. Nothing had ever been taught him except the Latin catechism; he had had nothing to make a pet of except the fat carp, supposed to be four hundred years old, in the tank; he had nothing to play with except a gala coral with bells by Benvenuto Cellini, which Duke Balthasar Maria had sent him on his eighth birthday. He had never had anything except a Grandfather, and had never been outside the Red Palace.

Now, after the loss of the tapestry, the disappearance of the plants and flowers and birds and beasts on its borders, and the departure of the kind knight on the horse and the dear golden-haired Snake Lady, Alberic became aware that he had always hated both his grandfather and the Red Palace.

The whole world, indeed, were agreed that Duke Balthasar was the most magnanimous and fascinating of monarchs, and that the Red Palace of Luna was the most magnificent and delectable of residences. But the knowledge of this universal opinion, and the consequent sense of his own extreme unworthiness, merely exasperated Alberic's detestation, which, as it grew, came to identify the Duke and the Palace as the personification and visible manifestation of each other. He knew now—oh, how well!—every time that he walked on the terrace or in the garden (at the hours when no one else ever entered them) that he had always abominated the brilliant tomato-colored plaster which gave the palace its name: such a pleasant, gay color, people would remark, particularly against the blue of the sky. Then there were the Twelve Caesars—they were the Twelve Caesars, but multiplied over and over again—busts with flying draperies and spiky garlands, one over every first-floor window, hundreds of them,

25

all fluttering and grimacing round the place. Alberic had always thought them uncanny; but now he positively avoided looking out of the window, lest his eye should catch the stucco eyeball of one of those Caesars in the opposite wing of the building. But there was one thing more especially in the Red Palace, of which a bare glimpse had always filled the youthful Prince with terror, and which now kept recurring to his mind like a nightmare. This was no other than the famous grotto of the Court of Honor. Its roof was ingeniously inlaid with oyster-shells, forming elegant patterns, among which you could plainly distinguish some colossal satyrs; the sides were built of rockery, and in its depths, disposed in a most natural and tasteful manner, was a herd of life-size animals all carved out of various precious marbles. On holidays the water was turned on, and spurted about in a gallant fashion. On such occasions persons of taste would flock to Luna from all parts of the world to enjoy the spectacle. But ever since his earliest infancy Prince Alberic had held this grotto in abhorrence. The oyster-shell satyrs on the roof frightened him into fits, particularly when the fountains were playing; and his terror of the marble animals was such that a bare allusion to the Porphyry Rhinoceros, the Giraffe of Cipollino, and the Verde Antique Monkeys, set him screaming for an hour. The grotto, moreover, had become associated in his mind with the other great glory of the Red Palace, to wit, the domed chapel in which Duke Balthasar Maria intended erecting monuments to his immediate ancestors, and in which he had already prepared a monument for himself. And the whole magnificent palace, grotto, chapel and all, had become mysteriously connected with Alberic's grandfather, owing to a particularly terrible dream. When the boy was eight years old, he was taken one day to see his grandfather. It was the feast of St. Balthasar, one of the Three Wise Kings from the East, as is well-known. There had been firing of mortars and ringing of bells ever since daybreak. Alberic had his hair curled, was put into new clothes (his usual raiment being somewhat tattered), a large nosegay was placed in his hand, and he and his nurse were conveyed by complicated relays of lackeys and of pages up to the ducal apartments. Here, in a crowded outer room, he was separated from his nurse and received by a gaunt person in a long black robe like a sheath, and a long shovel hat, whom Alberic identified many years later as his grandfather's Jesuit Confessor. He smiled a long smile, discovering a prodigious number of teeth, in a manner which froze the child's blood; and lifting an embroidered curtain, pushed Alberic into his grandfather's presence. Duke Balthasar Maria, called in all Italy the Ever Young Prince, was at his toilet. He was wrapped in a green Chinese wrapper, embroidered with gold pagodas, and round his head was tied an orange scarf of delicate fabric. He was listening to the performance of some fiddlers, and of a lady dressed as a nymph, who was singing the birthday ode with many shrill trills and quavers; and meanwhile his face, in the hands of a valet, was being plastered with a variety of brilliant colors. In his green and gold wrapper and orange headdress, with the strange patches of vermilion and white on his cheeks, Duke Balthasar looked to the diseased fancy of his nephew as if he had been made of various precious metals, like the celebrated effigy he had erected of himself in the great burial-chapel. But, just as Alberic was mustering up courage and approaching his magnificent grandparent, his eye fell upon a sight so mysterious and terrible that he fled wildly out of the ducal presence. For through an open door he could see in an adjacent closet a man dressed in white, combing the long flowing locks of what he recognized as his grandfather's head, stuck on a short pole in the light of a window.

That night Alberic had seen in his dreams the Ever Young Duke Balthasar Maria descend from his niche in the burial-chapel; and, with his Roman lappets and corslet visible beneath the green bronze cloak embroidered with gold pagodas, march down the great staircase into the Court of Honor, and ascend to the empty place at the end of the rockery grotto (where, as a matter of fact, a statue of Neptune, by a pupil of Bernini, was placed some months later), and there, raising his scepter, receive the obeisance of all the marble animals—the Giraffe, the Rhinoceros, the Stag, the Peacock, and the Monkeys. And behold! suddenly his well-known features waxed dim, and beneath the great curly peruke there was a round blank thing—a barber's block!

Alberic, who was an intelligent child, had gradually learned to disentangle this dream from reality; but its grotesque terror never vanished from his mind, and became the core of all his feelings towards Duke Balthasar Maria and the Red Palace.

III

The news—which was kept back as long as possible—of the destruction of Susanna and the Elders threw Duke Balthasar Maria into a most violent rage with his grandson. The boy should be punished by exile, and exile to a terrible place; above all, to a place where there was no furniture to destroy. Taking due counsel with his Jesuit, his Jester, and his

Dwarf, Duke Balthasar decided that in the whole Duchy of Luna there was no place more fitted for the purpose than the Castle of Sparkling Waters.

For the Castle of Sparkling Waters was little better than a ruin, and its sole inhabitants were a family of peasants. The original cradle of the House of Luna, and its principal bulwark against invasion, the castle had been ignominiously discarded and forsaken a couple of centuries before, when the dukes had built the rectangular town in the plain; after which it had been used as a quarry for ready-cut stone, and the greater part carted off to rebuild the town of Luna, and even the central portion of the Red Palace. The castle was therefore reduced to its outer circuit of walls, enclosing vineyards and orange-gardens, instead of moats and yards and towers, and to the large gate tower, which had been kept, with one or two smaller buildings, for the housing of the farmer, his cattle, and his stores.

Thither the misguided young Prince was conveyed in a carefully shuttered coach and at a late hour of the evening, as was proper in the case of an offender at once so illustrious and so criminal. Nature, moreover, had clearly shared Duke Balthasar Maria's legitimate anger, and had done her best to increase the horror of this just though terrible sentence. For that particular night the long summer broke up in a storm of fearful violence; and Alberic entered the ruined castle amid the howling of wind, the rumble of thunder, and the rush of torrents of rain.

But the young Prince showed no fear or reluctance; he saluted with dignity and sweetness the farmer and his wife and family, and took possession of his attic, where the curtains of an antique and crazy four-poster shook in the draft of the unglazed windows, as if he were taking possession of the gala chambers of a great palace. "And so," he merely remarked, looking round him with reserved satisfaction, "I am now in the castle which was built by my ancestor and namesake, the Marquis Alberic the Blond."

He looked not unworthy of such illustrious lineage, as he stood there in the flickering light of the pine-torch: tall for his age, slender and strong, with abundant golden hair falling about his very white face.

That first night at the Castle of Sparkling Waters, Alberic dreamed without end about his dear, lost tapestry. And when, in the radiant autumn morning, he descended to explore the place of his banishment and captivity, it seemed as if those dreams were still going on. Or had the tapestry been removed to this spot, and become a reality in which he himself was running about?

The gate tower in which he had slept was still intact and chivalrous. It had battlements, a drawbridge, a great escutcheon with the arms of Luna, just like the castle in the tapestry. Some vines, quite loaded with grapes, rose on the strong cords of their fibrous wood from the ground to the very roof of the town, exactly like those borders of leaves and fruit which Alberic had loved so much. And, between the vines, all along the masonry, were strung long narrow ropes of maize, like garlands of gold. A plantation of orange-trees filled what had once been the moat; lemons were spalliered against the delicate pink brickwork. There were no lilies, indeed, but big carnations hung down from the tower windows, and a tall oleander, which Alberic mistook for a special sort of rose-tree, shed its blossoms on to the drawbridge. After the storm of the night, birds were singing all round; not indeed as they sang in spring, which Alberic, of course, did not know, but in a manner quite different from the canaries in the ducal aviaries at Luna. Moreover, other birds, wonderful white and gold creatures, some of them with brilliant tails and scarlet crests, were pecking and strutting and making curious noises in the yard. And—could it be true?—a little way further up the hill, for the castle walls climbed steeply from the seaboard, in the grass beneath the olive-trees, white creatures were running in and out—white creatures with pinkish lining to their ears, undoubtedly—as Alberic's nurse had taught him on the tapestry—undoubtedly rabbits.

Thus Alberic rambled on, from discovery to discovery, with the growing sense that he was in the tapestry, but that the tapestry had become the whole world. He climbed from terrace to terrace of the steep olive-yard, among the sage and the fennel tufts, the long red walls of the castle winding ever higher on the hill. And on the very top of the hill was a high terrace surrounded by towers, and a white shining house with columns and windows, which seemed to drag him upwards.

It was, indeed, the citadel of the place, the very center of the castle.

Alberic's heart beat strangely as he passed beneath the wide arch of delicate ivy-grown brick, and clambered up the rough-paved path to the topmost terrace. And there he actually forgot the tapestry. The terrace was laid out as a vineyard, the vines trellised on the top of stone columns; at one end stood a clump of trees, pines, and a big ilex and a walnut, whose shriveled leaves already strewed the grass. To the back stood a tiny little house all built of shining marble, with two large rounded windows divided by delicate pillars, of the sort (as Alberic later learned) which people built in the barbarous days of the Goths. Among the vines, which formed a vast arbor, were growing, in open spaces, large orange and lemon trees, and flowering bushes of rosemary, and pale pink roses. And in front of the house, under a great umbrella pine, was a well, with an arch over it and a bucket hanging to a chain.

Alberic wandered about in the vineyard, and then slowly mounted the marble staircase which flanked the white house. There was no one in it. The two or three small upper chambers stood open, and on their blackened floor were heaped sacks, and faggots, and fodder, and all manner of colored seeds. The unglazed windows stood open, framing in between their white pillars a piece of deep blue sea. For there, below, but seen over the tops of the olive-trees and the green leaves of the oranges and lemons, stretched the sea, deep blue, speckled with white sails, bounded by pale blue capes, and arched over by a dazzling pale blue sky. From the lower story there rose faint sounds of cattle, and a fresh, sweet smell as of grass and herbs and coolness, which Alberic had never known before. How long did Alberic stand at that window? He was startled by what he took to be steps close behind him, and a rustle as of silk. But the rooms were empty, and he could see nothing moving among the stacked up fodder and seeds. Still, the sounds seemed to recur, but now outside, and he thought he heard someone in a very low voice call his name. He descended into the vineyard; he walked round every tree and every shrub, and climbed upon the broken masses of rose-colored masonry, crushing the scented ragwort and peppermint with which they were overgrown. But all was still and empty. Only, from far, far below, there rose a stave of peasant's song.

The great gold balls of oranges, and the delicate yellow lemons, stood out among their glossy green against the deep blue of the sea; the long bunches of grapes hung, filled with sunshine, like clusters of rubies and jacinths and topazes, from the trellis which patterned the pale blue sky. But Alberic felt not hunger, but sudden thirst, and mounted the three broken marble steps of the well. By its side was a long narrow trough of marble, such as stood in the court at Luna, and which, Alberic had been told, people had used as coffins in pagan times. This one was evidently intended to receive water from the well, for it had a mark in the middle, with a spout; but it was quite dry and full of wild herbs, and even of pale, prickly roses. There were garlands carved upon it, and people with twisted snakes about them; and the carving was picked out with golden brown minute mosses. Alberic looked at it, for it pleased him greatly; and then he lowered the bucket into the deep well, and drank. The well was very, very deep. Its inner sides were covered, as far as you could see, with long delicate weeds like pale green hair, but this faded away in the darkness. At the bottom was a bright space, reflecting the sky, but looking like some subterranean country. Alberic, as he bent over, was startled by suddenly seeing what seemed a face filling up part of that shining circle; but he remembered it must be his own reflection, and felt ashamed. So, to give himself courage, he bent over again, and sang his own name to the image. But instead of his own boyish voice he was answered by wonderful tones, high and deep alternately, running through the notes of a long, long cadence, as he had heard them on holidays at the Ducal Chapel at Luna.

When he had slaked his thirst, Alberic was about to unchain the bucket, when there was a rustle hard by, and a sort of little hiss, and there rose from the carved trough, from among the weeds and roses, and glided on to the brick of the well, a long, green, glittering thing. Alberic recognized it to be a snake; only, he had no idea it had such a flat, strange little head, and such a long forked tongue, for the lady on the tapestry was a woman from the waist upwards. It sat on the opposite side of the well, moving its long neck in his direction, and fixing him with its small golden eyes. Then, slowly, it began to glide round the well circle towards him. Perhaps it wants to drink, thought Alberic, and tipped the bronze pitcher in its direction. But the creature glided past, and came around, and rubbed itself against Alberic's hand. The boy was not afraid, for he knew nothing about snakes; but he started, for, on this hot day, the creature was icy cold. But then he felt sorry. "It must be dreadful to be always so cold," he said; "come, try and get warm in my pocket."

But the snake merely rubbed itself against his coat, and then disappeared back into the carved sarcophagus.

IV

Duke Balthasar Maria, as we have seen, was famous for his unfading youth, and much of his happiness and pride was due to this delightful peculiarity. Any comparison, therefore, which might diminish it, was distasteful to the Ever Young sovereign of Luna; and when his son had died with mysterious suddenness, Duke Balthasar Maria's grief had been tempered by the consolatory fact that he was now the youngest man at his own court. This very natural feeling explains why the Duke of Luna had put behind him for several years the fact of having a grandson, painful because implying that he

31

was of an age to be a grandfather. He had done his best, and succeeded not badly, to forget Alberic while the latter abode under his own roof; and now that the boy had been sent away to a distance, he forgot him entirely for the space of several years.

But Balthasar Maria's three chief counselors had no such reason for forgetfulness; and so, in turn, each unknown to the other, the Jesuit, the Dwarf, and the Jester sent spies to the Castle of Sparkling Waters, and even secretly visited that place in person. For by the coincidence of genius, the mind of each of these profound politicians had been illuminated by the same remarkable thought, to wit: that Duke Balthasar Maria, unnatural as it seemed, would some day have to die, and Prince Alberic, if still alive, become duke in his stead. Those were the times of subtle statecraft; and the Jesuit, the Dwarf, and the Jester were notable statesmen even in their day. So each of them had provided himself with a scheme, which, in order to be thoroughly artistic, was twofold and, so to speak, double-barreled. Alberic might live or he might die, and therefore Alberic must be turned to profit in either case. If, to invert the chances, Alberic should die before coming to the throne, the Jesuit, the Dwarf, and the Jester had each privately determined to represent this death as purposely brought about by himself for the benefit of one of the three Powers which would claim the duchy in case of extinction of the male line. The Jesuit had chosen to attribute the murder to devotion to the Holy See; the Dwarf had preferred to appear active in favor of the King of Spain; and the Jester had decided that he would lay claim to the gratitude of the Emperor. The very means which each would pretend to have used had been thought out: poison in each case, only while the Dwarf had selected henbane, taken through a pair of perfumed gloves, and the Jester pounded diamonds mixed in champagne, the Jesuit had modestly adhered to the humble cup of chocolate, which, whether real or fictitious, had always stood his order in such good stead. Thus did each of these wily courtiers dispose of Alberic in case he should die.

There remained the alternative of Alberic continuing to live; and for this the three rival statesmen were also prepared. If Alberic lived, it was obvious that he must be made to select one of the three as his sole minister, and banish, imprison, or put to death the other two. For this purpose it was necessary to secure his affection by gifts, until he should be old enough to understand that he had actually owed his life to the passionate loyalty of the Jesuit, or the Dwarf, or the Jester, each of whom had saved him from the atrocious enterprises of the other two counselors of Balthasar

32

Maria—nay, who knows? perhaps from the malignity of Balthasar Maria himself.

In accordance with these subtle machinations, each of the three statesmen determined to outwit his rivals by sending young Alberic such things as would appeal most strongly to a poor young Prince living in banishment among peasants, and wholly unsupplied with pocket-money. The Jesuit expended a considerable sum on books, magnificently bound with the arms of Luna; the Dwarf prepared several suits of tasteful clothes; and the Jester selected, with infinite care, a horse of equal and perfect gentleness and mettle. And, unknown to one another, but much about the same period, each of the statesmen sent his present most secretly to Alberic. Imagine the astonishment and wrath of the Jesuit, the Dwarf, and the Jester, when each saw his messenger come back from Sparkling Waters with his gift returned, and the news that Prince Alberic was already supplied with a complete library, a handsome wardrobe, and not one, but two horses of the finest breed and training; nay, more unexpected still, that while returning the gifts to their respective donors, he had rewarded the messengers with splendid liberality.

The result of this amazing discovery was much the same in the mind of the Jesuit, the Dwarf, and the Jester. Each instantly suspected one or both of his rivals; then, on second thoughts, determined to change the present to one of the other items (horse, clothes, or books, as the case might be), little suspecting that each of them had been supplied already; and, on further reflection, began to doubt the reality of the whole business, to suspect connivance of the messengers, intended insult on the part of the Prince; and, therefore, decided to trust only to the evidence of his own eyes in the matter.

Accordingly, within the same few months, the Jesuit, the Dwarf, and the Jester, feigned grievous illness to their Ducal Master, and while everybody thought them safe in bed in the Red Palace at Luna, hurried, on horseback, or in a litter, or in a coach, to the Castle of Sparkling Waters.

The scene with the peasant and his family, young Alberic's host, was identical on the three occasions; and, as the farmer saw that each of these personages was willing to pay liberally for absolute secrecy, he very consistently swore to supply that desideratum to each of the three great functionaries. And similarly, in all three cases, it was deemed preferable to see the young Prince first from a hiding-place, before asking leave to pay their respects.

The Dwarf, who was the first in the field, was able to hide very conveniently in one of the cut velvet plumes which

33

surmounted Alberic's four-post bedstead, and to observe the young Prince as he changed his apparel. But he scarcely recognized the Duke's grandson. Alberic was sixteen, but far taller and stronger than his age would warrant. His figure was at once manly and delicate, and full of grace and vigor of movement. His long hair, the color of floss silk, fell in wavy curls, which seemed to imply almost a woman's care and coquetry. His hands also, though powerful, were, as the Dwarf took note, of princely form and whiteness. As to his garments, the open doors of his wardrobe displayed every variety that a young Prince could need; and, while the Dwarf was watching, he was exchanging a russet and purple hunting-dress, cut after the Hungarian fashion with cape and hood, and accompanied by a cap crowned with peacock's feathers, for a habit of white and silver, trimmed with Venetian lace, in which he intended to honor the wedding of one of the farmer's daughters. Never, in his most genuine youth, had Balthasar Maria, the ever young and handsome, been one-quarter as beautiful in person or as delicate in apparel as his grandson in exile among poor country folk.

The Jesuit, in his turn, came to verify his messenger's extraordinary statements. Through the gap between two rafters he was enabled to look down on to Prince Alberic in his study. Magnificently bound books lined the walls of the closet, and in their gaps hung valuable prints and maps. On the table were heaped several open volumes, among globes both terrestrial and celestial; and Alberic himself was leaning on the arm of a great chair, reciting the verses of Virgil in a most graceful chant. Never had the Jesuit seen a better-appointed study nor a more precocious young scholar.

As regards the Jester, he came at the very moment that Alberic was returning from a ride; and, having begun life as an acrobat, he was able to climb into a large ilex which commanded an excellent view of the Castle yard.

Alberic was mounted on a splendid jet-black barb, magnificently caparisoned in crimson and gold Spanish trappings. His groom—for he had even a groom—was riding a horse only a shade less perfect: it was white and he was black—a splendid negro such as only great princes own. When Alberic came in sight of the farmer's wife, who stood shelling peas on the doorstep, he waved his hat with infinite grace, caused his horse to caracole and rear three times in salutation, picked an apple up while cantering round the Castle yard, threw it in the air with his sword and cut it in two as it descended, and did a number of similar feats such as are taught only to the most brilliant cavaliers. Now, as he was going to dismount, a branch of the ilex cracked, the black barb

34

reared, and Alberic, looking up, perceived the Jester moving in the tree.

"A wonderful parti-colored bird!" he exclaimed, and seized the fowling-piece that hung to his saddle. But before he had time to fire the Jester had thrown himself down and alighted, making three somersaults, on the ground.

"My Lord," said the Jester, "you see before you a faithful subject who, braving the threats and traps of your enemies, and, I am bound to add, risking also your Highness's sovereign displeasure, had been determined to see his Prince once more, to have the supreme happiness of seeing him at last clad and equipped and mounted—"

"Enough!" interrupted Alberic sternly. "You need say no more. You would have me believe that it is to you I owe my horses and books and clothes, even as the Dwarf and the Jesuit tried to make me believe about themselves last month. Know, then, that Alberic of Luna requires gifts from none of you. And now, most miserable counselor of my unhappy grandfather, begone!"

The Jester checked his rage, and tried, all the way back to Luna, to get at some solution of this intolerable riddle. The Jesuit and the Dwarf—the scoundrels—had been trying *their* hand then! Perhaps, indeed, it was their blundering which had ruined his own perfectly-concocted scheme. But for their having come and claimed gratitude for gifts they had not made, Alberic would perhaps have believed that the Jester had not merely offered the horse which was refused, but had actually given the two which had been accepted, and the books and clothes (since there had been books and clothes given) into the bargain. But then, had not Alberic spoken as if he were perfectly sure from what quarter all his possessions had come? This reminded the Jester of the allusion to the Duke Balthasar Maria; Alberic had spoken of him as unhappy. Was it, could it be, possible that the treacherous old wretch had been keeping up relations with his grandson in secret, afraid—for he was a miserable old coward at bottom—both of the wrath of his three counselors, and of the hatred of his grandson? Was it possible, thought the Jester, that not only the Jesuit and the Dwarf, but the Duke of Luna also, had been intriguing against him round young Prince Alberic? Balthasar Maria was quite capable of it; he might be enjoying the trick he was playing his three masters—for they were his masters; he might be preparing to turn suddenly upon them with his long neglected grandson like a sword to smite them. On the other hand, might this not be a mere mistaken supposition on the part of Prince Alberic, who, in his silly dignity, preferred to believe in the liberality of his ducal

35

grandfather than in that of his grandfather's servants? Might the horses, and all the rest, not really be the gift of either the Dwarf or the Jesuit, although neither had got the credit for it? "No, no," exclaimed the Jester, for he hated his fellow-servants worse than his master, "anything better than that! Rather a thousand times that it were the Duke himself who had outwitted them."

Then, in his bitterness, having gone over the old arguments again and again, some additional circumstances returned to his memory. The black groom was deaf and dumb, and the peasants, it appeared, had been quite unable to extract any information from him. But he had arrived with those particular horses only a few months ago; a gift, the peasants had thought, from the old Duke of Luna. But Alberic, they had said, had possessed other horses before, which they had also taken for granted had come from the Red Palace. And the clothes and books had been accumulating, it appeared, ever since the Prince's arrival in his place of banishment. Since this was the case, the plot, whether on the part of the Jesuit or the Dwarf, or on that of the Duke himself, had been going on for years before the Jester had bestirred himself! Moreover, the Prince not only possessed horses, but he had learned to ride, he not only had books, but he had learned to read, and even to read various tongues; and finally, the Prince was not only clad in princely garments, but he was every inch of him a Prince. He had then been consorting with other people than the peasants at Sparkling Waters. He must have been away—or—some one must have come. He had not been living in solitude.

But when—how—and above all, who?

And again the baffled Jester revolved the probabilities concerning the Dwarf, the Jesuit, and the Duke. It must be—it could be no other—it evidently could only be—.

"Ah!" exclaimed the unhappy diplomatist; "if only one could believe in magic!"

And it suddenly struck him, with terror and mingled relief, "Was it magic?"

But the Jester, like the Dwarf and the Jesuit, and the Duke of Luna himself, was altogether superior to such foolish beliefs.

V

The young Prince of Luna had never attempted to learn the story of Alberic the Blond and the Snake Lady. Children sometimes conceive an inexplicable shyness, almost a dread, of knowing more on some subject which is uppermost in their thoughts; and such had been the case of Duke Balthasar Maria's grandson. Ever since the memorable morning when the ebony crucifix had been removed from in front of the faded tapestry, and the whole figure of the Snake Lady had been for the first time revealed, scarcely a day had passed without their coming to the boy's mind: his nurse's words about his ancestors Alberic and the Snake Lady Oriana. But, even as he had asked no questions then, so he had asked no questions since shrinking more and more from all further knowledge of the matter. He had never questioned his nurse; he had never questioned the peasants of Sparkling Waters, although the story, he felt quite sure, must be well-known among the ruins of Alberic the Blond's own castle. Nay, stranger still, he had never mentioned the subject to his dear Godmother, to whom he had learned to open his heart about all things, and who had taught him all that he knew.

For the Duke's Jester had guessed rightly that, during these years at Sparkling Waters, the young Prince had not consorted solely with peasants. The very evening after his arrival, as he was sitting by the marble well in the vineyard, looking towards the sea, he had felt a hand placed lightly on his shoulder, and looked up into the face of a beautiful lady dressed in green.

"Do not be afraid," she had said, smiling at his terror. "I am not a ghost, but alive like you; and I am, though you do not know it, your Godmother. My dwelling is close to this castle, and I shall come every evening to play and talk with you, here by the little white palace with the pillars, where the fodder is stacked. Only, you must remember that I do so against the wishes of your grandfather and all his friends, and that if ever you mention me to anyone, or allude in any way to our meetings, I shall be obliged to leave the neighborhood, and you will never see me again. Some day when you are big you will learn why; till then you must take me on trust. And now what shall we play at?"

And thus his Godmother had come every evening at sunset, just for an hour and no more, and had taught the poor solitary little Prince to play (for he had never played) and to read, and to manage a horse, and, above all, to love: for, except the old tapestry in the Red Palace, he had never loved anything in the world.

Alberic told his dear Godmother everything, beginning with the story of the two pieces of tapestry, the one they had taken away and the one he had cut to pieces; and he asked her about all the things he ever wanted to know, and she was always able to answer. Only about two things they were silent: she never told him her name nor where she lived, nor whether Duke Balthasar Maria knew her (the boy guessed that she had been a friend of his father's); and Alberic never revealed the fact that the tapestry had represented his ancestor and the beautiful Oriana; for, even to his dear Grandmother, and most perhaps to her, he found it impossible even to mention Alberic the Blond and the Snake Lady.

But the story, or rather the name of the story he did not know, never loosened its hold in Alberic's mind. Little by little, as he grew up, it came to add to his life two friends, of whom he never told his Godmother. They were, to be sure, of such sort, however different, that a boy might find it difficult to speak about without feeling foolish. The first of the two friends was his own ancestor, Alberic the Blond; and the second that large tame grass snake whose acquaintance he had made the day after his arrival at the castle. About Alberic the Blond he knew indeed but little, save that he had reigned in Luna many hundreds of years ago, and that he had been a very brave and glorious Prince indeed, who had helped to conquer the Holy Sepulcher with Godfrey and Tancred and the other heroes of Tasso. But, perhaps in proportion to this vagueness, Alberic the Blond served to personify all the notions of chivalry which the boy had learned from his Godmother, and those which bubbled up in his own breast. Nay, little by little the young Prince began to take his unknown ancestor as a model, and in a confused way, to identify himself with him. For was he not fair-haired too, and Prince of Luna, *Alberic,* third of the name, as the other had been first? Perhaps for this reason he could never speak of this ancestor with his Godmother. She might think it presumptuous and foolish; besides, she might perhaps tell him things about Alberic the Blond which would hurt him; the poor young Prince, who had compared the splendid reputation of his own grandfather with the miserable reality, had grown up precociously skeptical. As to the Snake, with whom he played every day in the grass, and who was his only companion during the many hours of his Godmother's absence, he would willingly have spoken of her, and had once been on the point of doing so, but he had noticed that the mere name of such creatures seemed to be odious to his Godmother. Whenever, in their readings, they came across any mention of serpents, his Godmother would exclaim, "Let us skip that," with a look of intense pain in her usually cheerful countenance. It was a pity, Alberic thought, that so lovely and dear a lady should feel such hatred towards any living creature, particularly towards a kind which, like his own tame grass snake, was perfectly harmless. But he loved her too much to dream of thwarting her; and he was very grateful to his tame snake for having the tact never to show herself at the hour of his Godmother's visits.

But to return to the story represented on the dear, faded tapestry in the Red Palace.

When Prince Alberic, unconscious to himself, was beginning to turn into a full-grown and gallant-looking youth, a change began to take place in him, and it was about the story of his ancestor and the Lady Oriana. He thought of it more than ever, and it began to haunt his dreams; only it was now a vaguely painful thought; and, while dreading still to know more, he began to experience a restless, miserable craving to know all. His curiosity was like a thorn in his flesh, working its way in and in; and it seemed something almost more than curiosity. And yet, he was still shy and frightened of the subject; nay, the greater his craving to know, the greater grew a strange certainty that the knowing would be accompanied by evil. So, although many people could have answered—the very peasants, the fishermen of the coast, and first and foremost, his Godmother—he let months pass before he asked the question.

It, and the answer, came of a sudden.

There came occasionally to Sparkling Waters an old man, who united in his tattered person the trades of mending crockery and reciting fairy tales. He would seat himself in summer, under the spreading fig tree in the Castle yard, and in winter by the peasants' deep, black chimney, alternately boring holes in pipkins, or gluing plate edges, and singing, in a cracked, nasal voice, but not without dignity and charm of manner, the stories of the King of Portugal's Cowherd, of the Feathers of the Griffin, or some of the many stanzas of *Orlando* or *Jerusalem Delivered* which he knew by heart. Our young Prince had always avoided him, partly from a vague fear of a mention of his ancestor and the Snake Lady, and partly because of something vaguely sinister in the old man's eye. But now he awaited with impatience the vagrant's periodical return, and on one occasion, summoned him to his own chamber.

"Sing me," he commanded, "the story of Alberic the Blond and the Snake Lady."

The old man hesitated, and answered with a strange look—"My Lord, I do not know it."

A sudden feeling, such as the youth had never experienced before, seized hold of Alberic. He did not recognize himself. He saw and heard himself, as if it were someone else, nod first at some pieces of gold, of those his Godmother had given him, and then at his fowling-piece hung on the wall;

and as he did so he had a strange thought: "I must be mad."
But he merely said, sternly—

"Old man, that is not true. Sing that story at once, if you
value my money and your safety."

The vagrant took his white-bearded chin in his hand,
mused, and then, fumbling among the files and drills and
pieces of wire in his tool-basket, which made a faint metallic
accompaniment, he slowly began to chant the following stanzas:—

VI

Now listen, courteous Prince, to what befell your ancestor,
the valorous Alberic, returning from the Holy Land.

Already a year had passed since the strongholds of
Jerusalem had fallen beneath the blows of the faithful, and
since the Sepulcher of Christ had been delivered from the
worshipers of Macomet. The great Godfrey was enthroned as
its guardian, and the mighty barons, his companions, were
wending their way homewards—Tancred, and Bohemund,
and Reynold, and the rest.

The valorous Alberic, the honor of Luna, after many
perilous adventures, brought by the anger of the Wizard
Macomet, whom he had offended, was shipwrecked on his
homeward way, and cast, alone of all his great army, upon
the rocky shore of an unknown island. He wandered long
about, among woods and pleasant pastures, but without ever
seeing any signs of habitation, nourishing himself solely on
berries and clear water, and taking his rest in the green grass
beneath the trees. At length, after some days of wandering,
he came to a dense forest, the like of which he had never
seen before, so deep was its shade and so tangled were its
boughs. He broke the branches with his iron-gloved hand,
and the air became filled with the croaking and screeching of
dreadful night-birds. He pushed his way with shoulder and
knee, trampling the broken leafage under foot, and the air
was filled with the roaring of monstrous lions and tigers. He
grasped his sharp double-edged sword and hewed through the
interlaced branches, and the air was filled with the shrieks
and sobs of a vanquished city. But the Knight of Luna went
on, undaunted, cutting his way through the enchanted wood.
And behold! as he issued thence, there was before him a
lordly castle, as of some great Prince, situate in a pleasant
meadow among running streams. And as Alberic approached, the portcullis was raised, and the drawbridge lowered: and there arose sounds of fifes and bugles, but nowhere
should he descry any living wight around. And Alberic entered

the castle, and found therein guardrooms full of shining arms, and chambers spread with rich stuffs, and a banqueting-hall, with a great table laid and a chair of state at the end. And as he entered a concert of invisible voices and instruments greeted him sweetly, and called him by name, and bid him be welcome; but not a living soul did he see. So he sat him down at the table, and as he did so, invisible hands filled his cup and his plate, and ministered to him with delicacies of all sorts. Now, when the good knight had eaten and drunken his fill, he drank to the health of his unknown host, declaring himself the servant thereof with his sword and heart. After which, weary with wandering, he prepared to take rest on the carpets which strewed the ground; but invisible hands unbuckled his armor, and clad him in silken robes, and led him to a couch all covered with rose leaves. And when he had lain himself down, the concert of invisible singers and players put him to sleep with their melodies.

It was the hour of sunset when the valorous Baron awoke, and buckled on his armor, and hung on his thigh the great sword Brillamorte; and invisible hands helped him once more.

The Knight of Luna went all over the enchanted castle, and found all manner of rarities, treasures of precious stones, such as great kings possess, and stores of gold and silver vessels, and rich stuffs, and stables full of fiery coursers ready caparisoned; but never a human creature anywhere. And, wondering more and more, he went forth into the orchard, which lay within the castle walls. And such another orchard, sure, was never seen, since that in which the hero Hercules found the three golden apples and slew the great dragon. For you might see in this place fruit-trees of all kinds, apples and pears, and peaches and plums, and the goodly orange, which bore at the same time fruit and delicate and scented blossom. And all around were set hedges of roses, whose scent was even like heaven; and there were other flowers of all kinds, those into which the vain Narcissus turned through love of himself, and those which grew, they tell us, from the blood-drops of fair Venus's minion; and lilies of which that Messenger carried a sheaf who saluted the Meek Damsel, glorious above all womankind. And in the trees sang innumerable birds; and others, of unknown breed, joined melody in hanging cages and aviaries. And in the orchard's midst was set a fountain, the most wonderful e'er made, its waters running in green channels among the flowered grass. For that fountain was made in the likeness of twin naked maidens, dancing together, and pouring water out of pitchers as they did so; and the maidens were of fine silver, and the pitchers of wrought gold, and the whole so cunningly contrived by magic art that the maidens really moved and danced with the waters they were pouring out—a wonderful work, most truly. And when the Knight of Luna had feasted his eyes upon this marvel, he saw among the grass, beneath a flowering almond-tree, a sepulcher of marble, cunningly carved and gilded, on which was written, "Here is imprisoned the Fairy Oriana, most miserable of all fairies, condemned for no fault, but by envious powers, to a dreadful fate,"—and as he read, the inscription changed, and the sepulcher showed these words: "O Knight of Luna, valorous Alberic, if thou wouldst show thy gratitude to the hapless mistress of this castle, summon up thy redoubtable courage, and, whatsoever creature issue from my marble heart, swear thou to kiss it three times on the mouth, that Oriana may be released."

And Alberic drew his great sword, and on its hilt, shaped like a cross, he swore.

Then wouldst thou have heard a terrible sound of thunder, and seen the castle walls rock. But Alberic, nothing daunted, repeats in a loud voice, "I swear," and instantly that sepulcher's lid upheaves, and there issues thence and rises up a great green snake, wearing a golden crown, and raises itself and fawns toward the valorous Knight of Luna. And Alberic starts and recoils in terror. For rather, a thousand times, confront alone the armed hosts of all the heathen, than put his lips to that cold, creeping beast! And the serpent looks at Alberic with great gold eyes, and big tears issue thence, and it drops prostrate on the grass; and Alberic summons courage and approaches; but when the serpent glides along his arm, a horror takes him, and he falls back, unable. And the tears stream from the snake's golden eyes, and moans come from its mouth.

And Alberic runs forward, and seizes the serpent in both arms, and lifts it up, and three times presses his warm lips against its cold and slippery skin, shutting his eyes in horror. And when the Knight of Luna opens them again, behold! O wonder! in his arms no longer a dreadful snake, but a damsel, richly dressed and beautiful beyond compare.

VII

Young Alberic sickened that very night, and lay for many days raging with fever. The peasant's wife and a good neighboring priest nursed him unhelped, for when the messenger they sent arrived at Luna, Duke Balthasar was busy rehearsing a grand ballet in which he himself danced the part of Phoebus Apollo; and the ducal physician was therefore dispatched to Sparkling Waters only when the young Prince was already recovering.

Prince Alberic undoubtedly passed through a very bad illness and went fairly out of his mind for fever and ague.

He raved so dreadfully in his delirium about enchanted tapestries and terrible grottoes, Twelve Caesars with rolling eyeballs, barbers' blocks with perukes on them, monkeys of verde antique, and porphyry rhinoceroses, and all manner of hellish creatures, that the good priest began to suspect a case of demoniac possession, and caused candles to be kept lighted all day and all night, and holy water to be sprinkled, and a printed form of exorcism, absolutely sovereign in such trouble, to be nailed against the bedpost. On the fourth day the young Prince fell into a profound sleep, from which he awaked in apparent possession of his faculties.

"Then you are not the Porphyry Rhinoceros?" he said, very slowly, as his eye fell upon the priest; "and this is my own dear little room at Sparkling Waters, though I do not understand all those candles. I thought it was the great hall in the Red Palace, and that all those animals of precious marbles, and my grandfather, the Duke, in his bronze and gold robes, were beating me and my tame snake to death with harlequins' laths. It was terrible. But now I see it was all fancy and delirium."

The poor youth gave a sigh of relief, and feebly caressed the rugged old hand of the priest, which lay upon his counterpane. The Prince stayed for a long while motionless, but gradually a strange light came into his eyes, and a smile onto his lips. Presently he made a sign that the peasants should leave the room, and taking once more the good priest's hand, he looked solemnly in his eyes, and spoke in an earnest voice. "My father," he said, "I have seen and heard strange things in my sickness, and I cannot tell for certain now what belongs to the reality of my previous life, and what is merely the remembrance of delirium. On this I would fain be enlightened. Promise me, my father, to answer my questions truly, for this is a matter of the welfare of my soul, and therefore of your own."

The priest nearly jumped on his chair. So he had been right. The demons had been trying to tamper with the poor young Prince, and now he was going to have a fine account of it all.

"My son," he murmured, "as I hope for the spiritual welfare of both of us, I promise to answer all your interrogations to the best of my powers. Speak without reticence."

Alberic hesitated for a moment, and his eyes glanced from one long lit taper to the other.

43

"In that case," he said slowly, "let me conjure you, my father, to tell me whether or not there exists a certain tradition in my family, of the loves of my ancestor, Alberic the Blond, with a certain Snake Lady, and how he was unfaithful to her, and failed to disenchant her, and how a second Alberic, also my ancestor, loved this same Snake Lady, but failed before the ten years of fidelity were over, and became a monk. . . . Does such a story exist, or have I imagined it all during my sickness?"

"My son," replied the good priest testily, for he was most horribly disappointed by this speech, "it is scarce fitting that a young Prince but just escaped from the jaws of death—and, perhaps, even from the insidious onslaught of the Evil One— should give his mind to idle tales like these."

"Call them what you choose," answered the Prince gravely, "but remember your promise, father. Answer me truly, and presume not to question my reasons."

The priest started. What a hasty ass he had been! Why, these were probably the demons talking out of Alberic's mouth, causing him to ask silly irrelevant questions in order to prevent a good confession. Such were notoriously among their stock tricks! But he would outwit them. If only it were possible to summon up St. Paschal Baylon, that new fashionable saint who had been doing such wonders with devils lately! But St. Paschal Baylon required not only that you should say several rosaries, but that you should light four candles on a table and lay a supper for two; after that there was nothing he would not do. So the priest hastily seized two candlesticks from the foot of the bed, and called to the peasant's wife to bring a clean napkin and plates and glasses; and meanwhile endeavored to detain the demons by answering the poor Prince's foolish chatter, "Your ancestors, the two Alberics—a tradition in your Serene family—yes, my Lord—there is such—let me see, how does the story go?—ah yes—this demon, I mean this Snake Lady was a—what they call a fairy—or witch, malefica or strix is, I believe, the proper Latin expression—who had been turned into a snake for her sins—good woman, woman, is it possible you cannot be a little quicker in bringing those plates for His Highness's supper? The Snake Lady—let me see—was to cease altogether being a snake if a cavalier remained faithful to her for ten years, and at any rate turned into a woman every time a cavalier was found who had the courage to give her a kiss as if she were not a snake—a disagreeable thing, besides being mortal sin. As I said just now, this enabled her to resume temporarily her human shape, which is said to have been fair enough; but how can one tell? I believe she was allowed to

44

change into a woman for an hour at sunset, in any case and without anybody kissing her, but only for an hour. A very unlikely story, my Lord, and not a very moral one, to my thinking!"

And the good priest spread the tablecloth over the table, wondering secretly when the plates and glasses for St. Paschal Baylon would make their appearance. If only the demon could be prevented from beating a retreat before all was ready! "To return to the story about which Your Highness is pleased to inquire," he continued, trying to gain time by pretending to humor the demon who was asking questions through the poor Prince's mouth, "I can remember hearing a poem before I took orders—a foolish poem too, in a very poor style, if my memory is correct—that related the manner in which Alberic the Blond met this Snake Lady, and disenchanted her by performing the ceremony I have alluded to. The poem was frequently sung at fairs and similar resorts of the uneducated, and, as remarked, was a very inferior composition indeed. Alberic the Blond afterwards came to his senses, it appears, and after abandoning the Snake Lady fulfilled his duty as a Prince, and married the Princess. I cannot exactly remember what Princess, but it was a very suitable marriage, no doubt, from which Your Highness is of course descended.

"As regards the Marquis Alberic, second of the name, of whom it is accounted that he died in odor of sanctity (and indeed it is said that the facts concerning his beatification are being studied in the proper quarters), there is a mention in a life of St. Fredevaldus, bishop and patron of Luna, printed at the beginning of the present century at Venice, with Approbation and Licence of the Authorities and Inquisition, a mention of the fact that this Marquis Alberic the second had contracted, having abandoned his lawful wife, a left-handed marriage with this same Snake Lady (such evil creatures not being subject to natural death), she having induced him thereunto in hope of his proving faithful ten years, and by this means restoring her altogether to human shape. But a certain holy hermit, having got wind of this scandal, prayed to St. Fredevaldus as patron of Luna, whereupon St. Fredevaldus took pity on the Marquis Alberic's sins, and appeared to him in a vision at the end of the ninth year of his irregular connection with the Snake Lady, and touched his heart so thoroughly that he instantly forswore her company, and handing the Marquisate over to his mother, abandoned the world and entered the order of St. Romwald, in which he died, as remarked, in odor of sanctity, in consequence of which the present Duke, Your Highness's magnificent grandfather, is at this moment, as befits so pious a Prince, employing his influence with the Holy Father for the beatification of so glorious an ancestor. And now, my son," added the good priest, suddenly changing his tone, for he had got the table ready, and lighted the candles, and only required to go through the preliminary invocation of St. Paschal Baylon—"and now, my son, let your curiosity trouble you no more, but endeavor to obtain some rest, and if possible—"

But the Prince interrupted him.

"One word more, good father," he begged, fixing him with earnest eyes; "is it known what has been the fate of the Snake Lady?"

The impudence of the demons made the priest quite angry, but he must not scare them before the arrival of St. Paschal, so he controlled himself, and answered slowly by gulps, between the lines of the invocation he was mumbling under his breath:

"My Lord—it results from the same life of St. Fredevaldus, that (in case of property lost, fire, flood, earthquake, plague) that the Snake Lady (thee we invoke, most holy Paschal Baylon!)—the Snake Lady being of the nature of fairies, cannot die unless her head be severed from her trunk, and is still haunting the world, together with other evil spirits, in hopes that another member of the house of Luna (Thee we invoke, most holy Paschal Baylon!)—may succumb to her arts and be faithful to her for the ten years needful to her disenchantments—(most holy Paschal Baylon!—and most of all—on thee we call—for aid against the)—"

But before the priest could finish his invocation, a terrible shout came from the bed where the sick Prince was lying—

"O Oriana, Oriana!" cried Prince Alberic, sitting up in his bed with a look which terrified the priest as much as his voice. "O Oriana, Oriana!" he repeated, and then fell back exhausted and broken.

"Bless my soul!" cried the priest, almost upsetting the table; "why, the demon has already issued out of him! Who would have guessed that St. Paschal Baylon performed his miracles as quick as that?"

VIII

Prince Alberic was awakened by the loud trill of a nightingale. The room was bathed in moonlight, in which the tapers, left burning round the bed to ward off evil spirits, flickered yellow and ineffectual. Through the open casement came, with the scent of freshly-cut grass, a faint concert of nocturnal sounds: the silvery vibration of the cricket, the reedlike quavering notes of the leaf frogs, and, every now and then, the soft note of an owlet, seeming to stroke the silence as the downy wings growing out of the temples of the Sleep God might stroke the air. The nightingale had paused; and Alberic listened breathless for its next burst of song. At last, and when he expected it least, it came, liquid, loud, and triumphant; so near that it filled the room and thrilled through his marrow like an unison of Cremona viols. It was singing on the pomegranate close outside, whose first buds must be opening into flame-colored petals. For it was May. Alberic listened; and collected his thoughts, and understood. He arose and dressed, and his limbs seemed suddenly strong, and his mind strangely clear, as if his sickness had been but a dream. Again the nightingale trilled out, and again stopped. Alberic crept noiselessly out of his chamber, down the stairs and into the open. Opposite, the moon had just risen, immense and golden, and the pines and the cypresses of the hill, the furthest battlements of the castle walls, were printed upon it like delicate lace. It was so light that the roses were pink, and the pomegranate flower scarlet, and the lemons pale yellow, and the vines bright green, only differently colored from how they looked by day, and as if washed over with silver. The orchard spread uphill, its twigs and separate leaves all glittering as if made of diamonds, and its tree-trunks and spalliers weaving strange black patterns of shadow. A little breeze shuddered up from the sea, bringing the scent of the irises grown for their root among the cornfields below. The nightingale was silent. But Prince Alberic did not stand waiting for its song. A spiral dance of fireflies, rising and falling like a thin gold fountain, beckoned him upwards through the dewy grass. The circuit of castle walls, jagged and battlemented, and with tufts of trees profiled here and there against the resplendent blue pallor of the moonlight, seemed twined and knotted like huge snakes around the world.

Suddenly, again, the nightingale sang—a throbbing, silver song. It was the same bird, Alberic felt sure; but it was in front of him now, and was calling him onwards. The fireflies wove their golden dance a few steps in front, always a few steps in front, and drew him uphill through the orchard.

As the ground became steeper, the long trellises, black and crooked, seemed to twist and glide through the blue moonlit grass like black gliding snakes, and, at the top, its marble pillarets clear in the light, slumbered the little Gothic palace of white marble. From the solitary sentinel pine broke the song of the nightingale. This was the place. A breeze had risen, and from the shining moonlit sea, broken into causeways and flotillas of smooth and fretted silver, came a faint briny smell, mingling with that of the irises and blossoming lemons, with the scent of vague ripeness and freshness. The moon hung like a silver lantern over the orchard; the wood of the trellises patterned the blue luminous heaven; the vine-leaves seemed to swim, transparent, in the shining air. Over the circular well, in the high grass, the fireflies rose and fell like a thin fountain of gold. And, from the sentinel pine, the nightingale sang.

Prince Alberic leaned against the brink of the well, by the trough carved with antique designs of serpent-bearing mae-nads. He was wonderfully calm, and his heart sang within him. It was, he knew, the hour and place of his fate.

The nightingale ceased: and the shrill song of the crickets was suspended. The silvery luminous world was silent.

A quiver came through the grass by the well, a rustle through the roses. And, on the well's brink, encircling its central blackness, glided the Snake.

"Oriana!" whispered Alberic. "Oriana!" She paused, and stood almost erect. The Prince put out his hand, and she twisted round his arm, extending slowly her chilly coil to his wrist and fingers.

"Oriana!" whispered Prince Alberic again. And raising his hand to his face, he leaned down and pressed his lips on the little flat head of the serpent. And the nightingale sang. But a coldness seized his heart, the moon seemed suddenly extin-guished, and he slipped away in unconsciousness.

When he awoke the moon was still high. The nightingale was singing its loudest. He lay in the grass by the well, and his head rested on the knees of the most beautiful of ladies. She was dressed in cloth of silver which seemed woven of moon mists, and shimmering moonlit green grass. It was his own dear Godmother.

IX

When Duke Balthasar Maria had got through the re-hearsals of the ballet called Daphne Transformed, and finally danced his part of Phoebus Apollo to the infinite delight and glory of his subjects, he was greatly concerned, being benignly humored, on learning that he had very nearly lost his grandson and heir. The Dwarf, the Jesuit, and the Jester, whom he delighted in pitting against one another, had sever-ally accused each other of disrespectful remarks about the dancing of that ballet; so Duke Balthasar determined to disgrace all three together and inflict upon them the hated presence of Prince Alberic. It was, after all, very pleasant to possess a young grandson, whom one could take to one's bosom and employ in being insolent to one's own favorites. It was time, said Duke Balthasar, that Alberic should learn the habits of a court and take unto himself a suitable princess.

The young Prince accordingly was sent for from Sparkling Waters, and installed at Luna in a wing of the Red Palace, overlooking the Court of Honor, and commanding an excellent view of the great rockery, with the Verde Antique Apes and the Porphyry Rhinoceros. He found awaiting him on the great staircase a magnificent staff of servants, a master of the horse, a grand cook, a barber, a hairdresser and assistant, a fencing-master, and four fiddlers. Several lovely ladies of the Court, the principal ministers of the Crown, and the Jesuit, the Dwarf, and the Jester, were also ready to pay their respects. Prince Alberic threw himself out of the glass coach before they had time to open the door, and bowing coldly, ascended the staircase, carrying under his cloak what appeared to be a small wicker cage. The Jesuit, who was the soul of politeness, sprang forward and signed to an officer of the household to relieve His Highness of this burden. But Alberic waved the man off; and the rumor went abroad that a hissing noise had issued from under the Prince's cloak, and, like lightning, the head and forked tongue of a serpent.

Half an hour later the official spies had informed Duke Balthasar that his grandson and heir had brought from Sparkling Waters no apparent luggage save two swords, a fowling-piece, a volume of Virgil, a branch of pomegranate blossom, and a tame grass snake.

Duke Balthasar did not like the idea of the grass snake; but wishing to annoy the Jester, the Dwarf, and the Jesuit, he merely smiled when they told him of it, and said: "The dear boy! What a child he is! He probably, also, has a pet lamb, white as snow, and gentle as spring, mourning for him in his old home! How touching is the innocence of childhood! Heigho! I was just like that myself not so very long ago." Whereupon the three favorites and the whole Court of Luna smiled and bowed and sighed: "How lovely is the innocence of youth!" while the Duke fell to humming the well-known air, "Thyrsis was a shepherd-boy," of which the ducal fiddlers instantly struck up the ritornel.

"But," added Balthasar Maria, with that subtle blending of majesty and archness in which he excelled all living Princes, "but it is now time that the Prince, my grandson, should learn"—here he put his hand on his sword and threw back slightly one curl of his jet-black peruke— "the stern exercises of Mars; and also, let us hope, the freaks and frolics of Venus."

49

Saying which, the old sinner pinched the cheek of a lady of the very highest quality, whose husband and father were instantly congratulated by the whole Court.

Prince Alberic was displayed next day to the people of Luna, standing on the balcony among a tremendous banging of mortars; while Duke Balthasar explained that he felt towards this youth all the fondness and responsibility of an elder brother. There was a grand ball, a gala opera, a review, a very high mass in the cathedral; the Dwarf, the Jesuit, and the Jester each separately offered his services to Alberic in case he wanted a loan of money, a love-letter carried, or in case even (expressed in more delicate terms) he might wish to poison his grandfather. Duke Balthasar Maria, on his side, summoned his ministers, and sent couriers, booted and liveried, to three great dukes of Italy, carrying each of them, in a morocco wallet emblazoned with the arms of Luna, an account of Prince Alberic's lineage and person, and a request for particulars of any marriageable princesses and dowries to be disposed of.

X

Prince Alberic did not give his grandfather that warm satisfaction which the old Duke had expected. Balthasar Maria, entirely bent upon annoying the three favorites, had said and had finally believed, that he intended to introduce his grandson to the delights and duties of life, and in the company of this beloved stripling, to dream that he, too, was a youth once more: a statement which the Court took with due deprecatory reverence, as the Duke was well known never to have ceased to be young.

But Alberic did not lend himself to so touching an idyl. He behaved, indeed, with the greatest decorum, and manifested the utmost respect for his grandfather. He was marvelously assiduous in the council chamber, and still more so in following the military exercises and learning the trade of a soldier. He surprised every one by his interest and intelligence in all affairs of state; he more than surprised the Court by his readiness to seek knowledge about the administration of the country and the condition of the people. He was a youth of excellent morals, courage, and diligence; but, there was no denying it, he had positively no conception of *sacrificing to the Graces*. He sat out, as if he had been watching a review, the delicious operas and superb ballets which absorbed half the revenue of the duchy. He listened, without a smile of comprehension, to the witty innuendos of the ducal table. But worst of all, he had absolutely no eyes, let alone a heart, for

50

the fair sex. Now Balthasar Maria had assembled at Luna a perfect bevy of lovely nymphs, both ladies of the greatest birth, whose husbands received most honorable posts, military and civil, and young females of humbler extraction, though not less expensive habits, ranging from singers and dancers to slave-girls of various colors, all dressed in their appropriate costume: a galaxy of beauty which was duly represented by the skill of celebrated painters on the walls of the Red Palace, where you may still see their faded charms, habited as Diana, or Pallas, or in the spangles of Columbine, or the turbans of Sibyls. These ladies were the object of Duke Balthasar's most munificently divided attentions; and in the delight of his newborn family affection, he had promised himself much tender interest in guiding the taste of his heir among such of these nymphs as had already received his own exquisite appreciation. Great, therefore, was the disappointment of the affectionate grandfather when his dream of companionship was dispelled, and it became hopeless to interest young Alberic in anything at Luna save dispatches and cannons.

The Court, indeed, found the means of consoling Duke Balthasar for this bitterness by extracting therefrom a brilliant comparison between the unfading grace, the vivacious, though majestic, character of the grandfather, and the gloomy and pedantic personality of the grandson. But, although Balthasar Maria would only smile at every new proof of Alberic's bearish obtuseness, and ejaculate in French, "Poor child! he was born old, and I shall die young!" the reigning Prince of Luna grew vaguely to resent the peculiarities of his heir.

In this fashion things proceeded in the Red Palace at Luna, until Prince Alberic had attained his twenty-first year.

He was sent, in the interval, to visit the principal courts of Italy, and to inspect its chief curiosities, natural and historical, as befitted the heir to an illustrious state. He received the golden rose from the Pope in Rome; he witnessed the festivities of Ascension Day from the Doge's barge at Venice; he accompanied the Marquis of Montferrat to the camp under Turin; he witnessed the launching of a galley against the Barbary corsairs by the Knights of St. Stephen in the port of Leghorn, and a grand bullfight and burning of heretics given by the Spanish Viceroy at Palermo; and he was allowed to be present when the celebrated Dr. Borri turned two brass buckles into pure gold before the Archduke at Milan. On all of which occasions the heir apparent of Luna bore himself with a dignity and discretion most singular in one so young. In the course of these journeys he was presented to several of the most promising heiresses in Italy, some of whom were of

51

so tender age as to be displayed in jeweled swaddling clothes on brocade cushions; and a great many possible marriages were discussed behind his back. But Prince Alberic declared for his part that he had decided to lead a single life until the age of twenty-eight or thirty, and that he would then require the assistance of no ambassadors or chancellors, but find for himself the future Duchess of Luna.

All this did not please Balthasar Maria, as indeed nothing else about his grandson did please him much. But, as the old Duke did not really relish the idea of a daughter-in-law at Luna, and as young Alberic's whimsicalities entailed no expense, and left him entirely free in his business and pleasure, he turned a deaf ear to the criticisms of his counselors, and letting his grandson inspect fortifications, drill soldiers, pore over parchments, and mope in his wing of the palace, with no amusement save his repulsive tame snake, Balthasar Maria composed and practiced various ballets, and began to turn his attention very seriously to the completion of the rockery grotto and of the sepulchral chapel, which, besides the Red Palace itself, were the chief monuments of his glorious reign.

It was the growing desire to witness the fulfillment of these magnanimous projects which led the Duke of Luna into unexpected conflict with his grandson. The wonderful enterprises above-mentioned involved immense expenses, and had periodically been suspended for lack of funds. The collection of animals in the rockery was very far from complete. A camelopard of spotted alabaster, an elephant of Sardinian jasper, and the entire families of a cow and sheep, all of correspondingly rich marbles, were urgently required to fill up the corners. Moreover, the supply of water was at present so small that the fountains were dry save for a couple of hours on the very greatest holidays; and it was necessary for the perfect naturalness of this ingenious work that an aqueduct twenty miles long should pour perennial streams from a high mountain lake into the grotto of the Red Palace.

The question of the sepulchral chapel was, if possible, even more urgent, for, after every new ballet, Duke Balthasar went through a fit of contrition, during which he fixed his thoughts on death; and the possibilities of untimely release, and of burial in an unfinished mausoleum, filled him with terrors. It is true that Duke Balthasar had, immediately after building the vast domed chapel, secured an effigy of his own person before taking thought for the monuments of his already buried ancestors, and the statue, twelve feet high, representing himself in coronation robes of green bronze brocaded with gold, holding a scepter, and bearing on his head, of purest silver, a spiky coronet set with diamonds, was one of the curiosities which travelers admired most in Italy. But this statue was unsymmetrical, and moreover, had a dismal suggestiveness, so long as surrounded by empty niches; and the fact that only one-half of the pavement was inlaid with discs of sardonyx, jasper, and carnelian, and that the larger part of the walls were rough brick without a vestige of the mosaic pattern of lapis lazuli, malachite, pearl, and coral, which had been begun round the one finished tomb, rendered the chapel as poverty-stricken in one aspect as it was magnificent in another. The finishing of the chapel was therefore urgent, and two more bronze statues were actually cast, those, to wit, of the Duke's father and grandfather, and mosaic workmen called from the Medicean works in Florence. But, all of a sudden, the ducal treasury was discovered to be empty, and the ducal credit to be exploded.

State lotteries, taxes on salt, even a sham crusade against the Dey of Algiers, all failed to produce any money. The alliance, the right to pass troops through the duchy, the letting out of the ducal army to the highest bidder, had long since ceased to be a source of revenue either from the Emperor, the King of Spain, or the Most Christian One. The Serene Republics of Venice and Genoa publicly warned their subjects against lending a single sequin to the Duke of Luna; the Dukes of Mantua and Modena began to worry about bad debts; the Pope himself had the atrocious taste to make complaints about suppression of church dues and interception of Peter's pence. There remained to the bankrupt Duke Balthasar Maria only one hope in the world—the marriage of his grandson.

There happened to exist at that moment a sovereign of incalculable wealth, with an only daughter of marriageable age. But this potentate, although the nephew of a recent Pope, by whose confiscations his fortunes were founded, had originally been a dealer in such goods as are comprehensively known as drysalting; and, rapacious as were the Princes of the Empire, each was too much ashamed of his neighbors to venture upon alliance with a family of so obtrusive an origin. Here was Balthasar Maria's opportunity: the Drysalter Prince's ducats should complete the rockery, the aqueduct, and the chapel; the drysalter's daughter should be wedded to Alberic of Luna, that was to be third of the name.

XI

Prince Alberic sternly declined. He expressed his dutiful wish that the grotto and the chapel, like all other enterprises undertaken by his grandparent, might be brought to an end worthy of him. He declared that the aversion to drysalters was a prejudice unshared by himself. He even went so far as to suggest that the eligible princess should marry, not the heir apparent, but the reigning Duke of Luna. But, as regarded himself, he intended, as stated, to remain for many years single. Duke Balthasar had never in his life before seen a man who was determined to oppose him. He felt terrified and became speechless in the presence of young Alberic.

Direct influence having proved useless, the Duke and his counselors, among whom the Jesuit, the Dwarf, and the Jester had been duly reinstated, looked round for means of indirect persuasion or coercion. A celebrated Venetian beauty was sent for to Luna—a lady frequently employed in diplomatic missions, which she carried through by her unparalleled grace in dancing. But Prince Alberic, having watched her for half an hour, merely remarked to his equerry that his own tame grass snake made the same movements as the lady infinitely better and more modestly. Whereupon this means was abandoned. The Dwarf then suggested a new method of acting on the young Prince's feelings. This, which he remembered to have been employed very successfully in the case of a certain Duchess of Malfi, who had given her family much trouble some generations back, consisted in dressing a number of domestics up as ghosts and devils, hiring some genuine lunatics from a neighboring establishment, and introducing them at dead of night into Prince Alberic's chamber. But the Prince, who was busy at his orisons, merely threw a heavy stool and two candlesticks at the apparitions; and, as he did so, the tame snake suddenly rose up from the floor, growing colossal in the act, and hissed so terrifically that the whole party fled down the corridor. The most likely advice was given by the Jesuit. This truly subtle diplomatist averred that it was useless trying to act upon the Prince by means which did not already affect him; instead of clumsily constructing a lever for which there was no fulcrum in the youth's soul, it was necessary to find out whatever leverage there might already exist.

Now, on careful inquiry, there was discovered a fact which the official spies, who always acted by precedent and pursued their inquiries according to the rules of the human heart as taught by the Secret Inquisition of the Republic of Venice, had naturally failed to perceive. This fact consisted in a rumor, very vague but very persistent, that Prince Alberic did not inhabit his wing of the palace in absolute solitude. Some of the pages attending on his person affirmed to have heard whispered conversations in the Prince's study, on entering which they had invariably found him alone; others maintained that, during the absence of the Prince from the palace, they had heard the sound of his private harpsichord, the one with the story of Orpheus and the view of Soracte on the cover, although he always kept its key on his person. A footman declared that he had found in the Prince's study, and among his books and maps, a piece of embroidery certainly not belonging to the Prince's furniture and apparel, moreover, half finished, and with a needle sticking in the canvas; which piece of embroidery the Prince had thrust into his pocket. But, as none of the attendants had ever seen any visitor entering or issuing from the Prince's apartments, and the professional spies had ransacked all possible hiding-places and modes of exit in vain, these curious indications had been neglected, and the opinion had been formed that Alberic being, as every one could judge, somewhat insane, had a gift of ventriloquism, a taste for musical boxes, and a proficiency in unmanly handicrafts which he carefully secreted.

These rumors had at one time caused great delight to Duke Balthasar; but he had got tired of sitting in a dark cupboard in his grandson's chamber, and had caught a bad chill looking through his keyhole; so he had stopped all further inquiries as officious fooling on the part of impudent lackeys.

But the Jesuit foolishly adhered to the rumor. "Discover *her*," he said, "and work through her on Prince Alberic." But Duke Balthasar, after listing twenty times to this remark with the most delighted interest, turned round on the twenty-first time and gave the Jesuit a look of Jove-like thunder. "My father," he said, "I am surprised—I may say more than surprised—at a person of your cloth descending so low as to make aspersions upon the virtue of a young Prince reared in my palace and born of my blood. Never let me hear another word about ladies of light manners being secreted within these walls." Whereupon the Jesuit retired, and was in disgrace for a fortnight, till Duke Balthasar woke up one morning with a strong apprehension of dying.

But no more was said of the mysterious female friend of Prince Alberic, still less was any attempt made to gain her intervention in the matter of the Drysalter Princess's marriage.

XII

More desperate measures were soon resorted to. It was given out that Prince Alberic was engrossed in study; and he was forbidden to leave his wing of the Red Palace, with no other view than the famous grotto with the Verde Antique Apes and the Porphyry Rhinoceros. It was published that Prince Alberic was sick; and he was confined very rigorously to a less agreeable apartment in the rear of the Palace, where he could catch sight of the plaster laurels and draperies, and the rolling plaster eyeball of one of the Twelve Caesars under the cornice. It was judiciously hinted that the Prince had entered into religious retreat; and he was locked and bolted into the State prison, alongside of the unfinished sepulchral chapel, whence a lugubrious hammering came as the only sound of life. In each of these places the recalcitrant youth was duly argued with by some of his grandfather's familiars, and even received a visit from the old Duke in person. But threats and blandishments were all in vain, and Alberic persisted in his refusal to marry.

It was now six months since he had seen the outer world, and six weeks since he had inhabited the State prison, every stage in his confinement, almost every day thereof, having systematically deprived him of some luxury, some comfort, or some mode of passing his time. His harpsichord and foils had remained in the gala wing overlooking the grotto. His maps and books had not followed him beyond the higher story with the view of the Twelfth Caesar. And now they had taken away from him his Virgil, his inkstand and paper, and left him only a book of hours.

Balthasar Maria and his counselors felt intolerably baffled. There remained nothing further to do; for if Prince Alberic were publicly beheaded, or privately poisoned, or merely left to die of want and sadness, it was obvious that Prince Alberic could no longer conclude the marriage with the Drysalter Princess, and that no money to finish the grotto and the chapel, or to carry on Court expenses, would be forthcoming.

It was a burning day of August, a Friday, thirteenth of that month, and after a long prevalence of enervating siroc- co, when the old Duke determined to make one last appeal to the obedience of his grandson. The sun, setting among ominous clouds, sent a lurid orange gleam into Prince Alber- ic's prison chamber, at the moment that his ducal grandfa- ther, accompanied by the Jester, the Dwarf, and the Jesuit, appeared on its threshold after prodigious clanking of keys and clattering of bolts. The unhappy youth rose as they entered, and making a profound bow, motioned his grandpar- ent to the only chair in the place.

Balthasar Maria had never visited him before in this his worst place of confinement; and the bareness of the room, the dust and cobwebs, the excessive hardness of the chair.

affected his sensitive heart; and, joined with irritation at his grandson's obstinacy and utter depression about the marriage, the grotto, and the chapel, actually caused this magnanimous sovereign to burst into tears and bitter lamentations.

"It would indeed melt the heart of a stone," remarked the Jester sternly, while his two companions attempted to soothe the weeping Duke—"to see one of the greatest, wisest, and most valorous Princes in Europe reduced to tears by the undutifulness of his child."

"Princes, nay kings and emperors' sons," exclaimed the Dwarf, who was administering Melissa water to the Duke, "have perished miserably for much less."

"Some of the most remarkable personages of sacred history are stated to have incurred eternal perdition for far slighter offences," added the Jesuit.

Alberic had sat down on the bed. The tawny sunshine fell upon his figure. He had grown very thin, and his garments were inexpressibly threadbare. But he was spotlessly neat, his lace band was perfectly folded, his beautiful blond hair flowed in exquisite curls about his pale face, and his whole aspect was serene and even cheerful. He might be twenty-two years old, and was of consummate beauty and stature.

"My Lord," he answered slowly, "I entreat Your Serene Highness to believe that no one could regret more deeply than I do such a spectacle as is offered me by the tears of a Duke of Luna. At the same time, I can only reiterate that I accept no responsibility."

A distant growling of thunder caused the old Duke to start, and interrupted Alberic's speech.

"Your obstinacy, my Lord," exclaimed the Dwarf, who was an excessively choleric person, "betrays the existence of a hidden conspiracy most dangerous to the state."

"It is an indication," added the Jester, "of a highly deranged mind."

"It seems to me," whispered the Jesuit, "to savor most undoubtedly of devilry."

Alberic shrugged his shoulders. He had risen from the bed to close the grated window, into which a shower of hail was suddenly blowing with unparalleled violence, when the old Duke jumped on his seat, and, with eyeballs starting with terror, exclaimed, as he tottered convulsively, "The serpent! the serpent!"

For there, in a corner, the tame grass snake was placidly coiled up, sleeping.

"The snake! the devil! Prince Alberic's pet companion!"

57

exclaimed the three favorites, and rushed towards that corner.

Alberic threw himself forward. But he was too late. The Jester, with a blow of his harlequin's lath, had crushed the head of the startled creature; and, even while he was struggling with him and the Jesuit, the Dwarf had given it two cuts with his Turkish scimitar.

"The snake! the snake!" shrieked Duke Balthasar, heedless of the desperate struggle.

The warders and equerries waiting outside thought that Prince Alberic must be murdering his grandfather and burst into prison and separated the combatants.

"Chain the rebel! the wizard! the madman!" cried the three favorites.

Alberic had thrown himself on the dead snake, which lay crushed and bleeding on the floor; and he moaned piteously.

But the Prince was unarmed and overpowered in a moment. Three times he broke loose, but three times he was recaptured, and finally bound and gagged, and dragged away. The old Duke recovered from his fright, and was helped up from the bed on to which he had sunk. As he prepared to leave, he approached the dead snake, and looked at it for some time. He kicked its mangled head with his ribboned shoe, and turned away laughing.

"Who knows," he said, "whether you were not the Snake Lady? That foolish boy made a great fuss, I remember, when he was scarcely out of long clothes, about a tattered old tapestry representing that repulsive story."

And he departed to supper.

XIII

Prince Alberic of Luna, who should have been third of his name, died a fortnight later, it was stated, insane. But those who approached him maintained that he had been in perfect possession of his faculties; and that if he refused all nourishment during his second imprisonment, it was from set purpose. He was removed at night from his apartments facing the grotto with the Verde Antique Monkeys and the Porphyry Rhinoceros, and hastily buried under a slab, which remained without any name or date, in the famous mosaic sepulchral chapel.

Duke Balthasar Maria survived him only a few months. The old Duke had plunged into excesses of debauchery with a view, apparently, to dismissing certain terrible thoughts and images which seemed to haunt him day and night, and against which no religious practices or medical prescription were of any avail. The origin of these painful delusions was probably connected with a very strange rumor, which grew to a tradition at Luna, to the effect that when the prison room occupied by Prince Alberic was cleaned, after that terrible storm of the 13th August of the year 1700, the persons employed found in a corner, not the dead grass snake, which they had been ordered to cast into the palace drains, but the body of a woman, naked, and miserably disfigured with blows and saber cuts.

Be this as it may, history records as certain that the house of Luna became extinct in 1701, the duchy lapsing to the Empire. Moreover, that the mosaic chapel remained for ever unfinished, with no statue save the green bronze and gold one of Balthasar Maria above the nameless slab covering Prince Alberic. The rockery also was never completed; only a few marble animals adorning it besides the Porphyry Rhinoceros and the Verde Antique Apes, and the water-supply being sufficient only for the greatest holidays. These things the traveler can report. Also that certain chairs and curtains in the porter's lodge of the now long-deserted Red Palace are made of the various pieces of an extremely damaged arras, having represented the story of Alberic the Blond and the Snake Lady.

THE WHITE WOLF OF THE HARTZ MOUNTAINS

Frederick Marryat

I

Before noon Philip and Krantz had embarked, and made sail in the peroqua.

They had no difficulty in steering their course; the islands by day, and the clear stars by night, were their compass. It is true that they did not follow the more direct track, but they followed the more secure, working up the smooth waters, and gaining to the northward more than to the west. Many times they were chased by the Malay proas, which infested the islands, but the swiftness of their little peroqua was their security; indeed, the chase was, generally speaking, abandoned as soon as the smallness of the vessel was made out by the pirates, who expected that little or no booty was to be gained.

One morning, as they were sailing between the isles, with less wind than usual, Philip observed—

"Krantz, you said that there were mysterious events in your life, or connected with it. Will you now tell me to what you referred?"

"Certainly," replied Krantz; "I have often thought of doing so, but one circumstance or another has hitherto prevented me; this is, however, a fitting opportunity. Prepare therefore to listen to a strange story. I take it for granted that you have heard people speak of the Hartz Mountains," observed Krantz.

"I have never heard people speak of them, that I can recollect," replied Philip; "but I have read of them in some books, and of the strange things which have occurred there."

"It is indeed a wild region," rejoined Krantz, "and many strange tales are told of it; but strange as they are, I have good reason for believing them to be true.

"My father was not born, or originally a resident, in the Hartz Mountains; he was a serf of an Hungarian nobleman, of great possessions, in Transylvania; but although a serf, he was not by any means a poor or illiterate man. In fact, he was rich, and his intelligence and respectability were such,

60

that he had been raised by his lord to the stewardship; but whoever may happen to be born a serf, a serf must he remain, even though he become a wealthy man: such was the condition of my father. My father had been married for about five years; and by his marriage had three children—my eldest brother Caesar, myself (Hermann), and a sister named Marcella. You know, Philip, that Latin is still the language spoken in that country; and that will account for our high-sounding names. My mother was a very beautiful woman, unfortunately more beautiful than virtuous: she was seen and admired by the lord of the soil; my father was sent away upon some mission; and during his absence, my mother, flattered by the attentions, and won by the assiduities, of this nobleman, yielded to his wishes. It so happened that my father returned very unexpectedly, and discovered the intrigue. The evidence of my mother's shame was positive: he surprised her in the company of her seducer! Carried away by the impetuosity of his feelings, he watched the opportunity of a meeting taking place between them, and murdered both his wife and her seducer. Conscious that, as a serf, not even the provocation which he had received would be allowed as a justification of his conduct, he hastily collected together what money he could lay his hands upon, and, as we were then in the depth of winter, he put his horses to the sleigh, and taking his children with him, he set off in the middle of the night, and was far away before the tragical circumstance had transpired. Aware that he would be pursued, and that he had no chance of escape if he remained in any portion of his native country (in which the authorities could lay hold of him), he continued his flight without intermission until he had buried himself in the intricacies and seclusions of the Hartz Mountains. Of course, all that I have now told you I learned afterwards. My oldest recollections are knit to a rude, yet comfortable cottage, in which I lived with my father, brother, and sister. It was on the confines of one of those vast forests which cover the northern part of Germany; around it were a few acres of ground, which, during the summer months, my father cultivated, and which, though they yielded a doubtful harvest, were sufficient for our support. In the winter we remained much indoors, for, as my father followed the chase, we were left alone, and the wolves during that season incessantly prowled about. My father had purchased the cottage, and the land about it, of one of the rude foresters, who gain their livelihood partly by hunting, and partly by burning charcoal, for the purpose of smelting the ore from the neighbouring mines; it was distant about two miles from any other habitation. I can call to mind the whole landscape now; the tall pines which rose up on the mountain above us, and the wide expanse of the forest beneath, on the topmost boughs and heads of whose trees we looked down from our cottage, as the mountain below us rapidly descended into the distant valley. In summer time the prospect was beautiful: but during the severe winter a more desolate scene could not well be imagined.

"I said that, in the winter, my father occupied himself with the chase; every day he left us, and often would he lock the door, that we might not leave the cottage. He had no one to assist him, or to take care of us—indeed, it was not easy to find a female servant who would live in such a solitude; but, could he have found one, my father would not have received her, for he had imbibed a horror of the sex, as the difference of his conduct towards us, his two boys, and my poor little sister Marcella evidently proved. You may suppose we were sadly neglected; indeed, we suffered much, for my father, fearful that we might come to some harm, would not allow us fuel when he left the cottage; and we were obliged, therefore, to creep under the heaps of bears' skins, and there to keep ourselves as warm as we could until he returned in the evening, when a blazing fire was our delight. That my father chose this restless sort of life may appear strange, but the fact was, that he could not remain quiet; whether from the remorse for having committed murder, or from the misery consequent on his change of situation, or from both combined, he was never happy unless he was in a state of activity. Children, however, when left so much to themselves, acquire a thoughtfulness not common to their age. So it was with us; and during the short cold days of winter, we would sit silent, longing for the happy hours when the snow would melt and the leaves burst out, and the birds begin their songs, and when we should again be set at liberty.

"Such was our peculiar and savage sort of life until my brother Caesar was nine, myself seven, and my sister five years old, when the circumstances occurred on which is based the extraordinary narrative which I am about to relate.

"One evening my father returned home rather later than usual; he had been unsuccessful, and as the weather was very severe, and many feet of snow were upon the ground, he was not only very cold, but in a very bad humor. He had brought in wood, and we were all three gladly assisting each other in blowing on the embers to create a blaze, when he caught poor little Marcella by the arm and threw her aside; the child fell, struck her mouth, and bled very much. My brother ran to raise her up. Accustomed to ill-usage, and afraid of my father, she did not dare to cry, but looked up in

62

his face very piteously. My father drew his stool nearer to the hearth, muttered something in abuse of women, and busied himself with the fire, which both my brother and I had deserted when our sister was so unkindly treated. A cheerful blaze was soon the result of his exertions; but we did not, as usual, crowd round it. Marcella, still bleeding, retired to a corner, and my brother and I took our seats beside her, while my father hung over the fire gloomily and alone. Such had been our position for about half an hour, when the howl of a wolf, close under the window of the cottage fell on our ears. My father started up, and seized his gun; the howl was repeated; he examined the priming, and then hastily left the cottage, shutting the door after him. We all waited (anxiously listening), for we thought that if he succeeded in shooting the wolf, he would return in a better humor; and, although he was harsh to all of us, and particularly so to our little sister, still we loved our father, and loved to see him cheerful and happy, for what else had we to look up to? And I may here observe, that perhaps there never were three children who were fonder of each other; we did not, like other children, fight and dispute together; and if, by chance, any disagreement did arise, between my elder brother and me, little Marcella would run to us, and kissing us both, seal, through her entreaties, the peace between us. Marcella was a lovely, amiable child; I can recall her beautiful features even now. Alas! poor little Marcella."

"She is dead, then?" observed Philip.

"Dead! yes, dead! but how did she die?—But I must not anticipate, Philip; let me tell my story.

"We waited for some time, but the report of the gun did not reach us, and my elder brother then said, 'Our father has followed the wolf, and will not be back for some time. Marcella, let us wash the blood from your mouth, and then we will leave this corner and go to the fire to warm ourselves.'

"We did so, and remained there until near midnight, every minute wondering, as it grew later, why our father did not return. We had no idea that he was in any danger, but we thought that he must have chased the wolf for a very long time. 'I will look out and see if father is coming,' said my brother Caesar, going to the door. 'Take care,' said Marcella, 'the wolves must be about now, and we cannot kill them, brother.' My brother opened the door very cautiously, and but a few inches; he peeped out. 'I see nothing,' said he, after a time, and once more he joined us at the fire. 'We have had no supper,' said I, for my father usually cooked the meat as soon as he came home; and during his absence we had nothing but the fragments of the preceding day.

" 'And if our father comes home, after his hunt, Caesar,' said Marcella, 'he will be pleased to have some supper; let us cook it for him and for ourselves.' Caesar climbed upon the stool, and reached down some meat—I forget now whether it was venison or bear's meat, but we cut off the usual quantity, and proceeded to dress it, as we used to do under our father's superintendence. We were all busy putting it into the platters before the fire, to await his coming, when we heard the sound of a horn. We listened—there was a noise outside, and a minute afterwards my father entered, ushered in a young female and a large dark man in a hunter's dress.

"Perhaps I had better now relate what was only known to me many years afterwards. When my father had left the cottage, he perceived a large white wolf about thirty yards from him; as soon as the animal saw my father, it retreated slowly, growling and snarling. My father followed; the animal did not run, but always kept at some distance; and my father did not like to fire until he was pretty certain that his ball would take effect; thus they went on for some time, the wolf now leaving my father far behind, and then stopping and snarling defiance at him, and then, again, on his approach, setting off at speed.

"Anxious to shoot the animal (for the white wolf is very rare), my father continued the pursuit for several hours, during which he continually ascended the mountain.

"You must know, Philip, that there are peculiar spots on those mountains which are supposed, and, as mystery will prove, truly supposed, to be inhabited by the evil influences: they are well known to the huntsmen, who invariably avoid them. Now, one of these spots, an open space in the pine forest above us, had been pointed out to my father as dangerous on that account. But whether he disbelieved these wild stories, or whether, in his eager pursuit of the chase. he disregarded them, I know not; certain, however, it is, that he was decoyed by the white wolf to this open space, when the animal appeared to slacken her speed. My father approached, came close up to her, raised his gun to his shoulder and was about to fire, when the wolf suddenly disappeared. He thought that the snow on the ground must have dazzled his sight, and he let down his gun to look for the beast—but she was gone; how she could have escaped over the clearance, without his seeing her, was beyond his comprehension. Mortified at the ill-success of his chase, he was about to retrace his steps, when he heard the distant sound of a horn. Astonishment at such a sound—at such an hour—in such a wilderness, made him forget for the moment his disappointment, and he remained riveted to the spot. In a minute the horn was blown a second time, and at no great distance; my father stood still, and listened; a third time it was blown. I forget the term used to express it, but it was the signal which, my father well knew, implied that the party was lost in the woods. In a few minutes more my father beheld a man on horseback, with a female seated on the crupper, enter the cleared space, and ride up to him. At first, my father called to mind the strange stories which he had heard of the supernatural beings who were said to frequent these mountains; but the nearer approach of the parties satisfied him that they were mortals like himself. As soon as they came up to him, the man who guided the horse accosted him. 'Friend hunter, you are out late, the better fortune for us; we have ridden far, and are in fear of our lives, which are eagerly sought after. These mountains have enabled us to elude our pursuers; but if we find not shelter and refreshment, that will avail us little, as we must perish from hunger and the inclemence of the night. My daughter, who rides behind me, is now more dead than alive—say, can you assist us in our difficulty?'

" 'My cottage is some few miles distant,' replied my father, 'but I have little to offer you besides a shelter from the weather; to the little I have you are welcome. May I ask whence you come?'

" 'Yes, friend, it is no secret now; we have escaped from Transylvania, where my daughter's honor and my life were equally in jeopardy!'

"This information was quite enough to raise an interest in my father's heart. He remembered his own escape: he remembered the loss of his wife's honor, and the tragedy by which it was wound up. He immediately, and warmly, offered all the assistance which he could afford them.

" 'There is no time to be lost, then, good sir,' observed the horseman; 'my daughter is chilled with the frost, and cannot hold out much longer against the severity of the weather.'

" 'Follow me,' replied my father, leading the way towards his home.

" 'I was lured away in pursuit of a large white wolf,' observed my father; 'it came to the very window of my hut, or I should not have been out at this time of night.'

" 'The creature passed by us just as we came out of the wood,' said the female, in a silvery tone.

" 'I was nearly discharging my piece at it,' observed the hunter; 'but since it did us such good service, I am glad that I allowed it to escape.'

"In about an hour and a half, during which my father

walked at a rapid pace, the party arrived at the cottage, and, as I said before, came in.

" 'We are in good time, apparently,' observed the dark hunter, catching the smell of the roasted meat, as he walked to the fire and surveyed my brother and sister and myself. 'You have young cooks here, Meinheer.' 'I am glad that we shall not have to wait,' replied my father. 'Come, mistress, seat yourself by the fire; you require warmth after your cold ride.' 'And where can I put up my horse, Meinheer?' observed the huntsman. 'I will take care of him,' replied my father, going out of the cottage door.

"The female must, however, be particularly described. She was young, and apparently twenty years of age. She was dressed in a traveling dress, deeply bordered with white fur, and wore a cap of white ermine on her head. Her features were very beautiful, at least I thought so, and so my father has since declared. Her hair was flaxen, glossy, and shining, and bright as a mirror; and her mouth, although somewhat large when it was open, showed the most brilliant teeth I have ever beheld. But there was something about her eyes, bright as they were, which made us children afraid; they were so restless, so furtive; I could not at that time tell why, but I felt as if there was cruelty in her eye; and when she beckoned us to come to her, we approached her with fear and trembling. Still she was beautiful, very beautiful. She spoke kindly to my brother and myself, patted our heads and caressed us; but Marcella would not come near her; on the contrary, she slunk away, and hid herself in the bed, and would not wait for the supper, which half an hour before she had been so anxious for.

"My father, having put the horse into a close shed, soon returned, and supper was placed on the table. When it was over, my father requested the young lady would take possession of the bed, and he would remain at the fire, and sit up with her father. After some hesitation on her part, this arrangement was agreed to, and I and my brother crept into the other bed with Marcella, for we had as yet always slept together.

"But we could not sleep; there was something so unusual, not only in seeing strange people, but in having these people sleep at the cottage, that we were bewildered. As for poor little Marcella, she was quiet, but I perceived that she trembled during the whole night, and sometimes I thought that she was checking a sob. My father had brought out some spirits, which he rarely used, and he and the strange hunter remained drinking and talking before the fire. Our ears were ready to catch the slightest whisper—so much was our curiosity excited.

" 'You said you came from Transylvania?' observed my father.

" 'Even so, Meinheer,' replied the hunter. 'I was a serf to the noble house of ————; my master would insist upon my surrendering up my fair girl to his wishes; it ended in my giving him a few inches of my hunting-knife.'

" 'We are countrymen and brothers in misfortune,' replied my father, taking the huntsman's hand and pressing it warmly.

" 'Indeed! Are you then from that country?'

" 'Yes; and I too have fled for my life. But mine is a melancholy tale.'

" 'Your name?' inquired the hunter.

" 'Krantz.'

" 'What! Krantz of ————? I have heard your tale; you need not renew your grief by repeating it now. Welcome, most welcome, Meinheer, and, I may say, my worthy kinsman. I am your second cousin, Wilfred of Barnsdorf,' cried the hunter, rising up and embracing my father.

"They filled their horn-mugs to the brim, and drank to one another after the German fashion. The conversation was then carried on in a low tone; all that we could collect from it was that our new relative and his daughter were to take up their abode in our cottage, at least for the present. In about an hour they both fell back in their chairs and appeared to sleep.

" 'Marcella, dear, did you hear?' said my brother, in a low tone.

" 'Yes,' replied Marcella, in a whisper, 'I heard all. Oh! brother, I cannot bear to look upon that woman—I feel so frightened.'

"My brother made no reply, and shortly afterwards we were all three fast asleep.

"When we awoke the next morning, we found that the hunter's daughter had risen before us. I thought she looked more beautiful than ever. She came up to little Marcella and caressed her; the child burst into tears, and sobbed as if her heart would break.

"But not to detain you with too long a story, the huntsman and his daughter were accommodated in the cottage. My father and he went out hunting daily, leaving Christina with us. She performed all the household duties; was very kind to us children; and gradually the dislike even of little Marcella wore away. But a great change took place in my father; he appeared to have conquered his aversion to the sex, and was

67

most attentive to Christina. Often, after her father and we were in bed, would he sit up with her, conversing in a low tone by the fire. I ought to have mentioned that my father and the huntsman Wilfred slept in another portion of the cottage, and that the bed which he formerly occupied, and which was in the same room as ours, had been given up to the use of Christina. These visitors had been about three weeks at the cottage, when, one night, after we children had been sent to bed, a consultation was held. My father had asked Christina in marriage, and had obtained both her own consent and that of Wilfred; after this, a conversation took place, which was, as nearly as I can recollect, as follows:—

" 'You may take my child, Meinheer Krantz, and my blessing with her, and I shall then leave you and seek some other habitation—it matters little where.'

" 'Why not remain here, Wilfred?'

" 'No, no, I am called elsewhere; let that suffice, and ask no more questions. You have my child.'

" 'I thank you for her, and will duly value her; but there is one difficulty.'

" 'I know what you would say; there is no priest here in this wild country; true; neither is there any law to bind. Still must some ceremony pass between you, to satisfy a father. Will you consent to marry her after my fashion? If so, I will marry you directly.'

" 'I will,' replied my father.

" 'Then take her by the hand. Now, Meinheer, swear.'

" 'I swear,' repeated my father.

" 'By all the spirits of the Hartz Mountains—'

" 'Nay, why not by Heaven?' interrupted my father.

" 'Because it is not my humor,' rejoined Wilfred. 'If I prefer that oath, less binding, perhaps, than another, surely you will not thwart me.'

" 'Well, be it so, then; have your humor. Will you make me swear by that in which I do not believe?'

" 'Yet many do so, who in outward appearance are Christians,' rejoined Wilfred; 'say, will you be married, or shall I take my daughter away with me?'

" 'Proceed,' replied my father impatiently.

" 'I swear by all the spirits of the Hartz Mountains, by all their power for good or for evil, that I take Christina for my wedded wife; that I will ever protect her, cherish her, and love her; that my hand shall never be raised against her to harm her.'

"My father repeated the words after Wilfred.

" 'And if I fail in this my vow, may all the vengeance of the spirits fall upon me and upon my children; may they perish by the vulture, by the wolf, or other beasts of the forest; may their flesh be torn from their limbs, and their bones blanch in the wilderness: all this I swear.'

"My father hesitated, as he repeated the last words; little Marcella could not restrain herself, and as my father repeated the last sentence, she burst into tears. This sudden interruption appeared to discompose the party, particularly my father; he spoke harshly to the child, who controlled her sobs, burying her face under the bedclothes.

"Such was the second marriage of my father. The next morning, the hunter Wilfred mounted his horse and rode away.

"My father resumed his bed, which was in the same room as ours; and things went on much as before the marriage, except that our new mother-in-law did not show any kindness towards us; indeed, during my father's absence, she would often beat us, particularly little Marcella, and her eyes would flash fire, as she looked eagerly upon the fair and lovely child.

"One night my sister awoke me and my brother.

" 'What is the matter?' said Caesar.

" 'She has gone out,' whispered Marcella.

" 'Gone out!'

" 'Yes, gone out at the door, in her night-clothes,' replied the child; 'I saw her get out of bed, look at my father to see if he slept, and then she went out at the door.'

"What could induce her to leave her bed, and all undressed to go out, in such bitter wintry weather, with the snow deep on the ground, was to us incomprehensible; we lay awake, and in about an hour we heard the growl of a wolf close under the window.

" 'There is a wolf,' said Caesar. 'She will be torn to pieces.'

" 'Oh, no!' cried Marcella.

"In a few minutes afterwards our mother-in-law appeared; she was in her night-dress, as Marcella had stated. She let down the latch of the door, so as to make no noise, went to a pail of water and washed her face and hands, and then slipped into the bed where my father lay.

"We all three trembled—we hardly knew why; but we resolved to watch the next night. We did so; and not only on the ensuing night, but on many others, and always at about the same hour, would our mother-in-law rise from her bed and leave the cottage; and after she was gone we invariably heard the growl of a wolf under our window, and always saw her on her return wash herself before she retired to bed. We observed also that she seldom sat down to meals, and that when she did she appeared to eat with dislike; but when the meat was taken down to be prepared for dinner, she would often furtively put a raw piece into her mouth.

"My brother Caesar was a courageous boy; he did not like to speak to my father until he knew more. He resolved that he would follow her out, and ascertain what she did. Marcella and I endeavored to dissuade him from the project; but he would not be controlled; and the very next night he lay down in his clothes, and as soon as our mother-in-law had left the cottage he jumped up, took down my father's gun, and followed her.

"You may imagine in what a state of suspense Marcella and I remained during his absence. After a few minutes we heard the report of a gun. It did not awaken my father; and we lay trembling with anxiety. In a minute afterwards we saw our mother-in-law enter the cottage—her dress was bloody. I put my hand to Marcella's mouth to prevent her crying out, although I was myself in great alarm. Our mother-in-law approached my father's bed, looked to see if he was asleep, and then went to the chimney and blew up the embers into a blaze.

" 'Who is there?' said my father, waking up.

" 'Lie still, dearest,' replied my mother-in-law; 'it is only me; I have lighted the fire to warm some water; I am not quite well.'

"My father turned round, and was soon asleep; but we watched our mother-in-law. She changed her linen, and threw the garments she had worn into the fire; and we then perceived that her right leg was bleeding profusely, as if from a gun-shot wound. She bandaged it up, and then dressing herself, remained before the fire until the break of day.

"Poor little Marcella, her heart beat quick as she pressed me to her side—so indeed did mine. Where was our brother Caesar? How did my mother-in-law receive the wound unless from his gun? At last my father rose, and then for the first time I spoke, saying, 'Father, where is my brother Caesar?'

" 'Your brother?' exclaimed he; 'why, where can he be?'

" 'Merciful Heaven! I thought as I lay very restless last night,' observed our mother-in-law, 'that I heard somebody open the latch of the door; and, dear me, husband, what has become of your gun?'

"My father cast his eyes up above the chimney, and perceived that his gun was missing. For a moment he looked perplexed; then, seizing a broad axe, he went out of the cottage without saying another word.

"He did not remain away from us long; in a few minutes he returned, bearing in his arms the mangled body of my poor brother; he laid it down, and covered up his face.

"My mother-in-law rose up, and looked at the body, while Marcella and I threw ourselves by its side, wailing and sobbing bitterly.

" 'Go to bed again, children,' said she sharply. 'Husband,' continued she, 'your boy must have taken the gun down to shoot a wolf, and the animal has been too powerful for him. Poor boy! he has paid dearly for his rashness.'

"My father made no reply. I wished to speak—to tell all—but Marcella, who perceived my intention, held me by the arm, and looked at me so imploringly, that I desisted.

"My father, therefore, was left in his error; but Marcella and I, although we could not comprehend it, were conscious that our mother-in-law was in some way connected with my brother's death.

"That day my father went out and dug a grave; and when he laid the body in the earth he piled up stones over it, so that the wolves should not be able to dig it up. The shock of this catastrophe was to my poor father very severe; for several days he never went to the chase, although at times he would utter bitter anathemas and vengeance against the wolves.

"But during this time of mourning on his part, my mother-in-law's nocturnal wanderings continued with the same regularity as before.

"At last my father took down his gun to repair to the forest; but he soon returned, and appeared much annoyed.

" 'Would you believe it, Christina, that the wolves—perdition to the whole race!—have actually contrived to dig up the body of my poor boy, and now there is nothing left of him but his bones.'

" 'Indeed!' replied my mother-in-law. Marcella looked at me, and I saw in her intelligent eye all she would have uttered.

" 'A wolf growls under our window every night, father,' said I.

" 'Ay, indeed! Why did you not tell me, boy? Wake me the next time you hear it.'

"I saw my mother-in-law turn away; her eyes flashed fire, and she gnashed her teeth.

"My father went out again, and covered up with a larger pile of stones the little remains of my poor brother which the wolves had spared. Such was the first act of the tragedy.

"The spring now came on; the snow disappeared, and we were permitted to leave the cottage; but never would I quit for one moment my dear little sister, to whom, since the death of my brother, I was more ardently attached than ever; indeed, I was afraid to leave her alone with my mother-in-law, who appeared to have a particular pleasure in ill-treating the child. My father was now employed upon his little farm, and I was able to render him some assistance.

"Marcella used to sit by us while we were at work, leaving my mother-in-law alone in the cottage. I ought to observe that, as the spring advanced, so did my mother-in-law decrease her nocturnal rambles, and that we never heard the growl of the wolf under the window after I had spoken of it to my father.

"One day, when my father and I were in the field, Marcella being with us, my mother-in-law came out, saying that she was going into the forest to collect some herbs my father wanted, and that Marcella must go to the cottage and watch the dinner. Marcella went; and my mother-in-law soon disappeared in the forest, taking a direction quite contrary to that in which the cottage stood, and leaving my father and me, as it were, between her and Marcella.

"About an hour afterwards we were startled by shrieks from the cottage—evidently the shrieks of little Marcella. 'Marcella has burnt herself, father,' said I, throwing down my spade. My father threw down his, and we both hastened to the cottage. Before we could gain the door, out darted a large white wolf, which fled with the utmost celerity. My father had no weapon; he rushed into the cottage, and there saw poor little Marcella expiring. Her body was dreadfully mangled and the blood pouring from it had formed a large pool on the cottage floor. My father's first intention had been to seize his gun and pursue; but he was checked by this horrid spectacle; he knelt down by his dying child, and burst into tears. Marcella could just look kindly on us for a few seconds, and then her eyes were closed in death.

"My father and I were still hanging over my poor sister's body when my mother-in-law came in. At the dreadful sight she expressed much concern; but she did not appear to recoil from the sight of blood, as most women do.

"'Poor child!' said she, 'it must have been that great white wolf which passed me just now, and frightened me so. She's quite dead, Krantz.'

"'I know it!—I know it!' cried my father, in agony.

"I thought my father would never recover from the effects of this second tragedy; he mourned bitterly over the body of his sweet child, and for several days would not consign it to its grave, although frequently requested by my mother-in-law to do so. At last he yielded, and dug a grave for her close by that of my poor brother, and took every precaution that the wolves should not violate her remains.

"I was now really miserable as I lay alone in the bed which

I had formerly shared with my brother and sister. I could not help thinking that my mother-in-law was implicated in both their deaths, although I could not account for the manner; but I no longer felt afraid of her; my little heart was full of hatred and revenge.

"The night after my sister had been buried, as I lay awake, I perceived my mother-in-law get up and go out of the cottage. I waited some time, then dressed myself, and looked out through the door, which I half opened. The moon shone bright, and I could see the spot where my brother and my sister had been buried; and what was my horror when I perceived my mother-in-law busily removing the stones from Marcella's grave!

"She was in her white night-dress, and the moon shone full upon her. She was digging with her hands and throwing away the stones behind her with all the ferocity of a wild beast. It was some time before I could collect my senses and decide what I should do. At last I perceived that she had arrived at the body, and raised it up to the side of the grave. I could bear it no longer: I ran to my father and awoke him.

"'Father, father!' cried I, 'dress yourself, and get your gun.'

"'What!' cried my father, 'the wolves are there, are they?'

"He jumped out of bed, threw on his clothes, and in his anxiety did not appear to perceive the absence of his wife. As soon as he was ready I opened the door, he went out, and I followed him.

"Imagine his horror, when (unprepared as he was for such a sight) he beheld, as he advanced towards the grave, not a wolf, but his wife, in her night-dress, on her hands and knees, crouching by the body of my sister, and tearing off large pieces of the flesh, and devouring them with all the avidity of a wolf. She was too busy to be aware of our approach. My father dropped his gun; his hair stood on end, so did mine; he breathed heavily, and then his breath for a time stopped. I picked up the gun and put it into his hand. Suddenly he appeared as if concentrated rage had restored him to double vigor; he leveled his piece, fired, and with a loud shriek down fell the wretch whom he had fostered in his bosom.

"'God of heaven!' cried my father, sinking down upon the earth in a swoon, as soon as he had discharged his gun.

"I remained some time by his side before he recovered. 'Where am I?' said he, 'what has happened? Oh!—yes, yes! I recollect now. Heaven forgive me!'

"He rose and we walked up to the grave; what again was our astonishment and horror to find that, instead of the dead body of my mother-in-law, as we expected, there was lying over the remains of my poor sister a large white she-wolf.

" 'The white wolf,' exclaimed my father, 'the white wolf which decoyed me into the forest—I see it all now—I have dealt with the spirits of the Hartz Mountains.'

"For some time my father remained in silence and deep thought. He then carefully lifted up the body of my sister, replaced it in the grave, and covered it over as before, having struck the head of the dead animal with the heel of his boot, and raving like a madman. He walked back to the cottage, shut the door, and threw himself on the bed; I did the same, for I was in a stupor of amazement.

"Early in the morning we were both roused by a loud knocking at the door, and in rushed the hunter Wilfred.

" 'My daugher—man—my daughter!—where is my daughter?' cried he in a rage.

" 'Where the wretch, the fiend should be, I trust,' replied my father, starting up, and displaying equal choler: 'where she should be—in hell! Leave this cottage, or you may fare worse.'

" 'Ha—ha!' replied the hunter, 'would you harm a potent spirit of the Hartz Mountains? Poor mortal, who must needs wed a werewolf.'

" 'Out, demon! I defy thee and thy power.'

" 'Yet shall you feel it; remember your oath—your solemn oath—never to raise your hand against her to harm her.'

" 'I made no compact with evil spirits.'

" 'You did, and if you failed in your vow, you were to meet the vengeance of the spirits. Your children were to perish by the vulture, the wolf—'

" 'Out, out, demon!'

" 'And their bones blanch in the wilderness. Ha—ha!'

"My father, frantic with rage, seized his axe and raised it over Wilfred's head to strike.

" 'All this I swear,' continued the huntsman mockingly.

"The axe descended; but it passed through the form of the hunter, and my father lost his balance, and fell heavily on the floor.

" 'Mortal!' said the hunter, striding over my father's body, 'we have power over those only who have committed murder. You have been guilty of a double murder: you shall pay the penalty attached to your marriage vow. Two of your children are gone, the third is yet to follow—and follow them he will, for your oath is registered. Go—it were kindness to kill thee—your punishment is, that you live!'

"With these words the spirit disappeared. My father rose

from the floor, embraced me tenderly, and knelt down in prayer.

"The next morning he quitted the cottage for ever. He took me with him, and bent his steps to Holland, where we safely arrived. He had some little money with him; but he had not been many days in Amsterdam before he was seized with a brain fever, and died raving mad. I was put into the asylum, and afterwards was sent to sea before the mast. You now know all my history. The question is, whether I am to pay the penalty of my father's oath? I am myself perfectly convinced that, in some way or another, I shall."

II

On the twenty-second day the high land of the south of Sumatra was in view: as there were no vessels in sight, they resolved to keep their course through the Straits, and run for Pulo Penang, which they expected, as their vessel lay so close to the wind, to reach in seven or eight days. By constant exposure Philip and Krantz were now so bronzed, that with their long beards and Mussulman dresses, they might easily have passed off for natives. They had steered during the whole of the days exposed to a burning sun; they had lain down and slept in the dew of the night; but their health had not suffered. But for several days, since he had confided the history of his family to Philip, Krantz had become silent and melancholy; his usual flow of spirits had vanished, and Philip had often questioned him as to the cause. As they entered the Straits, Philip talked of what they should do upon their arrival at Goa; when Krantz gravely replied, "For some days, Philip, I have had a presentiment that I shall never see that city."

"You are out of health, Krantz," replied Philip.

"No, I am in sound health, body and mind. I have endeavored to shake off the presentiment, but in vain; there is a warning voice that continually tells me that I shall not be long with you. Philip, will you oblige me by making me content on one point? I have gold about my person which may be useful to you; oblige me by taking it, and securing it on your own."

"What nonsense, Krantz."

"It is no nonsense, Philip. You know that I have little fear in my composition, and that I care not about death; but I feel the presentiment which I speak of more strongly every hour."

"These are the imaginings of a disturbed brain, Krantz; why you, young, in full health and vigor, should not pass your days in peace, and live to a good old age, there is no cause for believing. You will be better tomorrow."

"Perhaps so," replied Krantz; "but you still must yield to my whim, and take the gold. If I am wrong, and we do arrive safe, you know, Philip, you can let me have it back," observed Krantz, with a faint smile—"but you forget, our water is nearly out, and we must look out for a rill on the coast to obtain a fresh supply."

"I was thinking of that when you commenced this unwelcome topic. We had better look out for the water before dark, and as soon as we have replenished our jars, we will make sail again."

At the time that this conversation took place, they were on the eastern side of the Strait, about forty miles to the northward. The interior of the coast was rocky and mountainous, but it slowly descended to low land of alternate forest and jungles, which continued to the beach; the country appeared to be uninhabited. Keeping close in to the shore, they discovered, after two hours' run, a fresh stream which burst in a cascade from the mountains, and swept its devious course through the jungle, until it poured its tribute into the waters of the Strait.

They ran close into the mouth of the stream, lowered the sails, and pulled the peroqua against the current, until they had advanced far enough to assure them that the water was quite fresh. The jars were soon filled, and they were again thinking of pushing off, when enticed by the beauty of the spot, the coolness of the fresh water, and wearied with their long confinement on board of the peroqua, they proposed to bathe—a luxury hardly to be appreciated by those who have not been in a similar situation. They threw off their Mussulman dresses, and plunged into the stream, where they remained for some time. Krantz was the first to get out; he complained of feeling chilled, and he walked on to the banks where their clothes had been laid. Philip also approached nearer to the beach, intending to follow him.

"And now, Philip," said Krantz, "this will be a good opportunity for me to give you the money. I will open my sash and pour it out, and you can put it into your own before you put it on."

Philip was standing in the water, which was about level with his waist.

"Well, Krantz," said he, "I suppose if it must be so, it must; but it appears to me an idea so ridiculous—however, you shall have your own way."

Philip quitted the run, and sat down by Krantz, who was

76

already busy in shaking the doubloons out of the folds of his sash; at last he said—

"I believe, Philip, you have got them all, now?—I feel satisfied."

"What danger there can be to you, which I am not equally exposed to, I cannot conceive," replied Philip; "however—"

Hardly had he said these words, when there was a tremendous roar—a rush like a mighty wind through the air—a blow which threw him on his back—a loud cry—and a contention. Philip recovered himself, and perceived the naked form of Krantz carried off with the speed of an arrow by an enormous tiger through the jungle. He watched with distended eyeballs; in a few seconds the animal and Krantz had disappeared.

"God of heaven! would that Thou hadst spared me this," cried Philip, throwing himself down in agony on his face. "O Krantz! my friend—my brother—too sure was your presentiment. Merciful God! have pity—but Thy will be done." And Philip burst into a flood of tears.

For more than an hour did he remain fixed upon the spot, careless and indifferent to the danger by which he was surrounded. At last, somewhat recovered, he rose, dressed himself, and then again sat down—his eyes fixed upon the clothes of Krantz, and the gold which still lay on the sand.

"He would give me that gold. He foretold his doom. Yes! yes! it was his destiny, and it has been fulfilled. *His bones will bleach in the wilderness,* and the spirit-hunter and his wolfish daughter are avenged."

ONE OF THE DEAD

William Wood

We couldn't have been more pleased. Deep in Clay Canyon we came upon the lot abruptly at a turn in the winding road. There was a crudely lettered board nailed to a dead tree which read, LOT FOR SALE—$1500 OR BEST OFFER, and a phone number.

"Fifteen hundred dollars—in Clay Canyon? I can't believe it," Ellen said.

"Or best offer," I corrected.

"I've heard you can't take a step without bumping into some movie person here."

"We've come three miles already without bumping into one. I haven't seen a soul."

"But there are the houses." Ellen looked about breathlessly.

There indeed were the houses—to our left and our right, to our front and our rear—low, ranch-style houses, unostentatious, prosaic, giving no hint of the gay and improbable lives we imagined went on inside them. But as the houses marched up the gradually climbing road there was not a single person to be seen. The cars—the Jaguars and Mercedeses and Cadillacs and Chryslers—were parked unattended in the driveways, their chrome gleaming in the sun; I caught a glimpse of one corner of a pool and a white diving board, but no one swam in the turquoise water. We climbed out of the car, Ellen with her rather large, short-haired head stooped forward as if under a weight. Except for the fiddling of a cicada somewhere on the hill, a profound hush lay over us in the stifling air. Not even a bird moved in the motionless trees.

"There must be something wrong with it," Ellen said.

"It's probably already been sold, and they just didn't bother to take down the sign. There was something here once, though." I had come across several ragged chunks of concrete that lay about randomly as if heaved out of the earth.

"A house, do you think?"

"It's hard to say. If it was a house it's been gone for years."

"Oh, Ted," Ellen cried. "It's perfect! Look at the view!" She pointed up the canyon toward the round, parched hills. Through the heat shimmering on the road they appeared to be melting down like wax.

"Another good thing," I said. "There won't be much to do to get the ground ready except for clearing the brush away. This place has been graded once. We save a thousand dollars right there."

Ellen took both my hands. Her eyes shone in her solemn face. "What do you think, Ted? What do you think?"

Ellen and I had been married four years, having both taken the step relatively late—in our early thirties—and in that time had lived in two different places, first an apartment in Santa Monica, then, when I was promoted to office manager, in a partly furnished house in the Hollywood Hills, always with the idea that when our first child came we would either buy or build a larger house of our own. But the child had not come. It was a source of anxiety and sadness to us both and lay between us like an old scandal for which each of us took on the blame.

Then I made an unexpected killing on the stock market and Ellen suddenly began agitating in her gentle way for the house. As we shopped around she dropped hints along the way—"This place is really too small for us, don't you think?" or "We'd have to fence off the yard of course"—that let me know that the house had become a talisman for her; she had conceived the notion that perhaps, in some occult way, if we went ahead with our accommodations for a child the child might come. The notion gave her happiness. Her face filled out, the gray circles under her eyes disappeared, the quiet gaiety, which did not seem like gaiety at all but a form of peace, returned.

As Ellen held on to my hands, I hesitated. I am convinced now that there was something behind my hesitation— something I felt then only as a quality of silence, a fleeting twinge of utter isolation. "It's so safe," she said. "There's no traffic at all."

I explained that. "It's not a through street. It ends somewhere up in the hills."

She turned back to me again with her bright, questioning eyes. The happiness that had grown in her during our months of house-hunting seemed to have welled into near rapture.

"We'll call the number," I said, "but don't expect too much. It must have been sold long ago."

We walked slowly back to the car. The door handle burned to the touch. Down the canyon the rear end of a panel truck disappeared noiselessly around a bend.

"No," Ellen said, "I have a feeling about this place. I think it was meant to be ours."

And she was right, of course.

Mr. Carswell Deeves, who owned the land, was called upon to do very little except take my check for $1500 and hand over the deed to us, for by the time Ellen and I met him we had already sold ourselves. Mr. Deeves, as we had suspected from the unprofessional sign, was a private citizen. We found his house in a predominantly Mexican section of Santa Monica. He was a chubby, pink man of indeterminate age dressed in white ducks and soft, white shoes, as if he had had a tennis court hidden away among the squalid, asphalt-shingled houses and dry kitchen gardens of his neighbors.

"Going to live in Clay Canyon, are you?" he said. "Ros Russell lives up there, or used to." So, we discovered, did Joel McCrea, Jimmy Stewart and Paula Raymond, as well as a cross-section of producers, directors and character actors. "Oh, yes," said Mr. Deeves, "it's an address that will look extremely good on your stationery."

Ellen beamed and squeezed my hand.

Mr. Deeves turned out to know very little about the land other than that a house had been destroyed by fire three years ago and that the land had changed hands many times since. "I myself acquired it in what may strike you as a novel way," he said as we sat in his parlor—a dark, airless box which smelled faintly of camphor and whose walls were obscured with yellowing autographed photographs of movie stars. "I won it in a game of hearts from a makeup man on the set of *Quo Vadis*. Perhaps you remember me. I had a close-up in one of the crowd scenes."

"That was a number of years ago, Mr. Deeves," I said. "Have you been trying to sell it all this time?"

"I've nearly sold it dozens of times," he said, "but something always went wrong somehow."

"What kind of things?"

"Naturally, the fire-insurance rates up there put off a lot of people. I hope you're prepared to pay a high premium——"

"I've already checked into that."

"Good. You'd be surprised how many people will let details like that go till the last minute."

"What other things have gone wrong?"

Ellen touched my arm to discourage my wasting any more time with foolish questions.

Mr. Deeves spread out the deed before me and smoothed it with his forearm. "Silly things, some of them. One couple found some dead doves."

"Dead doves?" I handed him the signed article. With one

80

pink hand Mr. Deeves waved it back and forth to dry the ink. "Five of them, if I remember correctly. In my opinion they'd sat on a wire and were electrocuted somehow. The husband thought nothing of it, of course, but his wife became so hysterical that we had to call off the transaction."

I made a sign at Mr. Deeves to drop this line of conversation. Ellen loves animals and birds of all kinds with a devotion that turns the loss of a household pet into a major tragedy, which is why, since the death of our cocker spaniel, we have had no more pets. But Ellen appeared not to have heard; she was watching the paper in Mr. Deeves' hand fixedly, as if she were afraid it might vanish.

Mr. Deeves sprang suddenly to his feet. "Well!" he cried. "It's all yours now. I know you'll be happy there."

Ellen flushed with pleasure. "I'm sure we will," she said, and took his pudgy hand in both of hers.

"A prestige address," called Mr. Deeves from his porch as we drove away. "A real prestige address."

Ellen and I are modern people. Our talk in the evenings is generally on issues of the modern world. Ellen paints a little and I do some writing from time to time—mostly on technical subjects. The house that Ellen and I built mirrored our concern with present-day aesthetics. We worked closely with Jack Salmanson, the architect and a friend, who designed a steel module house, low and compact and private, which could be fitted into the irregularities of our patch of land for a maximum of space. The interior *dècor* we left largely up to Ellen, who combed the home magazines and made sketches as if she were decorating a dozen homes.

I mention these things to show that there is nothing Gothic about my wife and me: We are as thankful for our common sense as for our sensibilities, and we flattered ourselves that the house we built achieved a balance between the aesthetic and the functional. Its lines were simple and clean; there were no dark corners, and it was surrounded on three sides by houses, none of which were more than eight years old.

There were, however, signs from the very beginning, ominous signs which can be read only in retrospect, though it seems to me now that there were others who suspected but said nothing. One was the Mexican who cut down the tree.

As a money-saving favor to us, Jack Salmanson agreed to supervise the building himself and hire small, independent contractors to do the labor, many of whom were Mexicans or Negroes with dilapidated equipment that appeared to run only by some mechanical miracle. The Mexican, a small, forlorn workman with a stringy moustache, had already burned out two chain-saw blades and still had not cut half-way through the tree. It was inexplicable. The tree, the same one on which Ellen and I had seen the original FOR SALE sign, had obviously been dead for years, and the branches that already lay scattered on the ground were rotted through.

"You must have run into a batch of knots," Jack said. "Try it again. If the saw gets too hot, quit and we'll pull it down with the bulldozer." As if answering to its name, the bulldozer turned at the back of the lot and lumbered toward us in a cloud of dust, the black shoulders of the Negro operator gleaming in the sun.

The Mexican need not have feared for his saw. He had scarcely touched it to the tree when it started to topple of its own accord. Startled, he backed away a few steps. The tree had begun to fall toward the back of the lot, in the direction of his cut, but now it appeared to arrest itself, its naked branches trembling as if in agitation; then with an awful rending sound it writhed upright and fell back on itself, gaining momentum and plunging directly at the bulldozer. My voice died in my throat, but Jack and the Mexican shouted, and the operator jumped and rolled on the ground just as the tree fell high on the hood, shattering the windshield to bits. The bulldozer, out of control and knocked off course, came directly at us, gears whining and gouging a deep trough in the earth. Jack and I jumped one way, the Mexican the other; the bulldozer lurched between us and ground on toward the street, the Negro sprinting after it.

"The car!" Jack shouted. "The car!"

Parked in front of the house across the street was a car, a car which was certainly brand-new. The bulldozer headed straight for it, its blade striking clusters of sparks from the pavement. The Mexican waved his chain saw over his head like a toy and shouted in Spanish. I covered my eyes with my hands and heard Jack grunt softly, as if he had been struck in the midsection, just before the crash.

Two women stood on the porch of the house across the street and gaped. The car had caved in at the center, its steel roof wrinkled like tissue paper; its front and rear ends were folded around the bulldozer as if embracing it. Then, with a low whoosh, both vehicles were enveloped in creeping blue flame.

"Rotten luck," Jack muttered under his breath as we ran into the street. From the corner of my eye I caught the curious sight of the Mexican on the ground, praying, his chain saw lying by his knees.

In the evening Ellen and I paid a visit to the Sheffits', Sondra and Jeff, our neighbors across the canyon road, where we met the owner of the ruined car, Joyce Castle, a striking blonde in lemon-colored pants. The shock of the accident itself wore off with the passing of time and cocktails, and the three of them treated it as a tremendous joke.

Mrs. Castle was particularly hilarious. "I'm doing better," she rejoiced. "The Alfa-Romeo only lasted two days, but I held on to this one a whole six weeks. I even had the permanent plates on."

"But you mustn't be without a car, Mrs. Castle," Ellen said in her serious way. "We'd be glad to loan you our Plymouth until you can—"

"I'm having a new car delivered tomorrow afternoon. Don't worry about me. A Daimler, Jeff, you'll be interested to know I couldn't resist after riding in yours. What about the poor bulldozer man? Is he absolutely wiped out?"

"I think he'll survive," I said. "In any case he has two other 'dozers."

"Then you won't be held up," Jeff said.

"I wouldn't think so."

Sondra chuckled softly. "I just happened to look out the window," she said. "It was just like a Rube Goldberg cartoon. A chain reaction."

"And there was my poor old Cadillac at the end of it," Mrs. Castle sighed.

Suey, Mrs. Castle's dog, who had been lying on the floor beside his mistress glaring dourly at us between dozes, suddenly ran to the front door barking ferociously, his red mane standing straight up.

"Suey!" Mrs. Castle slapped her knee. "Suey! Come here!"

The dog merely flattened its ears and looked from his mistress toward the door again as if measuring a decision. He growled deep in his throat.

"It's the ghost," Sondra said lightly. "He's behind the whole thing." Sondra sat curled up in one corner of the sofa and tilted her head to one side as she spoke, like a very clever child.

Jeff laughed sharply. "Oh, they tell some very good stories."

With a sigh Mrs. Castle rose and dragged Suey back by his collar. "If I didn't feel so self-conscious about it I'd take him to an analyst," she said. "Sit, Suey! Here's a cashew nut for you."

"I'm very fond of ghost stories," I said, smiling

"Oh, well," Jeff murmured, mildly disparaging.

"Go ahead, Jeff," Sondra urged him over the rim of her glass. "They'd like to hear it."

Jeff was a literary agent, a tall, sallow man with dark oily hair that he was continually pushing out of his eyes with his fingers. As he spoke he smiled lopsidedly as if defending against the probability of being taken seriously. "All I know is that back in the late seventeenth century the Spanish used to have hangings here. The victims are supposed to float around at night and make noises."

"Criminals?" I asked.

"Of the worst sort," said Sondra. "What was the story Guy Relling told you, Joyce?" She smiled with a curious inward relish that suggested she knew the story perfectly well herself.

"Is that Guy Relling, the director?" I asked.

"Yes," Jeff said. "He owns those stables down the canyon."

"I've seen them," Ellen said. "Such lovely horses."

Joyce Castle hoisted her empty glass into the air. "Jeff, love, will you find me another?"

"We keep straying from the subject," said Sondra gently. "Fetch me another too, darling"—she handed her glass to Jeff as he went by—"like a good boy. I didn't mean to interrupt, Joyce. Go on." She gestured toward us as the intended audience. Ellen stiffened slightly in her chair.

"It seems that there was one *hombre* of outstanding depravity," Joyce Castle said languidly. "I forget the name. He murdered, stole, raped ... one of those endless Spanish names with a 'Luis' in it, a nobleman I think Guy said. A charming sort. Mad, of course, and completely unpredictable. They hanged him at last for some unsavory escapade in a nunnery. You two are moving into a neighborhood rich with tradition."

We all laughed.

"What about the noises?" Ellen asked Sondra. "Have you heard anything?"

"Of course," Sondra said, tipping her head prettily. Every inch of her skin was tanned to the color of coffee from afternoons by the pool. It was a form of leisure that her husband, with his bilious coloring and lank hair, apparently did not enjoy.

"Everywhere I've ever lived," he said, his grin growing crookeder and more apologetic, "there were noises in the night that you couldn't explain. Here there are all kinds of wildlife—foxes, coons, possums—even coyotes up on the ridge. They're all active after sundown."

Ellen's smile of pleasure at this news turned to distress as Sondra remarked in her offhand way, "We found our poor kitty-cat positively torn to pieces one morning. He was all blood. We never did find his head."

"A fox," Jeff put in quickly. Everything he said seemed

hollow. Something came from him like a vapor. I thought it was grief.

Sondra gazed smugly into her lap as if hugging a secret to herself. She seemed enormously pleased. It occurred to me that Sondra was trying to frighten us. In a way it relieved me. She was enjoying herself too much, I thought, looking at her spoiled, brown face, to be frightened herself.

After the incident of the tree everything went well for some weeks. The house went up rapidly. Ellen and I visited it as often as we could, walking over the raw ground and making our home in our mind's eye. The fireplace would go here, the refrigerator here, our Picasso print there. "Ted," Ellen said timidly, "I've been thinking. Why don't we fix up the extra bedroom as a children's room?"

I waited.

"Now that we'll be living out here our friends will have to stay overnight more often. Most of them have young children. It would be nice for them."

I slipped my arm around her shoulders. She knew I understood. It was a delicate matter. She raised her face and I kissed her between her brows. Signal and countersignal, the keystones of our life together—a life of sensibility and tact.

"Hey, you two!" Sondra Sheffits called from across the street. She stood on her front porch in a pink bathing suit, her skin brown, her hair nearly white. "How about a swim?"

"No suits!"

"Come on, we've got plenty."

Ellen and I debated the question with a glance, settled it with a nod.

As I came out onto the patio in one of Jeff's suits, Sondra said, "Ted, you're pale as a ghost. Don't you get any sun where you are?" She lay in a chaise longue behind huge elliptical sunglasses encrusted with glass gems.

"I stay inside too much, writing articles," I said.

"You're welcome to come here any time you like"—she smiled suddenly, showing me a row of small, perfect teeth—"and swim."

Ellen appeared in her borrowed suit, a red one with a short, limp ruffle. She shaded her eyes as the sun, glittering metallically on the water, struck her full in the face.

Sondra ushered her forward as if to introduce my wife to me. "You look much better in that suit than I ever did." Her red nails flashed on Ellen's arm. Ellen smiled guardedly. The two women were about the same height, but Ellen was narrower in the shoulders, thicker through the waist and hips. As they came toward me it seemed to me that Ellen was the one I did not know. Her familiar body became strange. It looked out of proportion. Hairs that on Sondra were all but invisible except when the sun turned them to silver, lay flat and dark on Ellen's pallid arm.

As if sensing the sudden distance between us, Ellen took my hand. "Let's jump in together," she said gaily. "No hanging back."

Sondra retreated to the chaise longue to watch us, her eyes invisible behind her outrageous glasses, her head on one side.

Incidents began again and continued at intervals. Guy Relling, whom I never met but whose pronouncements on the supernatural reached me through others from time to time like messages from an oracle, claims that the existence of the living dead is a particularly excruciating one as they hover between two states of being. Their memories keep the passions of life forever fresh and sharp, but they are able to relieve them only at a monstrous expense of will and energy which leaves them literally helpless for months or sometimes even years afterward. This was why materializations and other forms of tangible action are relatively rare. There are of course exceptions, Sondra, our most frequent translator of Relling's theories, pointed out one evening with the odd joy that accompanied all of her remarks on the subject; some ghosts are terrifically active—particularly the insane ones who, ignorant of the limitations of death as they were of the impossibilities of life, transcend them with the dynamism that is exclusively the property of madness. Generally, however, it was Relling's opinion that a ghost was more to be pitied than feared. Sondra quoted him as having said, "The notion of a haunted house is a misconception semantically. It is not the house but the soul itself that is haunted."

On Saturday, August 6, a workman laying pipe was blinded in one eye by an acetylene torch.

On Thursday, September 1, a rockslide on the hill behind us dumped four tons of dirt and rock on the half-finished house and halted work for two weeks.

On Sunday, October 9—my birthday, oddly enough—while visiting the house alone, I slipped on a stray screw and struck my head on a can of latex paint which opened up a gash requiring ten stitches. I rushed across to the Sheffits'. Sondra answered the door in her bathing suit and a magazine in her hand. "Ted?" She peered at me. "I scarcely recognized you through the blood. Come in, I'll call the doctor. Try not to drip on the furniture, will you?"

I told the doctor of the screw on the floor, the big can of paint. I did not tell him that my foot had slipped because I had turned too quickly because the sensation had grown on me that there was someone behind me, close enough to touch me, perhaps, because something hovered there, fetid and damp and cold and almost palpable in its nearness; I remember shivering violently as I turned, as if the sun of this burning summer's day had been replaced by a mysterious star without warmth. I did not tell the doctor this nor anyone else.

In November Los Angeles burns. After the long drought of summer the sap goes underground and the baked hills seem to gasp in pain for the merciful release of either life or death—rain or fire. Invariably fire comes first, spreading through the outlying parts of the country like an epidemic, till the sky is livid and starless at night and overhung with dun-colored smoke during the day.

There was a huge fire in Tujunga, north of us, the day Ellen and I moved into our new house—handsome, severe, aggressively new on its dry hillside—under a choked sky the color of earth and a muffled, flyspeck sun. Sondra and Jeff came over to help, and in the evening Joyce Castle stopped by with Suey and a magnum of champagne.

Ellen clasped her hands under her chin. "What a lovely surprise!"

"I hope it's cold enough. I've had it in my refrigerator since four o'clock. Welcome to the canyon. You're nice people. You remind me of my parents. God, it's hot. I've been weeping all day on account of the smoke. You'll have air conditioning I suppose?"

Jeff was sprawled in a chair with his long legs straight in front of him in the way a cripple might put aside a pair of crutches. "Joyce, you're an angel. Excuse me if I don't get up. I'm recuperating."

"You're excused, doll, you're excused."

"Ted," Ellen said softly. "Why don't you get some glasses?"

Jeff hauled in his legs. "Can I give you a hand?"

"Sit still, Jeff."

He sighed. "I hadn't realized I was so out of shape." He looked more cadaverous than ever after our afternoon of lifting and shoving. Sweat had collected in the hollows under his eyes.

"Shall I show you the house, Joyce? While Ted is in the kitchen?"

"I love you, Ellen," Joyce said. "Take me on the whole tour."

Sondra followed me into the kitchen. She leaned against the wall and smoked, supporting her left elbow in the palm of her right hand. She didn't say a word. Through the open door I could see Jeff's outstretched legs from the calves down.

"Thanks for all the help today," I said to Sondra in a voice unaccountably close to a whisper. I could hear Joyce and Ellen as they moved from room to room, their voices swelling and dying: "It's all steel? You mean everything? Walls and all? Aren't you afraid of lightning?"

"Oh, we're all safely grounded, I think."

Jeff yawned noisily in the living room. Wordlessly Sondra put a tray on the kitchen table as I rummaged in an unpacked carton for the glasses. She watched me steadily and coolly, as if she expected me to entertain her. I wanted to say something further to break a silence which was becoming unnatural and oppressive. The sounds around us seemed only to isolate us in a ring of intimacy. With her head on one side Sondra smiled at me. I could hear her rapid breathing.

"What's this, a nursery? Ellen, love!"

"No, no! It's only for our friends' children."

Sondra's eyes were blue, the color of shallow water. She seemed faintly amused, as if we were sharing in a conspiracy—a conspiracy I was anxious to repudiate by making some prosaic remark in a loud voice for all to hear, but a kind of pain developed in my chest as the words seemed dammed there, and I only smiled at her foolishly. With every passing minute of silence, the more impossible it became to break through and the more I felt drawn in to the intrigue of which, though I was ignorant, I was surely guilty. Without so much as a touch she had made us lovers.

Ellen stood in the doorway, half turned away as if her first impulse had been to run. She appeared to be deep in thought, her eyes fixed on the steel, cream-colored doorjamb.

Sondra began to talk to Ellen in her dry, satirical voice. It was chatter of the idlest sort, but she was destroying, as I had wished to destroy, the absurd notion that there was something between us. I could see Ellen's confusion. She hung on Sondra's words, watching her lips attentively, as if this elegant, tanned woman, calmly smoking and talking of trifles, were her savior.

As for myself, I felt as if I had lost the power of speech entirely. If I joined in with Sondra's carefully innocent chatter I would only be joining in the deception against my wife; if I proclaimed the truth and ended everything by bringing it into the open. . . . but what truth? What was there in fact to bring into the open? What was there to end? A feeling in the air? An intimation? The answer was nothing, of course. I did not even like Sondra very much. There was something cold and unpleasant about her. There was nothing to proclaim because nothing had happened. "Where's Joyce?" I asked finally, out of a dry mouth. "Doesn't she want to see the kitchen?"

Ellen turned slowly toward me, as if it cost her a great effort. "She'll be here in a minute," she said tonelessly, and I became aware of Joyce's and Jeff's voices from the living room. Ellen studied my face, her pupils oddly dilated under the pinkish fluorescent light, as if she were trying to penetrate to the bottom of a great darkness that lay beneath my chance remark. Was it a code of some kind, a new signal for her that I would shortly make clear? What did it mean? I smiled at her and she responded with a smile of her own, a tentative and formal upturning of her mouth, as if I were a familiar face whose name escaped her for the moment.

Joyce came in behind Ellen. "I hate kitchens. I never go into mine." She looked from one to the other of us. "Am I interrupting something?"

At two o'clock in the morning I sat up in bed, wide awake. The bedroom was bathed in the dark red glow of the fire which had come closer in the night. A thin, autumnal veil of smoke hung in the room. Ellen lay on her side, asleep, one hand cupped on the pillow next to her face as if waiting for something to be put in it. I had no idea why I was so fully awake, but I threw off the covers and went to the window to check on the fire. I could see no flame, but the hills stood out blackly against a turgid sky that belled and sagged as the wind blew and relented.

Then I heard the sound.

I am a person who sets store by precision in the use of words—in the field of technical writing this is a necessity. But I can think of no word to describe that sound. The closest I can come with a word of my own invention is "vlump." It came erratically, neither loud nor soft. It was, rather, pervasive and without location. It was not a *solid* sound. There was something vague and whispering about it, and from time to time it began with the suggestion of a sigh—a shuffling dissipation in the air that seemed to take form and die in the same instant. In a way I cannot define, it was mindless, without will or reason, yet implacable. Because I could not explain it immediately I went to seek an explanation.

I stepped into the hall and switched on the light, pressing the noiseless button. The light came down out of a fixture set flush into the ceiling and diffused through a milky plastic like Japanese rice paper. The clean, indestructible walls rose perpendicularly around me. Through the slight haze of smoke came the smell of the newness, sweet and metallic—more like a car than a house. And still the sound went on. It seemed to be coming from the room at the end of the hall, the room we had designed for our friends' children. The door was open and I could see a gray patch that was a west window. Vlump ... vlump ... vlumpvlump. ...

Fixing on the gray patch, I moved down the hall while my legs made themselves heavy as logs, and all the while I repeated to myself, "The house is settling. All new houses settle and make strange noises." And so lucid was I that I believed I was not afraid. I was walking down the bright new hall of my new steel house to investigate a noise, for the house might be settling unevenly, or an animal might be up to some mischief—raccoons regularly raided the garbage cans, I had been told. There might be something wrong with the plumbing or with the radiant-heating system that warmed our steel and vinyl floors. And now, like the responsible master of the house, I had located the apparent center of the sound and was going responsibly toward it. In a second or two, very likely, I would know. Vlump, vlump. The gray of the window turned rosy as I came near enough to see the hillside beyond it: That black was underbrush and that pink the dusty swath cut by the bulldozer before it had run amok. I had watched the accident from just about the spot where I stood now, and the obliterated hole where the tree had been, laid firmly over with the prefabricated floor of the room whose darkness I would eradicate by touching with my right hand the light switch inside the door.

"Ted?"

Blood boomed in my ears. I had the impression that my heart had burst. I clutched at the wall for support. Yet of course I knew it was Ellen's voice, and I answered her calmly. "Yes, it's me."

"What's the matter?" I heard the bedclothes rustle.

"Don't get up, I'm coming right in." The noise had stopped. There was nothing. Only the almost inaudible hum of the refrigerator, the stirring of the wind.

Ellen was sitting up in bed. "I was just checking on the fire," I said. She patted my side of the bed and in the instant before I turned out the hall light I saw her smile.

"I was just dreaming about you," she said softly, as I climbed under the sheets. She rolled against me. "Why, you're trembling."

"I should have worn my robe."

"You'll be warm in a minute." Her fragrant body lay against mine, but I remained rigid as stone and just as cold, staring at the ceiling, my mind a furious blank. After a moment she said, "Ted?" It was her signal, always hesitant, always tremulous, that meant I was to roll over and take her in my arms.

Instead I answered, "What?" just as if I had not understood.

For a few seconds I sensed her struggling against her reserve to give me a further sign that would pierce my peculiar distraction and tell me she wanted love. But it was too much for her—too alien. My coldness had created a vacuum she was too unpracticed to fill—a coldness sudden and inexplicable, unless. . . .

She withdrew slowly and pulled the covers up under her chin. Finally she asked, "Ted, is there something happening that I should know about?" She had remembered Sondra and the curious scene in the kitchen. It took, I knew, great courage for Ellen to ask that question, though she must have known my answer.

"No, I'm just tired. We've had a busy day. Good-night, dear." I kissed her on the cheek and sensed her eyes, in the shadow of the fire, searching mine, asking the question she could not give voice to. I turned away, somehow ashamed because I could not supply the answer that would fulfill her need. Because there was no answer at all.

The fire was brought under control after burning some eight hundred acres and several homes, and three weeks later the rains came. Jack Salmanson came out one Sunday to see how the house was holding up, checked the foundation, the roof and all the seams and pronounced it tight as a drum. We sat looking moodily out the glass doors onto the patio—a flatland of grayish mud which threatened to swamp with a thin ooze of silt and gravel the few flagstones I had set in the ground. Ellen was in the bedroom lying down; she had got into the habit of taking a nap after lunch, though it was I, not she, who lay stark awake night after night explaining away sounds that became more and more impossible to explain away. The gagging sound that sometimes accompanied the vlump and the strangled expulsion of air that followed it were surely the result of some disturbance in the water pipes; the footsteps that came slowly down the hall and stopped outside our closed door and then went away again with something like a low chuckle were merely the night contracting of our metal house after the heat of the day. Through all this Ellen slept as if in a stupor; she seemed to have become addicted to sleep. She went to bed at nine and got up at ten the next morning; she napped in the afternoon and moved about lethargically the rest of the time with a Mexican shawl around her shoulders, complaining of the cold. The doctor examined her for mononucleosis but found nothing. He said perhaps it was her sinuses and that she should rest as much as she wanted.

After a protracted silence Jack put aside his drink and stood up. "I guess I'll go along."

"I'll tell Ellen."

"What the hell for? Let her sleep. Tell her I hope she feels better." He turned to frown at the room of the house he had designed and built. "Are you happy here?" he asked suddenly.

"Happy?" I repeated the word awkwardly. "Of course we're happy. We love the house. It's ... just a little noisy at night, that's all."

I stammered it out, like the first words of a monstrous confession, but Jack seemed hardly to hear it. He waved a hand. "House settling." He squinted from one side of the room to the other. "I don't know. There's something about it. ... It's not right. Maybe it's just the weather ... the light. ... It could be friendlier, you know what I mean? It seems cheerless."

I watched him with a kind of wild hope, as if he might magically fathom my terror—do for me what I could not do for myself, and permit it to be discussed calmly between two men of temperate mind. But Jack was not looking for the cause of the gloom but the cure for it. "Why don't you try putting down a couple of orange rugs in this room?" he said.

I stared at the floor as if two orange rugs were an infallible charm. "Yes," I said, "I think we'll try that."

Ellen scuffed in, pushing back her hair, her face puffy with sleep. "Jack," she said, "when the weather clears and I'm feeling livelier, you and Anne and the children must come and spend the night."

"We'd like that. After the noises die down," he added satirically to me.

"Noises? What noises?" A certain blankness came over Ellen's face when she looked at me now. The expression was the same, but what had been open in it before was now merely empty. She had put up her guard against me; she suspected me of keeping things from her.

"At night," I said. "The house is settling. You don't hear them."

When Jack had gone, Ellen sat with a cup of tea in the chair where Jack had sat, looking out at the mud. Her long purple shawl hung all the way to her knees and made her look armless. There seemed no explanation for the two white hands that curled around the teacup in her lap. "It's a sad thing," she said tonelessly. "I can't help but feel sorry for Sondra."

"Why is that?" I asked guardedly.

"Joyce was here yesterday. She told me that she and Jeff

have been having an affair off and on for six years." She turned to see how I would receive this news.

"Well, that explains the way Joyce and Sondra behave toward each other," I said, with a pleasant glance straight into Ellen's eyes; there I encountered only the reflection of the glass doors, even to the rain trickling down them, and I had the eerie sensation of having been shown a picture of the truth, as if she were weeping secretly in the depths of a soul I could no longer touch. For Ellen did not believe in my innocence; I'm not sure I still believed in it myself; very likely Jeff and Joyce didn't either. It is impossible to say what Sondra believed. She behaved as if our infidelity were an accomplished fact. In its way it was a performance of genius, for Sondra never touched me except in the most accidental or impersonal way; even her glances, the foundation on which she built the myth of our liaison, had nothing soft in them; they were probing and sly and were always accompanied by a furtive smile, as if we merely shared some private joke. Yet there was something in the way she did it—in the tilt of her head perhaps—that plainly implied that the joke was at everyone else's expense. And she had taken to calling me "darling."

"Sondra and Jeff have a feebleminded child off in an institution somewhere," Ellen said. "That set them against each other, apparently."

"Joyce told you all this?"

"She just mentioned it casually as if it were the most natural thing in the world—she assumed we must have known. . . . But I don't want to know things like that about my friends."

"That's show biz, I guess. You and I are just provincials at heart."

"Sondra must be a very unhappy girl."

"It's hard to tell with Sondra."

"I wonder what she tries to do with her life. . . . If she looks for anything—outside."

I waited.

"Probably not," Ellen answered her own question. "She seems very self-contained. Almost cold. . . ."

I was treated to the spectacle of my wife fighting with herself to delay a wound that she was convinced would come home to her sooner or later. She did not want to believe in my infidelity. I might have comforted her with lies. I might have told her that Sondra and I rendezvoused downtown in a cafeteria and made love in a second-rate hotel on the evenings when I called to say that I was working late. Then the wound would be open and could be cleaned and cured.

It would be painful of course, but I would have confided in her again and our old system would be restored. Watching Ellen torture herself with doubt, I was tempted to tell her those lies. The truth never tempted me: To have admitted that I knew what she was thinking would have been tantamount to an admission of guilt. How could I suspect such a thing unless it were true? And was I to explain my coldness by terrifying her with vague stories of indescribable sounds which she never heard?

And so the two of us sat on, dumb and chilled, in our watertight house as the daylight began to go. And then a sort of exultation seized me. What if my terror were no more real than Ellen's? What if both our ghosts were only ghosts of the mind which needed only a little common sense to drive them away? And I saw that if I could drive away my ghost, Ellen's would soon follow, for the secret that shut me away from her would be gone. It was a revelation, a triumph of reason.

"What's that up there?" Ellen pointed to something that looked like a leaf blowing at the top of the glass doors. "It's a tail, Ted. There must be some animal on the roof."

Only the bushy tip was visible. As I drew close to it I could see raindrops clinging as if by a geometrical system to each black hair. "It looks like a raccoon tail. What would a coon be doing out so early?" I put on a coat and went outside. The tail hung limply over the edge, ringed with white and swaying phlegmatically in the breeze. The animal itself was hidden behind the low parapet. Using the ship's ladder at the back of the house I climbed up to look at it.

The human mind, just like other parts of the anatomy, is an organ of habit. Its capabilities are bounded by the limits of precedent; it thinks what it is used to thinking. Faced with a phenomenon beyond its range it rebels, it rejects, sometimes it collapses. My mind, which for weeks had steadfastly refused to honor the evidence of my senses that there was Something Else living in the house with Ellen and me, something unearthly and evil, largely on the basis of insufficient evidence, was now forced to the subsequent denial by saying, as Jeff had said, "fox." It was, of course, ridiculous. The chances of a fox's winning a battle with a raccoon were very slight at best, let alone what had been done to this raccoon. The body lay on the far side of the roof. I didn't see the head at all until I had stumbled against it and it had rolled over and over to come to rest against the parapet where it pointed its masked, ferret face at me.

Only because my beleaguered mind kept repeating, like a voice, "Ellen mustn't know, Ellen mustn't know," was I able to take up the dismembered parts and hurl them with all my strength onto the hillside and answer when Ellen called out,

"What is it, Ted?" "Must have been a coon. It's gone now," in a perfectly level voice before I went to the back of the roof and vomited.

I recalled Sondra's mention of their mutilated cat and phoned Jeff at his agency. "We will discuss it over lunch," I told myself. I had a great need to talk, an action impossible within my own home, where every day the silence became denser and more intractable. Once or twice Ellen ventured to ask, "What's the matter, Ted?" but I always answered, "Nothing." And there our talk ended. I could see it in her wary eyes: I was not the man she had married; I was cold, secretive. The children's room, furnished with double bunks and wallpaper figured with toys, stood like a rebuke. Ellen kept the door closed most of the time, though once or twice, in the late afternoon, I had found her in there moving about aimlessly, touching objects as if half in wonder that they should still linger on after so many long, sterile months; a foolish hope had failed. Neither did our friends bring their children to stay. They did not because we did not ask them. The silence had brought with it a profound and debilitating inertia. Ellen's face seemed perpetually swollen, the features cloudy and amorphous, the eyes dull; her whole body had become bloated, as if an enormous cache of pain had backed up inside her. We moved through the house in our orbits like two sleepwalkers, going about our business out of habit. Our friends called at first, puzzled, a little hurt, but soon stopped and left us to ourselves. Occasionally we saw the Sheffitses. Jeff was looking seedier and seedier, told bad jokes, drank too much and seemed always ill at ease. Sondra did most of the talking, chattering blandly on indifferent subjects and always hinting by gesture, word or glance at our underground affair.

Jeff and I had lunch at the Brown Derby on Vine Street under charcoal caricatures of show folk. At a table next to ours an agent was eulogizing an actor in a voice hoarse with trumped-up enthusiasm to a large, purple-faced man who was devoting his entire attention to a bowl of vichyssoise.

"It's a crazy business," Jeff said to me. "Be glad you're not in it."

"I see what you mean," I replied. Jeff had not the faintest idea of why I had brought him there, nor had I given him any clue. We were "breaking the ice." Jeff grinned at me with that crooked trick of his mouth, and I grinned back. "We are friends"—presumably that is the message we were grinning at each other. Was he my friend? Was I his friend? He lived across the street; our paths crossed perhaps once a week; we joked together; he sat always in the same chair in

95

our living room that I preferred. Friendships have been founded on less, I suppose. Yet he had an idiot child locked off in an asylum somewhere and a wife who amused herself with infidelity by suggestion; I had a demon loose in my house and a wife gnawed with suspicion and growing remote and old because of it. And I had said, "I see what you mean." It seemed insufferable. I caught Jeff's eye. "You remember we talked once about a ghost?" My tone was bantering; perhaps I meant to make a joke.

"I remember."

"Sondra said something about a cat of yours that was killed."

"The one the fox got."

"That's what you said. That's not what Sondra said."

Jeff shrugged. "What about it?"

"I found a dead raccoon on our roof."

"Your roof!"

"Yes. It was pretty awful."

Jeff toyed with his fork. All pretense of levity was at an end. "No head?"

"Worse."

For a few moments he was silent. I felt him struggle with himself before he spoke. "Maybe you'd better move out, Ted," he said.

He was trying to help—I knew it. With a single swipe he had tried to push through the restraint that hung between us. He was my friend; he was putting out his hand to me. And I suppose I must have known what he'd suggest. But I could not accept it. It was not what I wanted to hear. "Jeff, I can't do that," I said tolerantly, as if he had missed my point. "We've only been living there five months. It cost me twenty-two thousand to build that place. We have to live in it at least a year under the GI loan."

"Well, you know best, Ted." The smile dipped at me again.

"I just wanted to talk," I said, irritated at the ease with which he had given in. "I wanted to find out what you knew about this ghost business."

"Not very much. Sondra knows more than I do."

"I doubt that you would advise me to leave a house I had just built for no reason at all."

"There seems to be some sort of jinx on the property, that's all. Whether there's a ghost or not I couldn't tell you," he replied, annoyed in his turn at the line the conversation was taking. "How does Ellen feel about this?"

"She doesn't know."

"About the raccoon?"

"About anything."

"You mean there's more?"

"There are noises—at night. . . ."

"I'd speak to Sondra if I were you. She's gone into this business much more deeply than I. When we first moved in, she used to hang around your land a good deal . . . just snooping . . . particularly after the cat was killed. . . ." He was having some difficulty with his words. It struck me that the conversation was causing him pain. He was showing his teeth now in a smiling grimace. Dangling an arm over the back of his chair he seemed loose to the point of collapse. We circled warily about his wife's name.

"Look, Jeff," I said, and took a breath, "about Sondra. . . ."

Jeff cut me off with a wave of his hand. "Don't worry, I know Sondra."

"Then you know there's nothing between us?"

"It's just her way of amusing herself. Sondra's a strange girl. She does the same thing with me. She flirts with me but we don't sleep together." He picked up his spoon and stared at it unseeingly. "It started when she became pregnant. After she had the boy, everything between us stopped. You knew we had a son? He's in a sanitarium in the Valley."

"Can't you do anything?"

"Sure. Joyce Castle. I don't know what I'd have done without her."

"I mean a divorce."

"Sondra won't divorce me. And I can't divorce her. No grounds." He shrugged as if the whole thing were of no concern at all to him. "What could I say? I want to divorce my wife because of the way she looks at other men? She's scrupulously faithful."

"To whom, Jeff? To you? To whom?"

"I don't know—to herself, maybe," he mumbled.

Whether with encouragement he might have gone on I don't know, for I cut him off. I sensed that with this enigmatic remark he was giving me my cue and that if I had chosen to respond to it he would have told me what I had asked him to lunch to find out—and all at once I was terrified; I did not want to hear it; I did not want to hear it at all. And so I laughed in a quiet way and said, "Undoubtedly, undoubtedly," and pushed it behind the closed door of my mind where I had stored all the impossibilities of the last months—the footsteps, the sounds in the night, the mutilated raccoon—or else, by recognizing them, go mad.

Jeff suddenly looked me full in the face; his cheeks were flushed, his teeth clamped together. "Look, Ted," he said, "can you take the afternoon off? I've got to go to the sanitarium and sign some papers. They're going to transfer the boy. He has fits of violence and does ... awful things. He's finally gotten out of hand."

"What about Sondra?"

"Sondra's signed already. She likes to go alone to visit him. She seems to like to have him to herself. I'd appreciate it, Ted—the moral support. . . . You don't have to come in. You can wait in the car. It's only about thirty miles from here, you'd be back by dinnertime. . . ." His voice shook, tears clouded the yellow-stained whites of his eyes. He looked like a man with fever. I noticed how shrunken his neck had become as it revolved in his collar, how his head caved in sharply at the temples. He fastened one hand on my arm, like a claw. "Of course I'll go, Jeff," I said. "I'll call the office. They can get along without me for one afternoon."

He collected himself in an instant. "I'd appreciate it, Ted. I promise you it won't be so bad."

The sanitarium was in the San Fernando Valley, a complex of new stucco buildings on a newly seeded lawn. Everywhere there were signs that read, PLEASE KEEP OFF, FOLKS. Midget saplings stood in discs of powdery earth along the cement walks angling white and hot through the grass. On these walks, faithfully observing the signs, the inmates strolled. Their traffic, as it flowed somnolently from one avenue to another, was controlled by attendants stationed at intersections, conspicuous in white uniforms and pith helmets.

After a time it became unbearably hot in the car, and I climbed out. Unless I wished to pace in the parking lot among the cars, I had no choice but to join the inmates and their visitors on the walks. I chose a nearly deserted walk and went slowly toward a building that had a yard attached to it surrounded by a wire fence. From the slide and the Jungle-gym in it I judged it to be for the children. Then I saw Jeff come into it. With him was a nurse pushing a kind of cart railed around like an oversized toddler. Strapped into it was "the boy."

He was human, I suppose, for he had all the equipment assigned to humans, yet I had the feeling that if it were not for the cart the creature would have crawled on his belly like an alligator. He had the eyes of an alligator too—sleepy, cold and soulless—set in a swarthy face and a head that seemed to run in a horizontal direction rather than the vertical, like an egg lying on its side. The features were devoid of any vestige of intelligence; the mouth hung open and the chin shone with saliva. While Jeff and the nurse talked, he sat under the sun inert and repulsive.

I turned on my heel and bolted, feeling that I had intruded on a disgrace. I imagined that I had been given a glimpse of a diseased universe, the mere existence of which constituted a threat to my life; the sight of that monstrous boy with his cold, bestial eyes made me feel as if, by stumbling on this shame, I somehow shared in it with Jeff. Yet I told myself that the greatest service I could do him was to pretend that I had seen nothing, knew nothing, and not place on him the hardship of talking about something which obviously caused him pain.

He returned to the car pale and shaky and wanting a drink. We stopped first at a place called Joey's on Hollywood Way. After that it was the Cherry Lane on Vine Street, where a couple of girls propositioned us, and then a stop at the Brown Derby again, where I had left my car. Jeff downed the liquor in a joyless, business-like way and talked to me in a rapid, confidential voice about a book he had just sold to Warner Brothers Studio for an exorbitant sum of money—trash in his opinion, but that was always the way—the parasites made it. Pretty soon there wouldn't be any good writers left: "There'll only be competent parasites and incompetent parasites." This was perhaps the third time we had had this conversation. Now Jeff repeated it mechanically, all the time looking down at the table where he was painstakingly breaking a red swizzle stick into ever tinier pieces.

When we left the restaurant, the sun had gone down, and the evening chill of the desert on which the city had been built had settled in. A faint pink glow from the vanished sun still lingered on the top of the Broadway Building. Jeff took a deep breath, then fell into a fit of coughing. "Goddam smog," he said. "Goddam city. I can't think of a single reason why I live here." He started toward his Daimler, tottering slightly.

"How about driving home with me?" I said. "You can pick your car up tomorrow."

He fumbled in the glove compartment and drew out a packet of small cigars. He stuck one between his teeth where it jutted unlit toward the end of his nose. "I'm not going home tonight, Ted friend," he said. "If you'll just drop me up the street at the Cherry Lane I'll remember you for life."

"Are you sure? I'll go with you if you want."

Jeff shook a forefinger at me archly.

"Ted, you're a gentleman and a scholar. But my advice to you is to go home and take care of your wife. No, seriously. Take care of her, Ted. As for myself I shall go quietly to seed in the Cherry Lane Cafe." I had started toward my car when Jeff called out to me again. "I just want to tell you, Ted friend. . . . My wife was once just as nice as your wife. . . ."

I had gone no more than a mile when the last glimmer of light left the sky and night fell like a shutter. The sky above the neon of Sunset Boulevard turned jet black, and a sickly half-moon rose and was immediately obscured by thick fog that lowered itself steadily as I traveled west, till at the foot of Clay Canyon it began to pat my windshield with little smears of moisture.

The house was dark, and at first I thought Ellen must have gone out, but then seeing her old Plymouth in the driveway I felt the grip of a cold and unreasoning fear. The events of the day seemed to crowd around and hover at my head in the fog; and the commonplace sight of that car, together with the blackness and silence of the house, sent me into a panic as I ran for the door. I pushed at it with my shoulder as if expecting it to be locked, but it swung open easily and I found myself in the darkened living room with no light anywhere and the only sound the rhythm of my own short breathing. "Ellen!" I called in a high, querulous voice I hardly recognized. "Ellen!" I seemed to lose my balance; my head swam; it was as if this darkness and silence were the one last iota that the chamber of horrors in my mind could not hold, and the door snapped open a crack, emitting a cloudy light that stank of corruption, and I saw the landscape of my denial, like a tomb. It was the children's room. Rats nested in the double bunks, mold caked the red wallpaper, and in it an insane Spanish don hung by his neck from a dead tree, his heels vlumping against the wall, his foppish clothes rubbing as he revolved slowly in invisible currents of bad air. And as he swung toward me, I saw his familiar reptile eyes open and stare at me with loathing and contempt.

I conceded: It is here and It is evil, and I have left my wife alone in the house with It, and now she has been sucked into that cold eternity where the dumb shades store their plasms against an anguished centenary of speech—a single word issuing from the petrified throat, a scream or a sign or a groan, syllables dredged up from a lifetime of eloquence to slake the bottomless thirst of living death.

And then a light went on over my head, and I found myself in the hall outside the children's room. Ellen was in her nightgown, smiling at me. "Ted? Why on earth are you standing here in the dark? I was just taking a nap. Do you want some dinner? Why don't you say something? Are you all right?" She came toward me; she seemed extraordinarily lovely; her eyes, a deeper blue than Sondra's, looked almost purple; she seemed young and slender again; her old serenity shone through like a restored beacon.

"I'm all right," I said hoarsely. "Are you sure you are?"

"Of course I am," she laughed. "Why shouldn't I be? I'm feeling much, much better." She took my hand and kissed it gaily. "I'll put on some clothes and then we'll have our dinner." She turned and went down the hall to our bedroom, leaving me with a clear view into the children's room. Though the room itself was dark, I could see by the hall light that the covers on the lower bunk had been turned back and that the bed had been slept in. "Ellen," I said. "Ellen, were you sleeping in the children's room?"

"Yes," she said, and I heard the rustle of a dress as she carried it from the closet. "I was in there mooning around, waiting for you to come home. I got sleepy and lay down on the bunk. What were *you* doing, by the way? Working late?"

"And nothing happened?"

"Why? What should have happened?"

I could not answer; my head throbbed with joy. It was over—whatever it was, it was over. All unknowing Ellen had faced the very heart of the evil and had slept through it like a child, and now she was herself again without having been tainted by the knowledge of what she had defeated; I had protected her by my silence, by my refusal to share my terror with this woman whom I loved. I reached inside and touched the light button; there was the brave red wallpaper scattered over with toys, the red-and-white curtains, the blue-and-red bedspreads. It was a fine room. A fine, gay room fit for children.

Ellen came down the hall in her slip. "Is anything wrong, Ted? You seem so distraught. Is everything all right at the office?"

"Yes, yes," I said. "I was with Jeff Sheffits. We went to see his boy in the asylum. Poor Jeff; he leads a rotten life." I told Ellen the whole story of our afternoon, speaking freely in my house for the first time since we had moved there. Ellen listened carefully as she always did, and wanted to know, when I had finished, what the boy was like.

"Like an alligator," I said with disgust. "Just like an alligator."

Ellen's face took on an unaccountable expression of private glee. She seemed to be looking past me into the children's room, as if the source of her amusement lay there. At the same moment I shivered in a breath of profound cold, the same clammy draft that might have warned me on my last birthday had I been other than what I am. I had a sense of sudden dehydration, as if all the blood had vanished from my veins. I felt as if I were shrinking. When I spoke, my voice seemed to come from a throat rusty and dry with disuse. "Is that funny?" I whispered.

And my wife replied, "Funny? Oh, no, it's just that I'm feeling so much better. I think I'm pregnant, Ted." She tipped her head to one side and smiled at me.

COUNT SZOLNOK'S ROBOTS

D. Scott-Moncrieff

IMRE NAGY was a displaced person. Admittedly he had displaced himself, but only just in time, for otherwise, having well over fifty percent Jewish blood in his veins, he would most certainly have been displaced, probably into the gas chambers at Auschwitz. By the time he was thirty he had already achieved some position as a novelist and journalist in Budapest. His work was not widely known abroad but he had got together a small balance of francs in Switzerland from the foreign sales of his work. Whatever happened he was in for trouble, for his writings had not only been consistently anti-German, but he had, he thought, put himself in some disfavor with the Russians by repeatedly demanding the return of Transylvania, Hungarian territory for eight hundred years.

Imre skipped, just in time in 1941, to Switzerland. Here he wrote a charming book of fairy stories that was a great success and enabled him before the European war ended, to get, via Portugal, to America. Two years after the outbreak of uneasy peace he was still writing in New York and making good money, but he was quite convinced that an atomic war between U. S. A. and Russia was only a matter of time. Imre had, remember, spent the greater part of his life in countries where the fear that haunted every man's night was war, war and war. So Imre decided that he would settle somewhere so remote and so unimportant that no one would bother to chuck an atom bomb at it, or even occupy it. He looked long and carefully at his map and decided that the ghost town of Manaos, one thousand miles up the Amazon, relic of a long defunct rubber boom, was the answer.

Manaos in the nineteenth century grew from a small trading town to a city built in the really fantastic bad taste of the period. But now the hideous false Parisian mansions with their mansard roofs are broken up into tenements and the gilt and plaster is flaking away in the vast florid mock-rococo opera house.

"Admittedly," reflected Imre, "it's incredibly shabby, provincial and isolated, but no one ever speaks of war, rumors of war and sudden death from the skies. Furthermore, living is cheap. I will make this my headquarters." So he settled in as a lodger with the Countess de Silva de Pereira de Pinto y Basto de la Ilha Verde. There was a great deal more to it than that but this was the irreducible minimum on which his skittish, lemon-colored landlady, of uncertain age, insisted. The house itself would lead one to suspect that an extremely knowledgeable curator of a museum had combed two hemispheres for pieces of inspired ugliness of the period 1880 to 1905, and staged an "exhibition du mauvais gôute." Although Imre with his Hungarian genius for languages had during his stay in Portugal achieved a fair command of the language, the Countess always insisted in conversing with him in her execrable French. But in spite of all these drawbacks Imre was most comfortable and the Mestizo cook was a real artist.

Imre Nagy, rejoicing for the first time in his life, in a feeling of real security, began to make friends, although he found the Countess's shabby genteel circle intensely wearying, with their eternal prattle of a vanished plutocracy and its shallow veneer of culture that it had imported from Europe in much the same spirit that it had imported its shiny victorias and broughams.

Magyars, like Scots, get around and Imre was in no way surprised to find that even in far Manaos there was another Hungarian. He was a dear old boy who, although well past sixty years old, was still foreman of the boiler department of the marine engineers down at the large docks, now handling not a twentieth part of the cargo for which they had been originally built. Just before the 1914 war young Kovacs, a charge hand in the boiler shop at the old Austro-Hungarian locomotive works at Tat was given a hint. He was told that his socialist speeches and trade union activities were not looked on with favor by the Bohemian policemen recruited by His Imperial Majesty Francis Joseph with the express object of stamping out that kind of nonsense. Now Kovacs was no fool, he wouldn't have been charge hand at thirty if he had been, and, within forty-eight hours of the "tip-off," Kovacs, Magda his wife, and Janos his infant son, were jolting down to Trieste in a third class railway carriage, their simple belongings stowed in bundles, and the few gold pieces they had saved sewn into Magda's many voluminous petticoats. The fact that they did not join the steady flow of "bohunks" to Pittsburgh, Chicago, or Buffalo is attributable to the fact that the day they arrived in Trieste a ship which would take steerage passengers was leaving for Bahia and they did not deem it wise to remain one hour longer than was necessary under the proud double-headed eagle of Austria-Hungary. In Bahia they learned of the vacancy at Manaos and there they settled. It was with this cosy working-class Hungarian family that Imre spent most of his spare time.

It was one grilling hot New Year's Eve that Imre was celebrating a true Hungarian "silvester" with roast goose and all the traditional trimmings at the Kovac's flat, that he first heard tell of the fabulous Count Szolnok.

"Are there," he asked, "no other Magyars in the neighborhood to join us at our silvester feast?"

"There used to be a dear old violin teacher," Magda Kovacs told him, "who celebrated with us every New Year since we came, but he died a couple of years back. There is not a Magyar nearer than Bahia, unless you count the high born Count Szolnok and you would hardly expect a cousin of the Emperor to sit down to our humble table." In spite of her early socialistic opinions the good Magda had never really got around to the fact that the Hapsburgs no longer ruled in the palace on Buda Hill and that the nobility were no longer something even further removed from the common people than the saints in the churches. It was too great an upheaval for her simple mind to compass. Imre Nagy thought grimly of the Hungarian aristocracy in the streets of shattered Budapest selling their silver and furs and fine English suits to buy meals, not one hundredth part as fine as the magnificent repast that Magda, true daughter of a Puszta farmer, had laid out.

This was the first mention Imre had ever heard of Count Szolnok. He knew that there had been a noble Hungarian family of that name: a family of great antiquity and legendary wealth. But he imagined that they had long been extinct.

"I doubt even if the old Count is still alive," said Kovacs. "A few years ago, before Pretzlik, his maintenance engineer, stopped coming to Manaos, he told me that, although his old master was still hale and hearty, he was within a year or two of his ninetieth birthday."

What follows was as much as old Kovacs knew of the story. It was in the 1880's a wonder that set every tongue between Bahia and Manaos awag. A huge steam yacht of some fifteen hundred tons passed Manaos and went on up the Amazon, all her fresh white paint and polished brass gleaming in the sun. Next, cargo steamers full of building materials and ship-loads of workmen discharged into shallow draft lighters and were towed upstream. It seemed that an apparently eccentric and boundlessly wealthy Count Szolnok had selected a site some way up a tributary of the Amazon which branched off two days' steaming beyond Manaos. The site, it was said, was on high healthy ground which lifted it out of the jungle, where a great waterfall thundered down. The masons, carpenters, carvers and craftsmen, brought from both England and Italy, were housed in wooden barracks, prefabricated and brought for the purpose. The Count, from what fragments of information could be picked up, was building himself a vast arabian nights palace, in the Palladian manner, with a tall pillared portico. This hearsay, and little more, could be gathered, for the workmen were conveyed direct to and from the site, and anyone visiting Manaos for any special reason was sworn to absolute secrecy under pain of instant dismissal. No one had actually seen anything, for over a hundred miles of impenetrable jungle made the approach impossible, except by water, and, though the great yacht could be seen anchored in the main stream, the only access to the work was by the Count's own special shallow draft lighters and steam tugs. All that was known were native reports by "bush telegraph" through the jungle, of a great white palace being completed in absolutely record time.

Presently the workmen were taken away in ships as they came, and the great steam yacht and most of the tugs and lighters went away downstream and were never seen again. With so little known, the mystery was soon exhausted as a subject of conversation and as rapidly forgotten. Next there was another development that caused surprise and comment. Engineering work on a large scale was in progress. Boatloads of engineers, mostly Swiss, but also French, German and Czech, or Bohemian as they were called in those days, by-passed Manaos and sailed up to the mysterious Count's property. Steamer load upon steamer load of cases of machinery were transhipped to lighters, and presently the greater part of the engineers well paid for their secrecy, disappeared as they had come. By the turn of the century, it was thought that not more than a few dozen specialist technicians remained. By the time Kovacs came on the scene, just before World War I, even they had all gone and it was said that but one maintenance engineer, Pretzlik, the Bohemian, who came into Manaos two or three times a year in the steam launch, remained. Few of the younger people, even in 1913, had ever heard of the fabled Count Szolnok.

Kovacs had only one positive light to throw on the story. When he first came to the company, the old electrician, now long dead, had told him that over twenty years earlier he had seen the most enormous hydro-electric generating plant, hundreds of times bigger than would be needed to light the largest house, being transhipped in sections into lighters. So huge was each individual section, that the operation was only performed with the greatest difficulty. In the old electrician's estimate this plant, presumably to be worked from the waterfall, would generate sufficient electricity to light a city far larger than Manaos itself.

This was all Kovacs could tell except that the jungle natives would never go within miles of the place because of a ridiculous superstition that the Count and Countess, who were never seen, had begotten some strange race of robots or mechanical men who tilled their fields and worked their farms.

Imre Nagy, trained newspaperman that he was, at once scented a good "story" here. These strange events of over half a century ago, should yield "feature" articles saleable to many of the better paying papers and periodicals. So, seeking the basis for an article, he did what any other intelligent reporter would have done, he went to the local newspaper and asked to see their files for the eighteen-eighties and nineties. Here he drew a complete blank, for although there were duplicate files, someone, presumably in the pay of Count Szolnok, had neatly clipped out every single reference to him! This of course made Imre Nagy all the keener to get the "story."

Old people in Manaos could repeat nothing but garbled versions of what Kovacs had already told him, and many frankly dismissed the story as an old wives' tale. He had little hope that the files of any of the Hungarian dailies, going back as far as 1880 would have survived that disastrous battle which Germans and Russians had just fought over their country. So, as the one point upon which people agreed seemed to be that the Countess Szolnok was the daughter of an English Duke, he cabled a friend in London to do some research for him. He was rewarded by receiving, by airmail, copies of articles in *The Times* newspaper and photostatic copies of engravings from the *Illustrated London News*.

The story it unfolded was a strange one. Born in 1856 the only son of the fabulously wealthy Count Szolnok, instead of following the usual procedure of his age and class and devoting his life to soldiering and sport, was determined from his earliest youth, to become an engineer. His father, most surprisingly, gave him the fullest support and had him educated in Switzerland where he took first place in every examination, and showed himself to be a student of absolutely exceptional brilliance and promise. The verdict of his professors appears to have been, "What a pity this young man will inherit such vast wealth and properties, for they are sure to divert him from being the most brilliant engineer of his generation." The young Count went on to work in the experimental department of a great engineering works in the Northern Midlands of England. His work here showed, in spite of his youth, the greatest promise. But, as far as the newspapers went, this was quite eclipsed by his wonderful mounts and dashing horsemanship on those occasions when he appeared in the hunting field. His engagement to the daughter, the only child, of one of the wealthiest coal-owning Dukes in the realm, was a nine days' wonder. For, as *The Times* newspaper says, "This young couple will command between them a fortune so vast that it will exceed that of several of the European Crowned Heads who will be arriving for the wedding."

The wedding itself far outshone any other social event in the lush year of 1880. And its terrible sequel made headlines in every newspaper in the world. As the open victoria carrying the radiant couple drew away from the church, a woman in the crowd, the mother of a miner who had been blinded at work in one of the Duke's pits, jumped on the carriage step and dashed a beaker of vitriol full in the face of the bride. By some miracle her eyesight was spared, but she was so hideously disfigured, that it was known that she would never permit any other human being except her husband ever to set eyes on her again. And that is all the English papers could tell Imre of Count and Countess Szolnok, except that, although Parliament were quite prepared to pass a special Bill that the woman might be hanged, the Countess wrote personally to Queen Victoria and asked that the woman should be committed to a madhouse. This was done. Some months later a small paragraph appeared in *The Times* reporting that the young Count and Countess were building in some secluded part of the Americas (unnamed) an exact replica of her old home in England built for her ancestor, the second Duke, by the architect and carver Inigo Jones. That was all.

The port and customs records at the mouth of the Amazon River, in reply to a letter, revealed that from 1881 for a period of about twenty years, ships chartered by Count Szolnok brought in goods to the value of several million pounds, and always returned empty.

Satisfied now that he was on the track of, if not exactly "hot news," an extremely sensational story, Imre bought a shallow draft motor launch. This he equipped with mosquito nets, beddings, and provisions, and set out. The journey was uneventful enough, and he easily spotted the disused wharf with a heavy rusting crane, that marked the entry of the tributary. After this it was hard going nosing against a five knot current over a foul unchartered bed. He punched the current for a day. When it got dark, he anchored in midstream, pulled down his mosquito curtains and turned in. It was far too tricky going to attempt in the dark. The next day he rounded a bend, the river widened out and he knew he had reached his goal. A large steam launch rocked at its moorings. The brass funnel was black from lack of cleaning, the paintwork had peeled away leaving the teak to bleach in the sun. The decks were foul with the droppings of birds, the windows opaque with dirt, and the anchor chains twisted and cluttered with weed. One thing was quite clear, she had lain there at her moorings for a good many years since Pretzlik had last taken her to Manaos. This Pretzlik, Kovacs had told him, had been an unattractive man, soapily humble in a Uriah Heapish way, but close as an oyster, and, there was no doubt about this, a really magnificent engineer. In all the years that Kovacs had known him, neither he nor anyone else had ever been able to get a single word out of him about his employer, or how they lived. By the well-built brick landing stage some shallow draft lighters had filled with rainwater and sunk. Imre made fast to the bollard, still above water, on one of these and raised his eyes. High up on the hill, standing in a parkland setting that made it look even more completely English, white as white in the morning sun, stood a lovely Palladian mansion with a tall portico. From where he was he could hear the steady thunder of a waterfall. "So far," said Imre to himself, "every word of the fantastic story seems to be true."

Grass was growing between the flagstones of the deserted wharf and another large crane was rusting on its rails. A broad pavé road led away to the great house, and a fork could be seen where a road branched off towards the water-fall, and, presumably, the power station. More grass and gay flowers were already growing up between the blocks of the pavé road.

Almost gleefully Imre started up the road, although, in spite of the thrill of the anticipated "story," he couldn't help, he didn't know why, experiencing a sense of chill foreboding. Presently the well graduated road rose beyond the jungle belt, and, to his surprise, Imre found himself in well culti-vated farm land. "This," he thought to himself, "is the first discrepancy with what I've heard. It was always said that the natives would not come within miles of the place, and yet the volume of labor to work these fields and orchards must be immense."

Then suddenly he caught sight of one of the things. It was picking fruit from a tree and putting the fruit carefully into a big basket. At first glance it was apparent that the thing wasn't human, if only for one reason; where its head should

have been there was a perfectly smooth cylindrical protu-
berance rounded at the edge, like a steam dome. Its body
conformed to the normal human shape and was quite naked,
covered, apparently, with some kind of smooth rubberoid
substance.

Imre stared and stared, but, before he had got over his
first shock, another of the creatures appeared through the
trees pushing a flat barrow with baskets of fruit on it. The
second creature deftly picked up the full basket, placed it
neatly on the barrow, left an empty basket on the ground,
and, turning, wheeled the barrow away the way it had come.
These smooth, sightless creatures, a uniform dark chocolate
colour, so human in their movements, yet so inhuman, filled
Imre with such a sense of loathing and repulsion that he lost
no time in hurrying on.

Everywhere he looked he could see the horrible things
toiling away at their appointed agricultural tasks. Passing by
some piggeries, he had another shock. One of the creatures
vaulted lightly into the pigsty, picked up an enormous sow in
its arms as easily as one would pick up a baby, straddled the
fence and carried it squealing away. Imre realized with a
shudder of horror that their strength must be ten times
greater than that of any human being. Like the others it
appeared completely unaware of Imre's presence.

Imre Nagy felt an irresistible desire to bolt back to the
motor launch and put as much distance as he could between
himself and these blood-curling creatures, but he reasoned
with himself, "During the war, when money was no object,
scientific developments that would normally take twenty
years took as many months. Why should not Count Szolnok,
himself an outstanding engineer, with unlimited funds and
half a century to do it in, have concentrated on and produced
the perfect robot. After all they are no more horrible to look
at than the still living victims of atomic radio activity, another logical outcome of scientific research. Besides, I've got the
story of a lifetime."

Steeling himself, he pressed on, out of the farming region,
through brilliantly colored shrubberies, up to the great front
door. His arrival must have operated a photo electric cell for
the door opened of its own accord. What he saw made him
feel chill even on this hot day. A robot with a synthetic face
was clad in sumptuous livery, but its hands had the same
rubberoid covering of a flesh color. "His Excellency does not
receive," it said, in Portuguese, and shut the door.

Imre was nothing if not quick-witted. As he came up the
drive he had passed close by a robot weeding the gravel
sweep. It had gone on weeding without showing any con-

sciousness of his presence. "It is quite clear," he told himself, "that they don't see and so they are presumably sensitive to sound and," he shuddered to think of it, "touch." He decided to try again. He retraced his steps and approached the door which was again opened by the same flunkey robot. "Good morning, my good fellow," he said haughtily in Hungarian. The thing bowed low and held the door open for him to pass, and a strange flat mechanical voice came out of it, returning his greeting in Hungarian, "Jo napot kivanok, kegyelmes." Other footmen-robots bowed their powdered heads in deep obeisance as he passed through the great hall. So great was his anxiety to get away from these creatures, that he barely noticed the priceless furniture and pictures. He could hardly restrain himself from breaking into a run towards a small door he saw at the far end, and which instinct told him, might well afford sanctuary from their dreadful presence. He could feel the perspiration running off him in streams as he fought down the panic thought, "Suppose I don't know how to control them and they close in on me." And he remembered the giant strength of the thing in the piggery.

With a sigh of relief, he gained the sanctuary of a room which, judging by its booklined walls must be the Count's library, and sank into a deep leather armchair. For a moment he relaxed, and then stiffened into horror when he realized that two more footmen-robots, or for all he knew, two of the ones from the hall, had approached absolutely silently with their rubber feet on the deep noiseless carpet, and were standing over him. Imre heard a voice he hardly recognized as his own say with the courage born of utter desperation, "Get me some coffee and a cigar." Silently the cat-footed golems went and returned with silver salvers, the finest old English Sheffield plate, bearing an old Irish silver coffee pot and a gold box of cigars. Then they retired as silently as they had come.

Relaxing over the fine coffee and superlative cigar, Imre thought that he had things fairly well sized. "The form seems to be," he told himself, "leave them severely alone, unless they notice me, then I tell them quickly in Hungarian to do something."

The Count was obviously a great diarist, for all round the walls, beautifully bound in the finest morocco leather, were his diaries, going back sixty years or more, but the one for the latest year was missing. Greatly heartened by his discovery, Imre roamed about the great house, lost in admiration of its beautiful furnishings. Count Szolnok had none of the debased decorative tastes of the latter half of the nineteenth century. His emissaries with ample purses had scoured the world for all the most perfect art treasures of a century and more earlier. The house-robots went silently about their menial tasks, and for all the interest they took, he might not have been there. Of the engineer-Count and his cruelly maimed Countess there was no sign.

Imre was fast gaining confidence. There were, he found, only two bedrooms. The vast state bedroom of the Count and Countess, and, tucked away right at the back of the house, a simple comfortable little bed-sitting room, which must have been where Pretzlik, the maintenance engineer, lived. The other rooms, which would normally have been bedrooms, were long disused laboratories and drawing offices. A glance through some of the Count's earlier diaries had revealed the reason for this. Even before he started to build the great house he wrote that his wife was showing increasing reluctance to have any human being except himself near her. "There is no reason," he says in the diary of 1881, "why, if research is resolutely prosecuted, we should not bring about and perfect the legend of a hundred years ago, the golems or mechanical homunculi, to serve us."

It was clear from the fact that twenty years later everyone except the maintenance engineer had departed, he had succeeded, and the wish of the Countess was gratified. Imre could get no clue as to what had become of the aged couple till he saw peeping out from under the great state bed the corner of a morocco-bound diary. The last entry was dated some years previously: it read, *"We are both too weak to leave our bed, but the nursing golems are functioning to perfection, even now they are bringing us bowls of hot nourishing goose soup and refilling our hot-water bottles. I have only one fear. Pretzlik has not returned from the wharf, and ill may have befallen him, so we have been unable to do the routine check of the burial golems. Pray God they do not come too soon."*

"Well," said Imre to himself, "Count Szolnok certainly seems to have thought of everything. Nursing golems to care for them in their dotage, and golems to bury them when they are dead." Then he remembered the sinister entry in the diary, and added with a shudder, "at least I hope they were dead." Dismissing the horrible thought from his mind, he went down through the great house, where the golems carried on as they had done for half a century, each in his appointed task. A savoury smell led him to the dining-room, where meals were served and cleared away daily, although for nearly five years now, there had been no one to eat them. Imre ate, and ordered a stately golem in rich livery, some inches taller than the others, who was clearly chief butler, to

111

bring him a glass of Tokay. The Tokay was brought, but the sight of the rubber-covered hand pouring it delicately into his glass made the fine wine turn sour for him.

After the meal Imre went to walk on the lawns, he told himself he had nothing to be afraid of, but somehow he felt safer in the open air. He could hardly believe his ears, he could have sworn he heard voices singing. He moved in the direction of the phantom voices and they became louder. He followed the singing, growing louder with every step. A turn in the shubbery revealed a small mortuary chapel, built in the "gothick romance" style. The door swung open to a touch, and he entered. Walking up the aisle, he could hardly repress a shudder at the cowled and hooded golems singing a solemn requiem mass. Every night and every morning he knew that they had sung mass since the death of the Count and Countess, almost five years ago. Every night and every morning they would go on singing until some date far in the future when a failure in the perfect machinery would cause every golem to stop suddenly immobile at whatever he was doing, never to work again. In front of the altar on two elaborate carved gilt, or possibly gold, stands, rested two glass coffins. Evidently they were electrically refrigerated by some hidden plant, for the bodies were in perfect condition, without a trace of decomposition. *One glance at the expression of agony and horror on the Count's noble grey face, his twisted tortured limbs and what was mirrored in his wide open eyes showed that his worst fear had been realized. The burial golems had come too soon. But when the journalist saw what had been once Countess Szolnok's face, he clapped his hand over his own, and stumbled shuddering between the rows of singing golems out of the mortuary chapel.*

Imre Nagy bit his lower lip till it bled in his terrible mental struggle not to bolt headlong down the broad paved road to the wharf. The warm, salty taste of blood in his mouth made him feel slightly better. He felt that he, at least, was a reasoning creature of flesh and blood in this bedlam of blind automata. He would, he reasoned with himself, go over the diaries, make a selection, and take them down to the launch with him, and be away from this hateful place at first morning light. To do him credit, he never thought for a moment of pocketing a single one of the smaller objets d'art, the sale of which would have made him wealthy for life.

The journalist settled in to the library, and started to sort out the diaries. There was so much that was of fascinating interest that it proved a far longer business than he expected. Then the storm broke, a cloudburst, in all its tropical intensity, a solid sheet of water, thunder and lightning. A brilliant flash of forked lightning revealed outside the library window one of the smooth naked primeval field-golems. The water ran easily off the horrid steam dome-like protuberance where its head should have been, and its chocolate coloured rubber skin. It was apparently quite unconscious of the deluge, which showed no signs of abating. Imre shuddered. Apart from the damage the wet would do to the diaries, he felt he could not bring himself to go out in the storm and the rapidly falling night among those sightless terrible automata. Then he had an idea, such a good one that for a moment he forgot his mounting sense of horror and laughed out aloud. He would spend the night, warm and snug and dry in Pretzlik's room, in Pretzlik's bed. When he had been exploring, a glance round the room showed him that the maintenance engineer evidently did not care to be, or was not permitted to be, waited on by the creatures that he serviced. There was ample evidence of that, a coffee percolator, a little electric cooking stove, an iron for pressing clothes and a hundred and one other indications that he was a bachelor well used to looking after himself. "Well," thought Imre, "that's the one place where I shan't see a single one of them tonight." The mere thought of them made gooseflesh rise on his forearms. A few more hours sorting out the diaries he wished to take, and making notes from the ones that he would leave behind, and Imre Nagy was deep asleep in Pretzlik's deep, comfortable bed, secure in the knowledge that no service-golem would enter into that room.

That night the burial golems came for Pretzlik, as indeed they came every night since Pretzlik had died of heart failure in the cabin of the steam launch. How did they know he was dead? That is a secret that died with Pretzlik and the old Count, and how were they, the burial golems, to know that the body in Pretzlik's bed was not the dead body of Pretzlik, the maintenance engineer, but Imre Nagy, the living journalist, deep asleep, exhausted with the day's terrors and discoveries?

Silently they came, and Imre awoke to find the inflexible rubber clad steel arms closing round him. The more he struggled, the tighter they gripped. He was held as firmly as in a vice, then, with overwhelming relief, he remembered how he had dealt with the other golems. He barked a sharp command in Hungarian. He shouted and cursed them and screamed till he was hoarse, and none of it had the slightest effect on the steel and rubber creatures that gripped him and bore him away. For burial golems are simply built to deal

113

with dead people who do not speak, and are therefore not equipped to be sensitive to sound.

Screwed into Pretzlik's coffin, Imre heard the hooded golems sing interminable masses over him. On and on it went, and although he had plenty of air the singing soothed him into a sort of coma of unreality. The first flat thud of a shovelful of earth landing fair and square on the coffin lid brought him screaming back to reality, and tearing at the thick smooth wood round him till his fingernails came off. But burial golems don't hear, and the spadefuls of earth fell faster and faster although now that there was a layer over the coffin they no longer sounded the same. It was not till there was a very slight rise in temperature that Imre realized that death by suffocation is not only terrible and painful, but very, very slow.

It was an ironical end for a man who had traveled so many thousand miles to avoid death.

PART 2

THE HUMAN

THE MAN AND THE SNAKE

Ambrose Bierce

IT IS of veritabyll report, and attested of so many that there be nowe of wyse and learned none to gaynsaye it, that ye serpente hys eye hath a magnetick propertie that whosoe falleth into its svasion is drawn forwards in despyte of his wille, and perisheth miserabyll by ye creature hys byte.

Stretched at ease upon a sofa, in gown and slippers, Harker Brayton smiled as he read the foregoing sentence in old Merryster's *Marvells of Science.* "The only marvel in the matter," he said to himself, "is that the wise and learned in Merryster's day should have believed such nonsense as is rejected by most of even the ignorant in ours."

A train of reflection followed—for Brayton was a man of thought—and he unconsciously lowered his book without altering the direction of his eyes. As soon as the volume had gone below the line of sight, something in an obscure corner of the room recalled his attention to his surroundings. What he saw, in the shadow under his bed, was two small points of light, apparently about an inch apart. They might have been reflections of the gas jet above him, in metal nail heads; he gave them but little thought and resumed his reading. A moment later something—some impulse which it did not occur to him to analyze—impelled him to lower the book again and seek for what he saw before. The points of light were still there. They seemed to have become brighter than before, shining with a greenish lustre that he had not at first observed. He thought, too, that they might have moved a trifle—were somewhat nearer. They were still too much in shadow, however, to reveal their nature and origin to an indolent attention, and again he resumed his reading. Suddenly something in the text suggested a thought that made him start and drop the book for the third time to the side of the sofa, whence, escaping from his hand, it fell sprawling to the floor, back upward. Brayton, half-risen, was staring intently into the obscurity beneath the bed, where the points of light shone with, it seemed to him, an added fire. His attention was

117

now fully aroused, his gaze eager and imperative. It disclosed, almost directly under the foot-rail of the bed, the coils of a large serpent—the points of light were its eyes! Its horrible head, thrust flatly forth from the innermost coil and resting upon the outermost, was directed straight toward him, the definition of the wide, brutal jaw and the idiot-like forehead serving to show the direction of its malevolent gaze. The eyes were no longer merely luminous points; they looked into his own with a meaning, a malign significance.

II

A snake in a bedroom of a modern city dwelling of the better sort is, happily, not so common a phenomenon as to make explanation altogether needless. Harker Brayton, a bachelor of thirty-five, a scholar, idler and something of an athlete, rich, popular and of sound health, had returned to San Francisco from all manner of remote and unfamiliar countries. His tastes, always a trifle luxurious, had taken on an added exuberance from long privation; and the resources of even the Castle Hotel being inadequate to their perfect gratification, he had gladly accepted the hospitality of his friend, Dr. Druring, the distinguished scientist. Dr. Druring's house, a large old-fashioned one in what is now an obscure quarter of the city, had an outer and visible aspect of proud reserve. It plainly would not associate with the contiguous elements of its altered environment, and appeared to have developed some of the eccentricities which come of isolation. One of these was a "wing," conspicuously irrelevant in point of architecture, and no less rebellious in matter of purpose; or it was a combination of laboratory, menagerie and museum. It was here that the doctor indulged the scientific side of his nature in the study of such forms of animal life as engaged his interest and comforted his taste—which, it must be confessed, ran rather to the lower types. For one of the higher nimbly and sweetly to recommend itself unto his gentle senses it had at least to retain certain rudimentary characteristics allying it to such "dragons of the prime" as toads and snakes. His scientific sympathies were distinctly reptilian; he loved nature's vulgarians and described himself as the Zola of zoölogy. His wife and daughters not having the advantage to share his enlightened curiosity regarding the works and ways of our ill-starred fellow-creatures, were with needless austerity excluded from what he called the Snakery and doomed to companionship with their own kind, though to soften the rigors of their lot he had permitted them out of his great wealth to outdo the reptiles in the gorgeousness of their surroundings and to shine with a superior splendor.

Architecturally and in point of "furnishing" the Snakery had a severe simplicity befitting the humble circumstances of its occupants, many of whom, indeed, could not safely have been intrusted with the liberty that is necessary to the full enjoyment of luxury, for they had the troublesome peculiarity of being alive. In their own apartments, however, they were under as little personal restraint as was compatible with their protection from the baneful habit of swallowing one another; and, as Brayton had thoughtfully been apprised, it was more than a tradition that some of them had at divers times been found in parts of the premises where it would have embarrassed them to explain their presence. Despite the Snakery and its uncanny associations—to which, indeed, he gave little attention—Brayton found life at the Druring mansion very much to his mind.

III

Beyond a smart shock of surprise and a shudder of mere loathing Mr. Brayton was not greatly affected. His first thought was to ring the call bell and bring a servant; but although the bell cord dangled within easy reach he made no movement toward it; it had occurred to his mind that the act might subject him to the suspicion of fear, which he certainly did not feel. He was more keenly conscious of the incongruous nature of the situation than affected by its perils; it was revolting, but absurd.

The reptile was of a species with which Brayton was unfamiliar. Its length he could only conjecture; the body at the largest visible part seemed about as thick as his forearm. In what way was it dangerous, if in any way? Was it venomous? Was it a constrictor? His knowledge of nature's danger signals did not enable him to say; he had never deciphered the code.

If not dangerous the creature was at least offensive. It was *de trop*—"matter out of place"—an impertinence. The gem was unworthy of the setting. Even the barbarous taste of our time and country, which had loaded the walls of the room with pictures, the floor with furniture and the furniture with bric-a-brac, had not quite fitted the place for this bit of the savage life of the jungle. Besides—insupportable thought!— the exhalations of its breath mingled with the atmosphere which he himself was breathing.

These thoughts shaped themselves with greater or less definition in Brayton's mind and begot action. The process is what we call consideration and decision. It is thus that we are wise and unwise. It is thus that the withered leaf in an autumn breeze shows greater or less intelligence than its fellows, falling upon the land or upon the lake. The secret of human action is an open one: something contracts our muscles. Does it matter if we give to the preparatory molecular changes the name of will?

Brayton rose to his feet and prepared to back softly away from the snake, without disturbing it if possible, and through the door. Men retire so from the presence of the great, for greatness is power and power is a menace. He knew that he could walk backward without error. Should the monster follow, the taste which had plastered the walls with paintings had consistently supplied a rack of murderous Oriental weapons from which he could snatch one to suit the occasion. In the mean time the snake's eyes burned with a more pitiless malevolence than before.

Brayton lifted his right foot free of the floor to step backward. That moment he felt a strong aversion to doing so.

"I am accounted brave," he thought; "is bravery, then, no more than pride? Because there are none to witness the shame shall I retreat?"

He was steadying himself with his right hand upon the back of a chair, his foot suspended.

"Nonsense!" he said aloud; "I am not so great a coward as to fear to seem to myself afraid."

He lifted the foot a little higher by slightly bending the knee and thrust it sharply to the floor—an inch in front of the other! He could not think how that occurred. A trial with the left foot had the same result; it was again in advance of the right. The hand upon the chair back was grasping it; the arm was straight, reaching somewhat backward. One might have said that he was reluctant to lose his hold. The snake's malignant head was still thrust forth from the inner coil as before, the neck level. It had not moved, but its eyes were now electric sparks, radiating an infinity of luminous needles.

The man had an ashy pallor. Again he took a step forward, and another, partly dragging the chair, which when finally released fell upon the floor with a crash. The man groaned; the snake made neither sound nor motion, but its eyes were two dazzling suns. The reptile itself was wholly concealed by them. They gave off enlarging rings of rich and vivid colors, which at their greatest expansion successively vanished like soap-bubbles; they seemed to approach his very face, and anon were an immeasurable distance away. He heard, somewhere, the continuous throbbing of a great drum, with desultory bursts of far music, inconceivably sweet, like the tones of an aeolian harp. He knew it for the sunrise melody of Memnon's statue, and thought he stood in the Nileside reeds hearing with exalted sense that immortal anthem through the silence of the centuries.

The music ceased; rather, it became by insensible degrees the distant roll of a retreating thunder-storm. A landscape, glittering with sun and rain, stretched before him, arched with a vivid rainbow framing in its giant curve a hundred visible cities. In the middle distance a vast serpent, wearing a crown, reared its head out of its voluminous convolutions and looked at him with his dead mother's eyes. Suddenly this enchanting landscape seemed to rise swiftly upward like the drop scene at a theatre, and vanished in a blank. Something struck him a hard blow upon the face and breast. He had fallen to the floor; the blood ran from his broken nose and his bruised lips. For a time he was dazed and stunned, and lay with closed eyes, his face against the floor. In a few moments he had rceovered, and then knew that this fall, by withdrawing his eyes, had broken the spell that held him. He felt that now, by keeping his gaze averted, he would be able to retreat. But the thought of the serpent within a few feet of his head, yet unseen—perhaps in the very act of springing upon him and throwing its coils about his throat—was too horrible! He lifted his head, stared again into those baleful eyes and was again in bondage.

The snake had not moved and appeared somewhat to have lost its power upon the imagination; the gorgeous illusions of a few moments before were not repeated. Beneath that flat and brainless brow its black, beady eyes simply glittered as at first with an expression unspeakably malignant. It was as if the creature, assured of its triumph, had determined to practice no more alluring wiles.

Now ensued a fearful scene. The man, prone upon the floor, within a yard of his enemy, raised the upper part of his body upon his elbows, his head thrown back, his legs extended to their full length. His face was white between its stains of blood; his eyes were strained open to their uttermost expansion. There was froth upon his lips; it dropped off in flakes. Strong convulsions ran through his body, making almost serpentile undulations. He bent himself at the waist, shifting his legs from side to side. And every movement left him a little nearer to the snake. He thrust his hands forward to brace himself back, yet constantly advanced upon his elbows.

Dr. Druring and his wife sat in the library. The scientist was in rare good humor.

"I have just obtained by exchange with another collector," he said, "a splendid specimen of the *ophiophagus*."

"And what may that be?" the lady inquired with a somewhat languid interest.

"Why, bless my soul, what profound ignorance! My dear, a man who ascertains after marriage that his wife does not know Greek is entitled to a divorce. The *ophiophagus* is a snake that eats other snakes."

"I hope it will eat all yours," she said, absently shifting the lamp. "But how does it get the other snakes? By charming them, I suppose."

"That is just like you, dear," said the doctor, with an affectation of petulance. "You know how irritating to me is any allusion to that vulgar superstition about a snake's power of fascination."

The conversation was interrupted by a mighty cry, which rang through the silent house like the voice of a demon shouting in a tomb! Again and yet again it sounded, with terrible distinctness. They sprang to their feet, the man confused, the lady pale and speechless with fright. Almost before the echoes of the last cry had died away the doctor was out of the room, springing up the stairs two steps at a time. In the corridor in front of Brayton's chamber he met some servants who had come from the upper floor. Together they rushed at the door without knocking. It was unfastened and gave way. Brayton lay upon his stomach on the floor, dead. His head and arms were partly concealed under the foot-rail of the bed. They pulled the body away, turning it upon the back. The face was daubed with blood and froth, the eyes were wide open, staring—a dreadful sight!

"Died in a fit," said the scientist, bending his knee and placing hand upon the heart. While in that position, he chanced to look under the bed. "Good God!" he added, "how did this thing get in here?"

He reached under the bed, pulled out the snake and flung it, still coiled, to the center of the room, whence with a harsh, shuffling sound it slid across the polished floor till stopped by the wall, where it lay without motion. It was a stuffed snake; its eyes were two shoe buttons.

THE HEADLESS MILLER OF KOBOLD'S KEEP

Irvin Ashkenazy

Mr. Abiathar Hall, Purchasing Director,
Americana Antiques, Inc., New York, N. Y.

Dear Mr. Hall:

I herewith tender my resignation, effective immediately. Maybe what I have seen tonight is all in my mind. Maybe it never really happened and the events that I believe to have occurred are but morbid hallucinations. If so, then I am the victim of the maddest cacodemonia a man's mind has ever been blasted with and all the more reason why I should resign this job and stop poking my nose into strange and unholy places. I'm through!

In all fairness to you, I suppose, I should give an account of what has occurred to bring me to this decision. I find it difficult to do so. I am no occultist. I have always scoffed at tales of spirits, ghosts, devils, or other spiritual manifestations. But tonight my faith in the fundamental reasonableness of God and Nature is shaken. Perhaps, as I've suggested already, I'm mad. After reading my account I suppose *you* will be sure of it!

How you ever suspected the existence of Kobold's Keep, even as only a legend, is a matter of wonder to me. It is marked on no map that I have ever seen. And I was practically on top of the place before I found anybody who'd ever heard of it.

I had dismissed the existence of Kobold's Keep as being, in fact, a legend, until one morning, while driving north along a narrow dirt road that wound among the mountains, I came to the village of Merlin.

While the attendant ministered to my gas tank at the hamlet's solitary filling station I sat back and took stock of my surroundings. The mountain peaks that serrated the skyline ahead seemed to be even loftier, craggier, more forbidding than the ones I had come over already. I wondered whether my brakes and bearings would hold out until I got to the next town. The sour-faced, close-mouthed hill-billy

123

who was pumping gasoline into my tank didn't impress me much as a possible repair man. And neither did the old fellow, whom I took to be his assistant, who was sitting at the base of the gas pump, knees drawn up under his chin, eyes shut tight, apparently fast asleep.

The old man caught my interest. He was, to say the least, an unusual type. His long, lank, dirty gray hair fell to his shoulders in two braids, like an Indian's. His face, weather-beaten and hairless, was broad and lean, the cheekbones as prominent as a cat's, his nose thin and hooked. I was about to question the station attendant whether the old fellow wasn't a member of some Indian reservation hereabouts that I hadn't heard of, when I noticed his hair more closely. At first glance it had seemed to be a dirty gray, but I saw now that it was actually red—a faded, nondescript, pinkish red, but red, nevertheless. I'd never heard of a red-headed Indian.

The ancient, red-headed anomaly yawned. I observed a curious, crescent-shaped swelling in the center of his fore-head. Its bottom border was fringed with little hairs, like misplaced eyelashes.

As if sensing my fixed stare, the old man's head lifted. I looked for his eyes to open. They seemed oddly sunken.

It was an unusually hot day. Yet, as I looked, I grew cold—cold and rigid, and a little sick; for the old man had opened his one, solitary, sky-blue eye. It was in the center of his forehead.

My horror must have been written on my face, for the old man's mouth slit in a frightful, toothless grin. I turned away hastily....

Of course, I'd heard of similar cases of persons born with cyclopean eye formations as recorded in medical history. But being faced with such an individual unexpectedly, even in broad daylight, is enough to give anyone a start.

I jerked my eyes away and tried to get a grip on myself—all the while being aware of that great, bulging, sky-blue orb fixed on me in dreadful contemplation.

"Have you ever," I asked the surly-faced attendant (as I had asked at every town, village, and hamlet in the state through which I'd passed), "have you ever heard of a place hereabouts called Kobold's Keep?"

The attendant, who was screwing my radiator cap back on, looked up suddenly. He stared at me a moment; then, averting his gaze, finished what he was doing.

"Naw," he growled, and knocked a tomato can into the ditch with a rifled stream of tobacco juice. "Never heered of it."

A nasal, cackling laugh clattered on the still air.

124

"Don't ye believe him, mister! He's lyin', Jim is! He's heered of the place all right!"

Torn between repulsion and a horrible fascination, I slowly turned and gazed on the dreadful face of the ancient mountain cyclops who sat by the gasoline pump. His bulging eye rolled, glistening in the bright sunlight. His toothless mouth writhed with crazy mirth.

"Don't pay him no mind," the attendant muttered sullenly. "He's crazy."

The old man slapped his thigh with a renewed spasm of hissing laughter.

"If that don't beat all! 'Don't pay him no mind,' he says! I'm outen my head, I am! What you want to lie to the feller for, Jim? Tell him!" He paused, subsiding reflectively, "But you can't go thataway, mister. You gotta leave your autymobile behind. It'll take more'n gasoline to git *that* thing over Black Knicht Pass!"

Black Knicht ... Black Knicht ... I stared at the old fellow curiously. Shockingly repulsive as he still was, most of the horror I'd experienced upon first laying eyes on him was fast evaporating. He was simply a freak. ... But what had he just said?

"Black Knicht Pass," he repeated, pronouncing the "Knicht" with the old Teutonic "ch" guttural—a sound that was dropped from modern English many centuries ago. "It's the on'y way ye kin git over the ridge into the Devil's Millhop."

"Black *Knight,* you mean, don't you?" I said curiously.

The bulging blue eye blinked.

"Knicht," the old man repeated, "Black Knicht.... It'll take ye over into the Millhop, and there—there ye'll find the thrivin' town of Kobold's Keep!" His eldritch laughter whistled and sucked between his toothless gums.

"Iffen you listen to that loon," the attendant spat, "you're fixin' to git yourself in a peck o' trouble. You want to stay outen Kobold's Keep, brother!"

Then there *was* such a place!

"Yeah," he growled sourly. "It's there, all right. And so is hell!"

At the moment I was puzzled and irritated because of the fellow's manifest reluctance to have me go to Kobold's Keep. After all, what business was it of his? I tried to discover some reason for his attitude.

"Don't be askin' no questions and you won't be gittin no lies," he responded discourteously. "You can't git to Kobold's Keep onless you walk or git a mule. And when you git there the main thing you'll be wantin' to do is to git out. So just drive on your way, brother, and forgit that you ever heered about the damned place!"

"But I've got to get there," I insisted. "I have business there."

One bushy black eyebrow lifted, "Business?" the mountaineer drawled incredulously. "Business in Kobold's Keep?"

"And why shouldn't he be havin' business there?" the old man cackled. "Kobold's Keep is a right smart town. Better'n this hole! Ye needn't be a'knockin', Jim, ye scut! Kobold's Keep is one o' the finest towns in these whole mountings!"

I began to lose patience. "I have business there! Damned important business! And if I can't get there by car, then I'd just as soon leave it here and rent a horse or a mule for the trip."

"Must be gosh-awful important," the attendant muttered.

"See here," I cried, "what the devil's the matter with the place? Why are you so damned anxious to have me stay away?"

He glanced at me out of the corner of his eye, and spat.

"Believe it or not, mister, I'm tryin' to keep you out for your own good."

"Oh, nonsense. What is there to be afraid of?"

"Wal," he drawled, "for one thing—the people."

"The people? What's the matter with the people?"

"Yah!" the old cyclops screeched. "Ain't nothin' the matter with 'em! Don't you listen to that damn' fool, mister! The citizens o' Kobold's Keep are right fine, upstandin' citizens!" And the glistening blue eye in his forehead blinked emphatically.

The attendant swept the freak with a lowering glance. He turned to me and jerked a thumb over his shoulder.

"*He* comes from Kobold's Keep. *He's* one of 'em. And he don't look so bad as the most of 'em. But that ain't the wust part."

He pulled a dirty rag out of his pocket and began to wipe the inside of my windshield.

"No?" I prompted.

"Naw," he drawled out of the corner of his mouth. "It ain't. The place is hexed. There's been a curse on it since the days when Injuns owned these mountings—afore the days o' my great-gran'pappy's great-gran'pappy, hunnerts and hunnerts o' year ago. That curse has been on it. And still is. I ain't askin' you to believe nothin', mister. I'm just tellin' you that no stranger who ever got into Kobold's Keep ever lived more'n a day after leavin' it!"

"Whut's that he's sayin'?" the old man drooled. "Is that lowdown dawg tellin' more lies about the Keep? Don't ye believe a word he says, mister! He's plumb loony, he is! Why, I'll guide ye to the Millhop myself, I will! And cheap, too!"

"You're hired!" I agreed promptly, and turned to the attendant. "Could I rent parking-space over in that shed for a couple of days?"

He shrugged. "You can. And, I reckon, you'll be wantin' a mule, too." He seemed to give up all efforts to dissuade me from visiting Kobold's Keep.

"*Two* mules," I corrected. "One for my guide."

He laughed shortly and with a grim significance that, at the moment, entirely escaped me.

"That'll be all right," the cyclops croaked hastily. "I won't be needin' no critter. I'd ruther lead ye afoot."

"And see that he allus keeps a good ten paces away f'om the mule," the attendant growled, "or the critter'll shy and throw ye as sure as God made little ducks!"

He sauntered around to the back of his shack behind the station and presently returned leading as ancient and woebe-gone-looking a beast as I've ever seen, alive or dead. He led the blind, spavined creature to within thirty feet of the old freak when the hobbling bag of bones suddenly snorted, as if he'd scented a mountain lion, reared up in terror, planted his front legs down with a crash, and refused to budge.

"Do ye git whut I mean?" the attendant leered.

Frankly, I didn't. But I could hardly afford to waste any more time trying to get around the patent stupidities of my filling-station mountaineer. I got down to business. How much did he want for the use of the mule for a couple of days? I was willing to pay a reasonable rental.

"*Rent* this mule?" he grinned sardonically. "I ain't rentin', mister. I'm sellin'. I ain't so sure you're coming back."

I flared with anger. Hadn't he my car as security?

He shrugged. "I'm sellin'. One hunnert dollars. Take it or leave it."

It was an outrageous price to pay for that moribund animal, but it was too early to be looking around and I was too much in a hurry, anyway. I took it.

He drove my car into the shed, then got out and threw a mildewed old saddle on the mule.

"Must be moughty important business you've got in Kobold's Keep," he muttered as he tightened the cinch strap.

"You've been there, I suppose?" I ventured casually.

He looked up—shook his head slowly.

"Naw, mister. Once, when I was a young sprout, I clumb to the top of the Pass and looked down into the Millhop. I could see the shacks of the place way off below. Yeah. I could even see some of the critters who live there. But I never went down to take a closer look. I got better sense."

"That doesn't sound reasonable!" I protested. "What's there to be scared of? What kind of people live there?"

He glanced at the cyclops. The great eye in the center of the freak's forehead winked weirdly, the toothless black gums showing in a lipless grin.

"Same kind as he is, I reckon. On'y this'n seems like the best-lookin' critter that ever came outen the Devil's Millhop. That's why he's still here now, I reckon. The others what tried it got kilt or chased back. There was no puttin' up with the sight of them!"

Black Knicht Pass ... the Devil's Millhop ... Kobold's Keep ... it all sounded like a Barnum's paradise. I guess I must have grinned, for the mountaineer scowled and I could get no further word out of him.

The cyclops hopped to his feet with surprising agility as I mounted my decrepit steed, and plunged down a steep embankment into a ravine that ran at right angles to the road. I hesitated, met the jaundiced sneer of the station attendant, then kicked the ribs of my blind mule so that he half slid, half dived down the road bank. The cyclops, turning, winked, then plunged into the woods, leading a good thirty feet or more.

Through silent, needle-cushioned pine forest, across dark and rocky mountain flanks, over verdant, flower-studded meadows the strange old fellow guided me. For all his apparent senility he was possessed of an astonishing vigor. His thin old legs skipped along with the spring and easy grace of youth. And when the country began to grow rougher, the grassy carpet sparser, and the rocks blacker and more cruelly sharp, he negotiated the difficult terrain with the supple, careless ease of a mountain goat, while my feeble old mule gasped and heaved and forced me to dismount and struggle along beside her over the crenellated rocks.

Our progress, however, was steady, and I found times during the smoother stretches in which to ponder certain strange peculiarities that I had noticed in the natives of this part of the state—and, more particularly, the peculiarities that I had observed in the eldritch fantasm who was my guide.

That he was a hybrid of some sort I had no doubt. Probably he was a Melungeon—one of those dark people who are descendants of early English settlers who took Indian wives. Still, I had never before met one who displayed such a combination of physical degeneracy with wiry stamina. As I contemplated his skipping figure, his pale pink braids waving in the air, his ragged overalls constantly on the verge of slipping off, I couldn't help but fancy that he wasn't exactly human—that he was, really, a cloven-footed goblin, an emanation of evil possessed of the immortality and deathless strength of Satan.

I smiled to myself. That was giving my fancy entirely too much leeway. For the world to me was a reasonable place—and belief in devils, evil spirits and such I took as a matter of course to be the products of sick minds and the spawn of ignorance.

The cyclops had called the mountain we would have to cross the "Black Knicht"—pronouncing it with the long unused Anglo-Saxon "ch" sound. Black Knicht! Why, the word "knight" hadn't been pronounced that way since the Fourteenth Century—a hundred years before America was officially discovered!

I knew that the mountaineers inhabiting these peaks are, perhaps, the purest bred stock in all America—fair, blue-eyed folk, descended from the earliest English settlers, being born, marrying among themselves, and dying within the radius of a few miles, generation after generation. I have met many who have never yet seen a railroad train, although I suspect aircraft passing overhead have become a familiar sight by now. I have found many a treasure of furniture and brassware among their mean huts—articles inherited from father to son down through the centuries.

Yet—Black Knicht! It worried me. Fourteenth Century stuff in Twentieth Century America! I concluded that the way he pronounced it must have been only a personal peculiarity.

Our ascent had become many degrees steeper. Then, quite abruptly, as we came to a looming wall of rock barring our way, the cyclops vanished. I soon discovered that he had disappeared into a narrow cleft in the raw stone—a cleft that rapidly widened into a wide, though unevenly graded, road. Overhead the sky gleamed like a crooked blue ribbon and thinned the shadows within the pass so that the figure of my guiding imp was a visible, though dim, silhouette. A cold, dank wind whispered about my ears and explored my summer clothes with chill fingers. I crouched close to my mule's neck for warmth.

Suddenly the path at the bottom of the crevasse grew straighter, smoother. Far ahead I could see the walls of the cleft fall away into sky, crystal-clear, a bright background framing the black silhouette of the cyclops, standing motionless, watching me like a monstrous, one-eyed ghoul. . . .

Thoughtlessly, I let my mule have its head, and it wasn't

until she suddenly snorted, reared, and flung me to the hard rock that I realized I'd let her approach the cyclops too closely. I still was seeing stars while the clattering gallop of my panic-stricken animal drummed in my ears, sounding more faintly with every hoofbeat.

I picked myself up and plodded painfully up to where the cyclops stood, his bulging eye sparkling giddily, his toothless jaws writhing in silent laughter.

We had reached the top of Black Knight Pass. I peered down and saw spread before me the panorama of the Devil's Millhop.

It resembles nothing so much as a huge black bowl with vertical sides, and almost perfectly circular. Perhaps it's as much as four miles in diameter. I could see absolutely not a single break in the great barrier of black cliffs that surround it. Then the ugly devil who was with me pointed to a precipitous path dropping away from the lip of the pass down the face of the cliff by a series of narrow, natural steps. I believe now that it's the only route by which a human being may enter or leave that frightful chasm.

The terrain of the Devil's Millhop, while showing patches of green here and there, seemed to be the same color as the rocks—basalt black. And though I scanned every section of the place, the only habitations I could discern were some curious hutches of black stones, almost invisible against the soot-like ground, grouped near the center of the bowl. A narrow waterfall splashed from the distant cliffs like a sliver of pale silver, and fed a brook coursing through the center of the Millhop. The brook, after speeding down a sink about a quarter of a mile in diameter that indented the bottom of the bowl, seemed to disappear into the ground.

"See yander?" the cyclops pointed, grinning. "In the sink, where the brook disappears ... see, that fine black mansion?"

I strained my eyes. Sure enough. It was quite pretentious, built in the style of—a castle? Anyway, I thought I could discern turrets. There seemed to be some kind of bulky affair hanging over the spot where the brook vanished—something that seemed suspended on an axis jutting from the building.

"Oh, that!" the cyclops cackled. "That's the mill! Gran'-pappy Kobolder called it the Keep. He had him a fancy house across the water that he called the Keep. So when he come here, he and his three sons they built this mill to grind the corn they larned to grow. And the ole man—he called it the Keep!" The eye winked.

"When did this happen?" Those curious stone dwellings offered food for speculation.

"Oh, long, long, long time ago, I reckon." The cyclops sat on his haunches and grinned spasmodically. "The ole folks down yander"—he jerked a thumb over his shoulder—"they sometimes mumble lies of whut *their* great-great-gran'pappy done tole 'em. Maybe some of it ain't lies, though."

The eye winked confidentially.

"Maybe it ain't a lie that Gran'pappy Kobolder was a boss man—a Knicht, they called 'em in those days. . . . Yeah—a Knicht. Funny, ain't it? He was a sinful man, murderin' and thievin'—yeah. . . . They chased him plumb outen the land over there 'cross the water . . . and he come here with a slew of people who, I reckon, had been sharecroppin' on his land. I reckon it was somethin' like that. . . . They come here and settle down. . . . But all that's a moughty long time ago, I reckon. Nobody knows how long. There's an old book made o' sheephide, seems-like, down yander in the Keep. Gran'pap wrote it hisself. He was full o' book-larnin', they say. A boss Knicht had to be, I reckon. But I don't figure it's in English. . . . Queer-lookin' printin'. Some furrin' language they spoke in them days, I guess. . . ."

The bulging blue eye regarded me contemplatively. I must have showed my excitement.

"Whut's on your mind?" he snarled, his black gums showing.

"Who owns that property?" I asked, trying to repress my eagerness. "Who is living there now?"

The old degenerate burst into a hilarious cackle.

" 'Who owns it?' he says! 'Who's livin' there now!' Hee, hee!"

I snapped, "What's so funny?"

"I'll tell you who owns it, mister! The feller that built it owns it! And the feller who built it is the feller who's still livin' in it right this very minute! It's old Robin Kobolder—the great-great-great-great gran'pappy of us all down yander!"

I didn't press the point. The fellow, of course, was quite mad.

The glistening eye studied me avidly.

"How come you're so all-fired set on comin' here?" he inquired. "What you so het up about Gran-pappy Kobold and his ole mill?"

I explained as patiently as I could that I might buy it if the price was right. Now that I was completely recovered and rested I was on pins and needles to be moving down before night overtook us.

The huge blue eye rolled with high humor.

"Let's get going," I broke into his cackling.

He scampered down the side of the precipice as nimbly as

any lemur. Evidently he knew every step, ridge and cranny by heart. I followed slowly, laboriously, clinging to the wall with trepidation, averting my eyes from the sheer drop below me, yet considering at the same time that it would require careful preparation and much delicate work with block and tackle to remove any possible purchase I might make in this strange crater.

When I got to the bottom I paused, sniffing disgustedly, for the smell of the ground was utterly fetid. I scuffed the soil with my boot, picked up a handful. It was loose, granular and flinty, reeking with an unpleasant chemical cacosmia. No wonder vast stretches of this bottom land were dark and barren. No possible thing might grow in it. Perhaps in some ancient day this had been the mouth of a monster volcano that had spewed up poisonous substances which, even today, carried the breath of death. . . .

A silence covered the valley like a choking blanket of dark swan's-down. An invisible cap seemed to seal the hole in the ground hermetically against the murmurs of life outside—the whisper of summer breezes, the song of birds, the rustle of trees. But as we strode toward the cluster of stone hutches on the farther side of the bowl I began to distinguish the sound of the waterfall—echoing and re-echoing like water splashing inside a bass drum. It accentuated the silence by its very solitude.

When I had viewed them from a distance I could have sworn I'd seen men moving about among the black stone hutches, but, as we approached, they appeared to be strangely deserted. The houses, thrown crudely together, were shockingly primitive and foul. They squatted in aimless clusters like a colony of filthy black bugs. The rock, I surmised, was their sole source of building material. As far as I could see, not a tree existed anywhere in this monstrous bowl. In fact, the only green things I saw growing were the infrequent garden patches that grew in hummocks of what was, quite evidently, imported soil.

The cyclops halted before one of the larger hutches.

"Funnel!" he screeched. "Open up, ye blabbermouth scound'el! It's me, Glim!"

There was no reply. Perhaps it was my nerves—but I could not escape the feeling that I was being watched; that eyes—many pairs of eyes—were peering at me covertly; eyes glinting from between stone chinks—peering from around corners. . . . I could catch fleeting glimpses of bodies from out of the corner of my eye now and then, but whenever I turned quickly there was—nothing.

Enraged, the cyclops was kicking the tall slate slab that

served as a door, and presently, slowly, inch by inch, the slab began to move outward. The cyclops stepped back, his huge blue eye blazing with wrath. A creature stuck its head out and peered at us.

I cannot adequately describe it. I can only say that Horror stared from that misshapen, rat-eared head. It was the head and face of a being scarcely three feet tall, capped with a matted bush of filthy black furze that straggled into the squinting, Mongoloid eyes. The creature had no nose. From where the nose was supposed to be the face shot out horizontally in a ghastly anostosis of the bone, both jaws opening forward and outward, the green-yellow fangs protruding beyond the lips like the mouth of a misshapen banshee.

"Git outen the door!" the cyclops screeched, and advancing a pace, grabbed the creature by the hair and jerked it out.

The tiny gargoyle had virtually no body at all. Its huge, chinless head sloped down to a scrawny infant's torso, a pair of crooked matchstick legs, and two tiny clubbed feet. Its bent toes and tiny fingers were webbed.

"That's Funnel," the cyclops said, nodding to the creature.

Glancing at the monstrous mouth, I understood the name. He stood there in the muted light, eyeing me, motionless. I stared a moment as the cyclops entered the foul-smelling hutch. Each slanting eye of the creature contained two beady pupils.

Within the rocky hutch a perpetual twilight reigned. The light filtered through the cracks and crannies between the slabs of the rock. In the center of the room was a table made of a single slab of slate supported by a block of hewn granite. Smaller blocks served as chairs. On the table were a broken clay crock and several clay mugs.

I followed the cyclops' example and sat down at the table. He poured a dark, heavy-odored liquor into two of the mugs and handed me one. I watched him drain his, then sniffed at mine. A rather sweetish, though flat, scent.

The bulging blue eye winked confidentially.

"Not bad, eh?" He smacked his lips and filled his mug again. "We make it outen honey. It goes down even better'n White Mule."

I tasted it—and was rather shaken by its strength. A hazy memory floated around the inner depths of my mind . . . the memory of tales of ancient Cornish feasting-halls, where warriors rolled under the benches, drunk with a fermented liquor made of honey, water, and spices . . . They called it mead. . . .

Idiocy writhed in the freak's gibbering mouth.

"Ole Gran'pappy Kobolder—we call him Kobold for short —wal, he was the one who fust mixed the fust mashpot full of this stuff. He mixed it up in Cornwall, and up in the fur North Country—and then he brought the idear with him here. He was a smart bugger, he was!"

My skin prickled.

"How do you know all this?" I asked.

But he didn't hear, apparently. And, presently, I remarked on the shyness of the populace around here.

The cyclops agreed. "They ain't used to visitors," he explained. "Shucks, the last time anybody come hereabouts was—wal, come to think of it, it was exactly a year ago to this very day. It were an old priest, I remember. Yeah. He crawled down Black Knicht and began prayin' for his salvation when he seen some of the ugly scound'els around here! I reckon he figured he'd come to an outcrop of Satan's kingdom!"

And the cyclops laughed with huge, nasal mirth, his rolling eye crinkling at the corners.

"I showed him around. Yeah. I took the holy scound'el down to the Keep itself! I showed him the furniture, the things that's been lyin' around untouched for hunnerts and hunnerts of years. Yeah. . . . But when I showed him Gran'pappy's ole book, blamed if the rascal didn't claim that it was a fake!"

"A fake!"

"Yeah. The blamed ole fool claimed that Gran'pappy never wrote it. Said it was a Bible printed by some feller named Caxton!"

You can understand how I thrilled to my very soul. A Bible by Caxton! William Caxton, date—1477! I realized that I was on the verge of a priceless discovery.

There was a stealthy scuffling of footfalls just outside the walls of the hutch—I'd been aware of them for several minutes now. I could almost feel the eyes peering at me through the chinks and envision the shapeless monstrosities crowding about the hutch to spy on me—to listen. My horror and disgust were giving way now to a misty sort of pity. Poor, hopeless, Godforsaken wretches! They were so desperately frightened of, yet hungry for, contact with the outside world. But, I sighed to myself, better that they stay here, unknown and unmolested. The milk of human kindness ran thin throughout the world. . . . Once I thought I heard a sound in the rear of the room—the dark threshold of what was probably a sleeping-chamber.

"Gran'pappy didn't cotton to that priest none," the cyclops was mouthing again. "When mornin' come, damn iffen we didn't find that priest lyin' in the door of the main room in the mill. His head was chopped clean off."

"Gran'pappy?" I repeated stupidly.

"Shore. Gran'pappy Kobold. He didn't like that old priest. He chopped his haid off!" He grinned more hideously than ever, and edged a little closer toward me. "Though, jes' between you and me, stranger, maybe the old priest stumbled against the door-jamb under which Gran'pappy's ax-head is hangin', and the shakin' made it fall so that it hit the priest in the neck and killed him. . . . Still"—he shrugged—"ye can't tell about sperrits. They say that them what see's Gran'pappy's sperrit walkin' dies on the spot. Or, anyways, within twenty-four hours. It ain't never failed yit, mister!"

I pressed him for details about Grandfather Kobolder.

He grinned nauseatingly, winked, and leaned forward.

"He was the Knicht. The big boss man. But he was gittin' old—old and the cold was criipin' into his bones. He began cotchin' young uns when their mammies weren't lookin'—and then cuttin' off their haids and drinkin' their blood. It kept him young, it did. Mebbe, if they'd let him alone, he could live for ever thataway. . . ." The lipless mouth receded from the black, gangrenous gums. "But no—they druv him off. He and his three sons and his three daughters had to skedaddle for their lives! They come here . . . they settled down. . . ."

The cyclops filled his mug and drained it at a gulp, his eye shining bright.

"Yeah," he rasped, "but soon the cold come again. . . . The ole man needed blood. He tried to git his youngest son—but the scound'el took the knife away f'om him, stabbed him daid, cut off his haid, sculped him, and hung it at the belt. The murderin' whelp!"

I stared, transfixed at the glaring rage suddenly contorting that evil face. It subsided slowly.

"You," I ventured timidly, "you are all his descendants?"

"Yeah. His chillen ma'ied 'mongst themselves, and *their* chillen ma'ied 'mongst themselves, I reckon. Later on mebbe there was an Injun gal or two to mix with. But not often. It's been mostly—jest us!"

My gorge rose. These amorphous creatures, a self-sustaining breed of compounded incests, had miraculously existed century after century through deepening shadows of insanity, through successive generations of horror and deformity, alone, shunned by the world, isolated from civilization, fit only for death!

A sudden weird mewing in the next room snatched up my shocked attention. I stared at the opening of the chamber.

My eyes slowly lowered to the Thing that appeared on the floor.

Rolling, squirming, writhing its way out of the opening was a naked, armless, legless, eyeless, earless Thing. It paused on the threshold, as if it sensed our presence, mewed once, like a frightened kitten, then continued its weirdly painful progress until it reached the door. The cyclops got up, opened the door, and it rolled out.

I rose, nauseated. Through the wide-open doorway I could see that the shadows had lengthened considerably; that, in fact, time had passed so swiftly that it was nearly twilight. The idea of spending the night here, which I'd originally entertained, now left me trembling.

"Let's get on down to the Keep!" I cried. "Let's get on down. I want to see these things, buy them if I can, and leave!"

The cyclops licked the edge of his mouth with a thick, coal-black tongue. I shoved some bills into his hand and we both sallied forth into the deepening dusk, walking briskly to the brook and following it down into the sink.

"Buy them!" the cyclops kept hissing to himself with thoughtful glee. "Buy them—and leave!" He seemed to mouth the words as if they tasted good.

As we approached the old mill I was struck with the similarity of its design to that of several old castles of Norman vintage that I had seen in England. The silent mill-wheel hung motionless on its broken, rust-eaten axis, the swift waters of the stream breaking about it futilely. As we came more closely toward the old mill house I was struck by the strength of the chemical vapors that swirled into my nostrils. I stopped, half suffocated.

The cyclops clutched my arm, grinning.

"Come on," he snarled, "come on."

We stumbled to the bottom of that dank, mephitic pit, waded across the brook, and stepped across the threshold into the open doorway of Kobold's Keep.

Its interior was a revelation. Though laden and crusted with filth, everything was, perhaps, as the owner had left it unknown centuries ago. The spacious chambers were timbered with Gothic arches and ornamented with gargoyles of wood. The furniture was of an undetermined period. Certainly it antedated any of the so-called "period" furniture that we recognize today—and antedated it, I'll swear, by centuries. As I scuffed through the strange and ancient old house a feeling that was nearly awe encompassed me. If the story of old Robin Kobolder's voyage to the New World could be authenticated a new chapter would be added to American history!

At first I was suspicious of the extraordinary state of preservation of the woodwork and, especially, of certain stiff damask draperies I saw still hanging there. I am now convinced, however, that these objects are entirely authentic. And the most reasonable conjecture I can offer as to their preservation is that the strong chemical exhalations rising from the ground have served as an effective bactericide, halting the process of decomposition through the centuries.

Presently I found myself in a large, nearly empty room, whose paneless windows gaped upon the teetering mill-wheel and the yawning pit into which the brook vanished. It had been, apparently, an armorer's workshop. A few blades of ancient design and all rust yet hung precariously on the walls. Glancing about, I perceived the huge bronze blade of a battle-ax hanging, edge downward like a guillotine, over the lintel of the door I had just entered. A black stain crusted the greater part of its surface.

A splintering crash!

I spun around, my heart beating wildly. The cyclops stood there, grinning at me, winking that ghastly eye of his. But when I saw what he had done my fright gave way to swift anger. He'd smashed one of those priceless chairs to fragments!

"You damned fool!" I yelled. "What did you do that for?" And, like a hen gathering in a lost chick, I fell on my knees and gathered together the pieces of the chair tenderly.

The cyclops shrugged. "We'll be needin' a fire, I reckon. We gotta have firewood!"

An authentic Fifteenth Century chair—firewood!

I warned him to keep his hands off the furniture while I prowled about.

The book lay on a huge work table near the center of the room. It was a Bible, all right—a Caxton Bible! My eyes devoured its priceless pages, my fingers infinitely tender, infinitely reverent. God! To find such a treasure in this dismal, miasmic hole, alone, uncared for!

Suddenly I was aware of the crackle of flames. I glanced up—leaped to my feet with an oath.

The deformed wretch had built a fire on the ancient hearth with the broken pieces of the chair!

I aimed a blow at his blinking eye, but he ducked and skipped away nimble, hissing like a frightened adder. But the flames had completely engulfed the fragments. It was too late to save them. . . . The dancing flames painted eery chiaroscuros of scarlet light and stygian shadows on the walls.

I was suddenly aware how late it had grown. So engrossed had I been in the book that night had already slipped over the Devil's Millhop like a swift-flowing black melena, catching me unawares.

To be forced to spend the night in this mephitic hermitage was no pleasant prospect. But the book provided consolation. I sat cross-legged on the floor near the fire, and read it slowly, critically, picking my way, as you may well imagine, with sheerest delight through its ornate typography.

The cyclops sat on his haunches beside me, his glistening eye pondering the flames hungrily.

How long I sat there wading through the pages of Caxton's Bible I cannot say. Suddenly I was aware of a strange sound—a squeaking and a thrashing, as of badly greased machinery stirring to activity.

Simultaneously there came a slow, crunching, grinding sound that shook the house in every rafter. It seemed to come from directly beneath me.

I leaped to my feet, scuttled to the window and peered out.

The ancient mill-wheel was turning! Slowly, at first, it began to pick up speed even as I stared and soon was spinning industriously, the blinding moonlight catching spray dancing from its paddles like spume of liquid silver.

Puzzled and, I must admit, scared by this inexplicable event, I turned to the cyclops—and found him on his feet, facing me, a long, curving blade of oriental design clenched in one fist.

"Where did you get that?" I rasped, startled.

"Funny thing," he grinned horridly, "but it was a-lyin' right there where I was a-settin'."

The firelight scintillated on the bright steel. "It doesn't look so very old," I commented, more to myself than anyone else.

The black gums bared. "I reckon it ain't so old. Only a mite over four hundred years, I reckon. This is the knife that old Kobold's whelp used to sculp his old dad—and to cut off his haid! Feel that edge."

He extended the blade to me. I drew back.

The cyclops cackled mockingly, "Gran'pap Kobold, he warn't feared of man nor devil!" The eye winked confidentially. "He'd as soon slit your throat as look at ye. That's the kind of man *he* was! Iron-fisted! He couldn't be puttin' up with the law. 'Cause he was the law hisself! That's why he come across the water. Not that he wanted to much, I reckon!" His laugh rattled through the room like loose bones. "But y' can't do much when the Devil sends a storm that blows ye across!"

The cyclops laughed hissingly and spat into the fire. His gaze swung back to my face with a sudden intensity.

"But, like I tole ye, he was a-needin' new blood . . . new blood. . . . The cold was a-creepin' into his bones." His taloned fingers curved and slowly clenched.

As I stared into that writhing face glistening with sweat, it seemed to take on a glow, an uncanny, greenish aura. The slack chin seemed to strengthen, to grow heavier, and in those grotesque, shriveled features burned a mad, brutal virility!

"But they caught him one night!" The cyclops' voice clattered with a harsh note of fury. A chill malaise crept over me as I stared into that terrible visage. "They caught him!" the cyclops snarled. "They caught him and drove him out! And we run, my boys and my three daughters—we run! And then—"

The great burning eye closed slowly. And as I stared in sick horror it seemed that it was not really an eye at all. No—no eye at all, but a swollen scar—a scar from whose ends stretched two finer, dead-white lines that completely encircled the base of his scalp—the mark of the scalper's knife!

"The young scound'el stabbed me!" the horror roared in a strange, deep voice—a voice that I heard as if through a vast stretch of space and time. "He stabbed me!" he screamed madly.

I stared into the sunken blank walls of flesh covering the eyesockets. And, even as I stared, they lifted and I was gazing into a pair of mad, burning, red-rimmed eyes.

The knife flashed, and before my very eyes the creature had slashed his own throat, sawing the knife back and forth until the head dropped off, hit the floor, and rolled across the boards. I stared at it as if in a dream. I remember vividly an instant of crowning horror when the head, as it came to rest on the floor, looking at me, closed one eye in a ribald wink.

How I got out of that accursed house, across the moonlit crater, up the face of the cliff, and back to civilization is a confused nightmare of terror and madness. I can recall only flashes of my mad flight—the gibing creaking of the spinning millwheel, the dull crash of some heavy object as I fled from the room—an object that brushed my coat-tails as I passed under the door-lintel—the goblin laughter of the brook, the searing pain of my hands and knees as I tore them on the cruel cliff rocks, the eerie moonlight sifting through a forest . . . gasping, stumbling, falling, plunging forward—ever forward . . . and, by some unfathomed miracle, the vision of a road sign which read in the bright moonlight: "You Are Now Entering the City of Merlin. Go slow."

I woke up the filling-station keeper. He didn't seem very

surprised to see me. His jaundiced grin swept me once; then, not waiting to hear my gasping explanations, he led me to a room—the room I am writing this letter in. . . .

It's no use trying to sleep. Sleep takes me back there. . . . The eye of the cyclops . . . the bleeding head . . . the ribald wink. . . .

If all these things are but the figments of a diseased mentality then I suppose I should be put away. . . . Maybe they didn't happen. . . . Maybe I'm crazy. . . .

I see dawn breaking over the hills. As soon as it gets a bit lighter I'm going to post this letter via the first bus.

Then I'm going to get in my car and drive like mad out of this accursed country!

> Faithfully yours,
> Robert Darnley.

The following newspaper clipping was included by Mr. Abiathar Hall with the manuscript of Mr. Darnley's letter:

May 5, 1936—The body of a man believed to be Robert Darnley, a professional art collector, was found in the wreckage of his automobile about three miles north of Merlin, Tenn. The car, which had sheared off a number of telegraph poles, had evidently been traveling at a high rate of speed. Glass from the shattered windshield had completely decapitated the body.

TIGER CAT

David H. Keller

THE MAN tried his best to sell me the house. He was confident that I would like it. He called my attention to the view repeatedly.

There was something in what he said about the scenery. The villa on the top of a mountain commanded a vision of the valley, vine-clad and cottage-studded. It was an irregular bowl of green, dotted with stone houses which were white-washed to almost painful brilliance.

The valley was three and a third miles at its greatest width. Standing at the front door of the house, an expert marksman with telescopic sight could have placed a rifle bullet in each of the white marks of cottages. They nestled like little pearls amid a sea of green grapevines.

"A wonderful panorama, *Signor*," the real-estate agent repeated. "That scene, at any time of year, is worth twice what I am asking for the villa."

"But I can see all this without buying," I argued.

"Not without trespassing."

"But the place is old. It has no running water."

"Wrong!" and he smiled expansively, showing a row of gold-filled teeth. "Listen."

We were silent.

There came to us the sound of bubbling water. Turning, I traced the sound. I found a marble Cupid spurting water in a most peculiar way into a wall basin. I smiled and commented:

"There is one like that in Brussels and another in Madrid. But this is very fine. However, I referred to running water in a modern bathroom."

"But why bathe when you can sit here and enjoy the view?"

He was impossible. So, I wrote a check, took his bill of sale and became the owner of a mountain, topped by a stone house that seemed to be half ruin. But he did not know, and I did not tell him that I considered the fountain alone worth the price I had paid. In fact, I had come to Italy to buy that fountain if I could; buy it and take it back to America with me. I knew all about that curious piece of marble. George Seabrook had written to me about it. Just one letter, and then he had gone on, goodness knows where. George was like that, always on the move. Now I owned the fountain and was already planning where I should place it in my New York home. Certainly not in the rose garden.

I sat on a marble bench and looked down into the valley. The real-estate man was right. It was a delicate, delicious piece of scenery. The surrounding mountains were high enough to throw a constant shadow on some part of the valley except at high noon. There was no sign of life, but I was sure that the vineyards were alive with husbandmen and their families.

Stretching myself, I gave one look at my car and then walked into the house. In the kitchen sat two peasants, an old man and an old woman. They rose as I entered.

"Who are you?" I asked in Italian.

"We serve," the man replied.

"Serve whom?"

"Whoever is the master."

"Have you been here long?"

"We have always been here. It is our home."

His statement amused me. "The masters come and go, but you remain?"

"It seems so."

"Many masters?"

"Alas! yes. They come and go. Nice young men, like you, but they do not stay. They buy and look at the view, and eat with us a few days and then they are gone."

"And then the villa is sold again?"

The man shrugged. "How should we know? We simply serve."

"Then prepare my dinner. And serve it outside, under the grapevine, where I can see the view."

The woman started to obey. The man drew nearer to me.

"Shall I carry your bags to the bedroom?"

"Yes. And I'll go with you and unpack."

He led me to a room on the second floor. There was a bed and a very old chest of drawers. The floor, everything about the room was spotlessly clean. The walls had been freshly whitewashed. Their smooth whiteness suggested wonderful possibilities for spoliation, the drawing of a picture, the writing of a poem, the careless writhing autograph that caused my relatives so much despair.

"Have all the masters slept here?" I asked carelessly.

"All."

"Was there one by the name of George Seabrook?"

142

"I think so. But they come and go and I am old and forget."

"And all these masters, none of them ever wrote on the walls?"

"Of a certainty. All wrote with pencil what they desired to write. Who might say they should not? For did not the villa belong to them while they were here? But always we prepared for the new master, and made the walls clean and beautiful again."

"You were always sure that there would be a new master?"

"Certainly. Someone must pay us our wages."

Gravely I laid a gold piece in his itching palm, asking, "What did they write on the walls?"

He looked at me with old, unblinking eyes, and said slowly, "Each wrote or drew as his fancy led him, for they were the masters and could do as they wished."

"But what were the words?"

"I cannot speak English, or read it."

Evidently, the man was not going to talk. To me the entire situation was most interesting. Same servants, same villa, many masters. They came and bought and wrote on the wall and left, and then my real-estate friend sold the house again. A fine racket!

Downstairs, under the grapevine, eating a good Italian meal, looking at the wonderful view, I came to laugh at my suspicions. I ate spaghetti, olives, dark bread, and wine. Silence hung heavily over the sullen sleepy afternoon. The sky became copper-colored. It was about to rain. The old man came and showed me a place to put my car, a recess in the wall of the house, open at one end, but sheltered from the weather. The stone floor was black with grease; more than one automobile had been kept there.

Back on the stone gallery I waited for the storm to break. At last it came in a solid wall of gray wetness across the valley. Nearer and nearer it came till it deluged my villa and drove me inside.

The woman was lighting candles. I took one from her hand.

"I want to look through the house," I explained.

She made no protest; so I started exploring the first floor. One room was evidently the sleeping-quarters for the servants; another was the kitchen, and the remaining two might have served in the old days for dining room and drawing room. There was little furniture, and the walls were gray with time and mold. One flight of stone stairs led upward to the bedroom, another to the cellar. I decided to go downstairs.

There were steps, not made of masonry, but apparently carved out of the living rock. The cellar was only a cubical hole in the mountain. It all looked very old. I had the uneasy feeling that originally the cellar had been a tomb and that later the house had been built over it. But, once at the bottom of the stairs there was nothing to indicate a sepulcher. A few small casks of wine, some junk, odds of rope and rusty iron were in the corners; otherwise, the room was empty and dusty.

"It is an odd room," I commented to myself. It seemed in some way out of place and out of shape and size for the villa rising above it. I had expected something more, something larger, gloomier. Walking around, I examined the walls, and then something came to my alert senses.

Three sides of the room were carved out of rock, but the remaining side was of masonry, and in that side there was a door. A door! Why should a door be there except to lead to another room? There was a door, and that presupposed something on the other side. And what a door it was! More of a barricade than a partition. The iron hinges were built to support weight and give complete defense and support. Also there was a keyhole, and if the key corresponded with the size of the hole, it was the largest that I had ever known.

Naturally, I wanted to open the door. As master of the villa, I had a right to do so. Upstairs, the old woman seemed unable to understand me and ended by telling me to see her husband. He, in turn, seemed incapable of following my stream of talk. At last, I took him to the door and pointed to the keyhole. In English, Italian, and sign language I told him emphatically that I wanted the key to that door. At last he was willing to admit that he understood my questions. He shook his head. He had never had the key to that door. Yes, he knew that there was such a door, but he had never been on the other side. It was very old. Perhaps his ancestors understood about it, but they were all dead. He made me tired, so much so that I rested by placing a hand on the butt of the upper hinge. I knew that he was deceiving me. Lived there all his life and never saw the door open!

"And you have no key to that door?" I repeated.

"No. I have no key."

"Who has the key?"

"The owner of the house."

"But I own it."

"Yes, you are the master; but I mean the one who owns it all the time."

"So, the various masters do not really buy the place?"

"They buy it, but they come and go."

144

"But the owner keeps on selling it and owning it?"

"Yes."

"Must be a profitable business. And who owns it?"

"Donna Marchesi."

"I think I met her yesterday in Sorona."

"Yes, that is where she lives."

The storm had passed. Sorona was only two miles away, on the other side of the mountain. The cellar, the door, the mysterious uncertainty on the other side intrigued me. I told the man that I would be back by supper, and I went to my bedroom to change, preparatory to making an afternoon call.

In the room I found my hand black with oil.

And that told me a good many things, as it was the hand that had rested against the upper hinge of the door. I washed, changed my clothes, and drove my car to Sorona.

Fortunately, the Donna Marchesi was at home. I might have met her before, but I now saw her ethereal beauty for the first time. At least, it seemed ethereal at the first moment. In some ways she was the most beautiful woman that I had ever seen: skin white as milk, tawny red hair piled in great masses on her head, and eyes of a peculiar green, with pupils that were slits instead of circles. She wore her nails long, and they were tinted red to match the Titian of her hair. She seemed surprised that I should call on her, and more surprised to hear of my errand.

"You bought the villa?" she asked.

"Yes. Though, when I bought it, I didn't know that you were the owner. The agent never said for whom he was acting."

"I know," she said with a smile. "Franco is peculiar that way. He always pretends he owns the place."

"No doubt he has used it more than once."

"I fear so. The place seems to be unfortunate. I sell it with a reserve clause. The owner must live there. And no one seems to want to stay; so the place reverts to me."

"It seems to be an old place."

"Very old. It has been in my family for generations. I have tried to get rid of it, but, what can I do when the young men will not stay?" She shrugged her shoulders expressively.

I countered with, "Perhaps if they knew, as I do, that you owned the property, they would be content to stay, forever, in Sorona."

"Prettily said," she answered. Then the room became silent, and I heard her heavy breathing, like the deep purr of a cat.

"I have come for the key," I said bluntly, "the key to the cellar door."

"Are you sure you want it?"

"Absolutely! It is my villa and my cellar and my door. I want the key. I want to see what is on the other side of the door."

And then it was I saw the pupils of her eyes narrow to livid slits. She looked at me for a second, for five, and then, opening a drawer in a cabinet near her chair, she took out the key and handed it to me. It was a tool worthy of the door that it was supposed to open, being fully eight inches long and a pound in weight.

Taking it, I thanked her and said goodbye. Fifteen minutes later I was back, profuse in my apologies: I was temperamental, I explained, and I frequently changed my mind. Whatever was on the other side of the door could stay there, as far as I was concerned. Then again I kissed her hand in farewell.

On the side street I passed through the doorway of a locksmith and waited while he completed a key. He was following a wax impression of the original key. An hour later I was on my way back to the villa, with the key in my pocket, a key that I was sure would unlock the door, and I was confident that the lady with the cat eyes felt sure that I had lost all interest in that door and what was beyond it.

The full moon was just appearing over the mountains when I drove my car up to the villa. I was tired, but happy. Taking the candlestick in my hand, which candlestick was handed to me with a deep bow by the old woman, I ascended the stairs to my bedroom. And soon I was fast asleep.

I awoke with a start. The moon was still shining. It was midnight. I heard, or thought I heard, a deep moaning. It sounded a little like waves beating on a rockbound coast. Then it ceased and was replaced by a musical element that rose in certain stately measures. Those sounds were in the room, but they came from far away; only by straining my senses to the utmost could I hear anything.

Slippers on my feet, flashlight in hand and the key in the pocket of my dressing-gown, I slowly descended the stairs. Loud snores from the servants' room told, or seemed to tell, of their deep slumbers. Down into the cellar I went and put the key into the hole of the lock. The key turned easily—no rust there—the springs and the tumblers had been well oiled, like the hinges. It was evident that the door had been used often. Turning the light on the hinges, I saw what had made my hand black with oil. Earnestly I damned the servants. They knew about the door. They knew what was on the other side!

Just as I was about to open the door I heard a woman's

voice singing in Italian; it sounded like a selection from an opera. The aria was followed by applause, and then a moaning, and one shrill cry, as though someone had been hurt. There was no doubt now as to where the sounds I had heard in my room had come from; they had come from the other side of the door. There lay a mystery for me to solve. But I was not yet ready to solve it; so I turned the key noiselessly, and with the door locked, tiptoed back to my bed.

Vainly I tried to put two and two together. They made five, seven, a hundred vague admixtures of impossible results, all filled with weird forebodings. But never did they make four, and till they did, I knew the answers to be wrong, for two and two had to make four.

Many changes of masters! One after another they came and bought and—disappeared. A whitewashed wall. What secrets were covered with that whitewash? A door in a cellar. And what deviltry went on behind it? A key and a well-oiled lock, and servants who knew everything. In vain the question came to me. *What is back of the door?* There was no ready answer. But Donna Marchesi knew! Was it her voice that I had heard? She knew almost everything about it, but there was one thing I knew and she did not. She did not know that I could pass through the door and find out what was on the other side. She did not know I had a key.

The next day I pleaded indisposition and spent most of the hours idling and drowsing in my chamber. Not till nearly midnight did I venture down. The servants were certainly asleep that time. A dose of chloral in their wine had insured the certainty of their slumbers. Fully dressed, with an automatic in my pocket, I descended to the cellar and opened the door. It swung noiselessly on its well-greased hinges. The darkness on the other side was the blackness of hell. An indescribable odor greeted me, a prison smell and with it the soft half sob, half laugh of sleeping children, dreaming in their sleep, and not happy.

I flashed the light around the room. It was not a room but a cavern, a cave that extended far into the distance, the roof supported by stone pillars, set at regular intervals. As far as my light would carry I saw the long rows of white columns.

And to each pillar a man was bound by chains. They were asleep. Snores, grunts, and weary sighs came from them, but not a single eyelid opened. Even when I flashed the light directly into their faces their eyes were shut.

And those faces sickened me; white and drawn and filled with the lines of deep suffering. All were covered with scars; long, narrow, deep scars, some fresh and red, blood-clotted, others old and dead-white. At last, the sunken eyelids and the inability to see my flashlight and respond told me the nauseating truth. Those men were all blind.

A pleasant sight: One blind man, looking eternally into the blackness of his life, and chained to a pillar of stone—that was bad enough; but multiply that by twenty! Was it worse? Could it be worse? Could twenty men suffer more than one man? And then a thought came to me, a terrible, impossible thought, so horrible that I doubted my logic. But now two and two were beginning to make four. Could those men be the masters? They came and bought and left—to go to the cellar and stay there!

"Oh! Donna Marchesi!" I whispered. "How about those cat-eyes? If you had a hand in this, you are not a woman. You are a tiger."

I thought that I understood part of it. The latest master came to her for the key to the cellar, and then, when he once passed through the door he never left. She and her servants were not there to welcome me that night, because she did not know that I had a key.

The thought came to me that perhaps one of those sleeping men was George Seabrook. He and I used to play tennis together and we knew each other like brothers. He had a large scar on the back of his right hand; a livid star-shaped scar. With that in mind, I walked carefully from sleeping man to sleeping man, looking at their right hands. And I found a right hand with a scar that was shaped like the one I knew so well. But that blind man, only a skin-covered skeleton, chained to a bed of stone! That could not be my gay young tennis player, George!

The discovery nauseated me. What did it mean? What *could* it mean? If the Donna Marchesi was the cause of all that misery, what was her motive?

Down the long cave-like room I went. There seemed to be no end to it, though many of the columns were surrounded with empty chains. Only those near the door had their human flies in the trap. In the opposite direction the rows of pillars stretched into deep oblivion. I thought that at the end there was the black mouth of a tunnel, but I could not be sure and dared not go that far to explore the truth. Then, out of that tunnel, I heard a voice, a singing voice. Slipping my shoes off, I ran back near the door and hid as best I could in a dark recess, back of a far piece of stone. I stood there in the darkness, my torch out, the butt of the revolver clutched in my hand.

The singing grew louder and louder, and then the singer came into view. It was none other than Donna Marchesi! She carried a lantern in one hand and a basket in the other.

Hanging the lantern on a nail, she took the basket and went from one sleeping man to another. With each her performance was the same; she awakened them with a kick in the face, and then, when they sat up crying with pain, she placed a hard roll of bread in each trembling, outstretched hand. With all fed, there was silence save for gnawing teeth breaking through the hard crusts. The poor devils were hungry, and slowly starving to death, and how they wolfed the bread! She laughed with animal delight as they cried for more. Standing under the lantern, a lovely devil in her décolleté dress, she laughed at them. I swear I saw her yellow eyes, dilated in the semi-darkness!

Suddenly she gave the command, "Up! you dogs, *up!*"

Like well-trained animals they rose to their feet, clumsily, but as fast as they could under the handicap of trembling limbs and heavy chains. Two were slow in obeying, and those she struck across the face with a small whip, lashing them until they whined with pain.

They stood in silence, twenty odd blind men, chained against as many pillars of stone; and then the woman, standing in the middle of them, began to sing. It was a well-trained voice, but metallic, and her high notes had in them the cry of a wild animal. No feminine softness there. She sang from an Italian opera, and I knew that I had heard that song before. While she sang, her audience waited silently. At last she finished, and they started to applaud. Shrunken hands beat noisily against shrunken hands.

She seemed to watch them carefully, as though she were measuring the degree of their appreciation. Evidently one man did not satisfy her. She went over and dug into his face with long strokes of those talon-like red nails until his face was red and her fingers bloody. And when she finished her second song that man clapped louder than any other. He had learned his lesson.

She ended by giving them each another roll and a dipper of water. Then, lantern and basket in her hands, she walked away and disappeared down the tunnel. The blind men, crying and cursing in their impotent rage, sank down on their stone beds.

I went to my friend, and took his hand.

"George! George Seabrook!" I whispered.

He sat up and cried, "Who calls me? Who is there?"

I told him, and he burst into tears. At last he became quiet enough to talk to me. What he told me, with slight variants, was the story of all the men there and all the men who had been there but who had died. Each man had been master for a day or a week. Each had found the cellar door and had come to the Donna Marchesi for the key. Some had been suspicious and had written their thoughts on the wall of the bedroom. But one and all had, in the end, found their curiosity more than they could resist and had opened the door. On the other side they had been overpowered and chained to a pillar, and there they had remained till they died. Some lived longer than others. Smith, of Boston, had been there over two years, though he was coughing badly and did not think that he could last much longer. Seabrook told me their names. They were the best blood of America, with three Englishmen and one Frenchman.

"And are you all blind?" I whispered, dreading the answer.

"Yes. That happens the first night we are here. She does it with her nails."

"And she comes every night?"

"Every night. She feeds us and sings to us and we applaud. When one of us dies, she unchains the body, and throws it down a hole somewhere. She talks to us about that hole sometimes and brags that she is going to fill it up before she stops."

"But who is helping her?"

"I think it is the real-estate man. Of course, the old devils upstairs help. I think that they must drug us. Some of the men say that they went to sleep in their beds and woke, chained to their posts."

My voice trembled as I bent over and whispered in his ear, "What would you do, George, if she came and sang, and you found that you were not chained? You and the other men not chained? What would you men do, George?"

"Ask them," he snarled. "Ask them, one at a time. But I know what I would do. I know!"

And he started to cry, because he could not do it the next second; cried from rage and helplessness till the tears ran from his empty sockets.

"Does she always come at the same time?"

"As far as I know. But time is nothing to us. We just wait for death."

"Are the chains locked?"

"Yes. And she must have the key. But we could file the links if only we had files. If only each of us had a file, we could get free. Perhaps the man upstairs has a key, but I hardly think so."

"Did you write on that pretty wall upstairs, the white-washed wall?"

"I did; I think we all did. One man wrote a sonnet to the woman, verses in her honor, telling about her beautiful eyes.

He raved about that poem for hours while he was dying. Did you ever see it on the wall?"

"I did not see it. The old people whitewash the walls before each new master comes."

"I thought so."

"Are you sure you would know what to do, George, if she sang to you and you were loose?"

"Yes, we would know."

So I left him, promising an end to the matter as soon as I could arrange it.

The next day saw me calling on the Donna Marchesi. I took her flowers that time, a corsage of vivid purple and scarlet orchids. She entertained me in her music room and I, taking the hint, asked her to sing. Shyly, almost with reluctance, she did as I asked. She sang the selection from the Italian opera that I knew so well. I was generous in my applause.

She smiled.

"You like to hear me sing?"

"Indeed! I want to hear you again. I could listen to you every day without being bored."

"You're nice," she purred. "Perhaps it could be arranged."

"You are much too modest. You have a wonderful voice. Why not go into opera?"

"I sang once in public," she sighed. "It was in New York, at a private musicale. Many men were there. Perhaps it was stage fright; my voice broke badly, and the audience, especially the men, were not kind. I am not sure, but I thought I heard some of them hiss."

"Surely not!" I protested.

"Indeed, so. But no man has hissed my singing since."

"I hope not!" I replied indignantly. "You have a wonderful voice, and, when I applauded you, I was sincere. By the way, may I change my mind and ask for the key to the door in the cellar?"

"Do you want it, really want it, my friend?"

"I'm sure I do. I may never use it, but it will please me to have it. Little things in life make me happy, and this key is a little thing."

"Then you shall have it. Will you do me a favor? Wait till Sunday to use it. Today is Friday, and you will not have to wait many hours."

"It will be a pleasure," I replied, kissing her hand. "Shall you sing again? May I come often to hear you sing?"

"I promise you that," she sighed. "I am sure that you will hear me sing very often. I feel that in some way our fates approach the same star."

I looked into her eyes, her yellow cat-eyes, and I was sure that she spoke the truth. Destiny had certainly brought me to find her in Sorona.

I bought two dozen rat-tailed files and dashed across the mountains to Milan. There I was closeted with the consuls of three nations: England, France, and my own. They didn't want to believe my story. I gave them names and they had to admit there had been inquiries, but felt that the main details were nightmares, resulting from an over-indulgence in Italian wines. But I insisted that I wasn't drunk with new wine. At last, they called in the chief of the detective bureau. He knew Franco, the real-estate agent; also the lady in question. And he had heard something of the villa; not much, but vague whisperings.

"We will be there Saturday night," he promised. "That leaves you tonight. The lady will not try to trap you till Sunday. Can you attend to the old people?"

"They will be harmless. See that Franco does not have a chance to escape. Here is the extra key to the door. I will go through before twelve. When I am ready, I will open the door. If I'm not out by one in the morning, you come through with your police. Do we all understand?"

"I understand," said the American consul. "But I still think you are dreaming."

Back at the villa, I again drugged the old people, not much, but enough to insure their sleep that night. They liked me. I was liberal with my gold, and carelessly I showed them where I kept my reserve.

Then I went through the door. Again I heard the Donna Marchesi sing to an audience that would never hiss her. She left, and I started to distribute the files. From one blind wretch to the next I went, whispering words of cheer and instruction for the next night. They were to cut through a link in the chain, but in such a way that the Tiger Cat would not suspect that they had gained their liberty. Were they pleased to have a hope of freedom? I am not sure, but they were delighted at another prospect.

The next night I doubled the tips to the old servants. With tears of gratitude in their eyes, they thanked me as they called me their dear master. I put them to sleep as though they were babies. In fact, I wondered at the time if they would ever recover from the dose of chloral I had given them. I did not even bother to tie them, but just tossed them on their beds.

At half past ten, automobiles with dimmed lights began to arrive. We had a lengthy conference, and soon after eleven I went through the door. I lost no time in making sure that each of the blind mice was a free man, but I insisted that they act as though bound till the proper time. They were trembling, but it was not from fear, not that time.

Back in my hiding-place I waited, and soon I heard the singing voice. Ten minutes later the Donna Marchesi had her lantern hung on the nail. Ah! She was more beautiful that night than I had ever seen her. Dressed in filmy white, her beautiful body, lovely hair, long lithe limbs would have bound any man to her through eternity. She seemed to sense that beauty, for, after giving out the first supply of rolls, she varied her program. She told her audience how she had dressed that evening for their special pleasure. She described her jewels and her costume. She became almost grandiose as she told of her beauty, and, driving in the dagger, she twisted it as she reminded them that never would they be able to see her, never touch her or kiss her hand. All they could do was to hear her sing, applaud and, at last, die.

Of all the terrible things in her life that little talk to those blind men was the climax.

And then she sang. I watched her closely, and I saw what I suspected. She sang with her eyes closed. Was she in fancy seeming that she was in an opera house before thousands of spellbound admirers? Who knows? But ever as she sang that night her eyes were closed, and even as she came to an end, waiting for the usual applause, her eyes were closed.

She waited in the silence for the clap of hands. It did not come. With terrific anger, she whirled to her basket and reached for her whip.

"Dogs!" she cried. "Have you so soon forgotten your lesson?"

And then she realized that the twenty blind men were closing in on her. They were silent, but their outstretched hands were feeling for something that they wanted very much. Even when her whip lashed and cut, they were silent. Then one man touched her. To her credit, there was no sign of fear. She knew what had happened. She must have known, but she was not afraid. Her single scream was nothing but the battle-cry of the tiger cat going into action.

There was a single cry, and that was all. In silence the men reached for what they wanted. For a while they were all a struggling group on their feet, but soon they were all on the ground. It was simply a mass, and under that mass was a biting, scratching, fighting, dying animal.

I couldn't stand it. I had planned it all, I wanted it all to happen, but when it came, I just couldn't stand it. Covered with the sweat of fear, I ran to the door and unlocked it. I swung it open, went through the doorway, closed it and locked it again. The men, waiting for me in the cellar, looked on with doubt. It seemed that they were right in thinking that my tale was an alcoholic one.

"Give me a whisky!" I gasped, as I dropped to the floor.

In a few minutes I had recovered.

"Open the door," I ordered. "And bring the blind men out."

One at a time they were brought to the kitchen, and identified. Some were terribly mutilated in the face, long deep scratches, and even pieces bitten out, and one had the corner of his mouth torn. Most of them were sobbing hysterically, but, in some way, though none said so, I judged that they were all happy.

"What's that?" asked the American consul, looking into the cellar.

"I think that is the Donna Marchesi," I replied. "She must have met with an accident."

CURIOUS ADVENTURE OF MR. BOND

Nugent Barker

MR. BOND climbed from the wooded slopes of the valley into broad moonlight. His Inverness cape, throwing his portly figure into still greater prominence against the floor of tree-tops at his back, was torn and soiled by twigs and thorns and leaves, and he stooped with prim concern to brush off the bits and pieces. After this, he eased his knapsack on his shoulder; and now he blinked his eyes upon the country stretching out before him.

Far away, across the tufted surface of the tableland, there stood a house, with its column of smoke, lighted and still, on the verge of a forest.

A house—an *inn*—he felt it in his very bones! His hunger returned, and became a source of gratification to him. Toiling on, and pulling the brim of his hat over his eyes, he watched the ruby gleam grow bigger and brighter; and when at last he stood beneath the sign, he cried aloud, scarcely able to believe in his good fortune.

"The Rest of the Traveler," he read; and there, too, ran the name of the landlord: "Crispin Sasserach."

The stillness of the night discouraged him, and he was afraid to tap at the curtained window. And now, for the first time, the full weight of his weariness fell upon the traveler. Staring into the black mouth of the porch, he imagined himself to be at rest, in bed, sprawled out, abundantly sleeping, drugged into forgetfulness by a full stomach. He shut his eyes, and drooped a little under his Inverness cape; but when he looked again into the entrance, there stood Crispin Sasserach, holding a lamp between their faces. Mr. Bond's was plump and heavy-jawed, with sagging cheeks, and eyes that scarcely reflected the lamp-light; the other face was smooth and large and oval, with small lips pressed into a smile.

"Come in, come in," the landlord whispered, "*do* come in. She is cooking a lovely broth tonight!"

He turned and chuckled, holding the lamp above his head.

Through the doorway of this lost, upland inn, Mr. Bond followed the monstrous back of his host. The passage widened and became a hall; and here, amongst the shadows that were gliding from their lurking-places as the lamp advanced, the landlord stopped, and tilted the flat of his hand in the air, as though enjoining his guest to listen. Then Mr. Bond disturbed the silence of the house with a sniff and a sigh. Not only could he smell the "lovely broth"—already, in this outer hall, he tasted it ... a complex and subtle flavor, pungent, heavy as honey, light as a web in the air, nipping him in the stomach, bringing tears into his eyes.

Mr. Bond stared at Crispin Sasserach, at the shadows beyond, and back again to Crispin Sasserach. The man was standing there with his huge, oval, hairless face upturned in the light of the lamp he carried; then, impulsively, and as though reluctant to cut short such sweet anticipation, he plucked the traveler by the cape, and led him to the cheerful living-room, and introduced him, with a flourish of the hand, to Myrtle Sasserach, the landlord's young and small and busy wife, who at that very moment was standing at a round table of great size, beneath the massive center-beam of the ceiling, her black hair gleaming in the light of many candles, her plump hand dipping a ladle soundlessly into a bowl of steam.

On seeing the woman, whose long lashes were once more directed towards the bowl, Mr. Bond drew his chin primly into his neckcloth, and glanced from her to Crispin Sasserach, and finally he fixed his eyes on the revolutions of the ladle. In a moment, purpose fell upon the living-room, and with swift and nervous gestures the landlord seated his guest at the table, seized the ladle from his wife, plunged it into the bowl, and thrust the brimming plate into the hands of Myrtle, who began at once to walk towards the traveler, the steam of the broth rising into her grave eyes.

After a muttered grace, Mr. Bond pushed out his lips as though he were whispering "spoon."

"Oh, what a lovely broth!" he murmured, catching a drip in his handkerchief.

Crispin Sasserach grinned with delight. "I always say it's the best in the world." Whereupon, with a rush, he broke into peals of falsetto laughter, and blew a kiss towards his wife. A moment later, the two Sasserachs were leaving their guest to himself, bending over their own platefuls of broth, and discussing domestic affairs, as though they had no other person sitting at their table. For some time their voices were scarcely louder than the sound of the broth-eating; but when the traveler's plate was empty, then, in a flash, Crispin Sasserach became again a loud and attentive host. "Now then, sir— another helping?" he suggested, picking up the ladle, and beaming down into the bowl, while Myrtle left her chair and walked a second time towards the guest.

Mr. Bond said that he would, and pulled his chair a little closer to the table. Into his blood and bones, life had returned with twice its accustomed vigor; his very feet were as light as though he had soaked them in a bath of pine needles.

"There you are, sir! Myrtle's coming! Lord a'mighty, how I wish I was tasting it for the first time!" Then, spreading his elbows, the landlord crouched over his own steaming plateful, and chuckled again. "This broth is a wine in itself! It's a wine in itself, b'God! It staggers a man!" Flushed with excitement, his oval face looked larger than ever, and his auburn hair, whirled into bellicose corkscrews, seemed to burn brighter, as though someone had brought the bellows to it.

Stirred by the broth, Mr. Bond began to describe minutely his journey out of the valley. His voice grew as prosy, his words as involved, as though he were talking at home amongst his own people. "Now, let me see—where was I?" he buzzed again and again. And later: "I was very glad to see your light, I can tell you!" he chuckled. Then Crispin jumped up from the table, his small mouth pouting with laughter.

The evening shifted to the fireside. Fresh logs cracked like pistol shots as Crispin Sasserach dropped them into the flames. The traveler could wish for nothing better than to sit here by the hearth, talking plangently to Crispin, and slyly watching Myrtle as she cleared away the supper things; though, indeed, amongst his own people, Mr. Bond was thought to hold women in low esteem. He found her downcast eyes modest and even pretty. One by one she blew the candles out; with each extinguishment she grew more ethereal, while reaping a fuller share of the pagan firelight. "Come and sit beside us now, and talk," thought Mr. Bond, and presently she came.

They made him very comfortable. He found a log fire burning in his bedroom, and a bowl of broth on the bedside table. "Oh, but they're overdoing it!" he cried aloud, petulantly; "they're crude, crude! They're nothing but school-children!"—and, seizing the bowl, he emptied it onto the shaggy patch of garden beneath his window. The black wall of the forest seemed to stand within a few feet of his eyes. The room was filled with the mingled light of moon, fire, and candle.

Mr. Bond, eager at last for the dreamless rest, the abandoned sleep, of the traveler, turned and surveyed the room in which he was to spend the night. He saw with pleasure the four-poster bed, itself as large as a tiny room; the heavy oaken chairs and cupboards; the tall, twisting candlesticks, their candles burnt half-way, no doubt, by a previous guest;

the ceiling, that he could touch with the flat of his hand. He touched it.

In the misty morning he could see no hint of the forest, and down the shallow staircase he found the hall thick with the odor of broth. The Sasserachs were seated already at the breakfast-table, like two children, eager to begin the day with their favorite food. Crispin Sasserach was lifting his spoon and pouting his lips, while Myrtle was stirring her ladle round the tureen, her eyes downcast; and Mr. Bond sighed inaudibly as he saw again the woman's dark and lustrous hair. He noticed also the flawless condition of the Sasserach skin. There was not a blemish to be seen on their two faces, on their four hands. He attributed this perfection to the beneficial qualities of the broth, no less than to the upland air; and he began to discuss, in his plangent voice, the subject of health in general. In the middle of this discourse Crispin Sasserach remarked, excitedly, that he had a brother who kept an inn a day's journey along the edge of the forest.

"Oh," said Mr. Bond, pricking up his ears, "so you have a brother, have you?"

"Certainly," whispered the innkeeper. "It is most convenient."

"Most convenient for what?"

"Why, for the inns. His name's Martin. We share our guests. We help each other. The proper brotherly spirit, b'God!"

Mr. Bond stared angrily into his broth. "They share their guests. . . . But what," he thought, "has that to do with me?" He said aloud: "Perhaps I'll meet him one day, Mr. Sasserach."

"Today!" cried Crispin, whacking his spoon on to the table. "I'm taking you there today! But don't you worry," he added, seeing the look on the other's face, and flattering himself that he had read it aright; "you'll be coming back to us. Don't you worry! Day after tomorrow—day after that— one of these days! Ain't that right, Myr? Ain't that right?" he repeated, bouncing up and down in his chair like a big child.

"Quite right," answered Myrtle Sasserach to Mr. Bond, whose eyes were fixed upon her with heavy attention.

A moment later the innkeeper was out of his chair, making for the hall, calling back to Myrtle to have his boots ready. In the midst of this bustle, Mr. Bond bowed stiffly to Myrtle Sasserach, and found his way with dignity to the back garden, that now appeared wilder than he had supposed—a fenced-in plot of grass reaching above his knees and scattered with burdock whose prickly heads clung to his clothes as he made for the gate in the fence at the foot of this wilderness.

He blinked his eyes, and walked on the rough turf that lay between him and the forest. By this time the sun was shining in an unclouded sky; a fine day was at hand; and Mr. Bond was sweeping his eye along the endless wall of the forest when he heard the innkeeper's voice calling to him in the stillness. "Mr. Bond! Mr. Bond!" Turning reluctantly, and stepping carefully through the garden in order to avoid the burrs of the burdock, the traveler found Crispin Sasserach on the point of departure, in a great bustle, with a strong horse harnessed to a two-wheeled cart, and his wife putting up her face to be kissed.

"Yes, I'll go with you," cried Mr. Bond, but the Sasserachs did not appear to hear him. He lingered for a moment in the porch, scowling at Myrtle's back, scowling at the large young horse that seemed to toss its head at him with almost human insolence; then he sighed, and, slinging his knapsack over his shoulder, sat himself beside the driver; the horse was uncommonly large, restless between the shafts, and in perfect fettle; and without a word from Crispin the animal began to plunge forward rapidly over the worn track.

For some time the two men drove in silence, on the second stage of Mr. Bond's adventure above the valley. The traveler sat up stiffly, inflating his lungs methodically, glaring through his small eyes, and forcing back his shoulders. Presently he began to talk about the mountain air, and received no answer. On his right hand the wall of the forest extended as far as his eyes could see; while on his left hand ran the brink of the valley, a mile away, broken here and there by rowan trees.

The monotony of the landscape, and the continued silence of the innkeeper, soon began to pall on Mr. Bond, who liked talking and was seldom at ease unless his eyes were busy picking out new things. Even the horse behaved with the soundless regularity of a machine; so that, besides the traveler, only the sky showed a struggle to make progress.

Clouds came from nowhere, shaped and broke, and at midday the sun in full swing was riding between white puffs of cloud, glistening by fits and starts on the moist coat of the horse. The forest beneath, and the stretch of coarse grass running to the valley, were constantly shining and darkening, yet Crispin Sasserach never opened his mouth, even to whisper, though sometimes, between his teeth, he spat soundlessly over the edge of the cart. The landlord had brought with him a casserole of the broth; and during one of these sunny breaks he pulled up the horse, without a word, and poured the liquor into two pannikins, which he proceeded to heat patiently over a spirit-stove.

In the failing light of the afternoon, when the horse was still making his top speed, when Crispin Sasserach was buzzing fitfully between his teeth, and sleep was flirting with the traveler, a shape appeared obscurely on the track ahead, and with it came the growing jingle of bells. Mr. Bond sat up and stared. He had not expected to meet, in such a God-forsaken spot, another cart, or carriage. He saw at length, approaching him, a four-wheeled buggy, drawn by two sprightly horses in tandem. A thin-faced man in breeches and a bowler hat was driving it. The two drivers greeted each other solemnly, raised their whips, but never slackened speed.

"Well—who was that?" asked Mr. Bond, after a pause.

"My brother Martin's manservant."

"Where is he going?" asked Mr. Bond.

"To 'The Rest of the Traveler', with news."

"Indeed? What news?" persisted Mr. Bond.

The landlord turned his head.

"News for my Myrtle," he whispered, winking at the traveler.

Mr. Bond shrugged his shoulders. "What is the use of talking to such a boor?" he thought, and fell once more into his doze; the harvest-moon climbed up again, whitening the earth; while now and then the landlord spat towards the forest, and never spoke another word until he came to Martin Sasserach's.

Then Crispin leapt to life.

"Out with you!" he cried. "Pst! Mr. Bond! Wake up! Get out at once! We've reached 'The Headless Man,' sir!"

Mr. Bond, staggered by so much energy, flopped to the ground. His head felt as large as the moon. He heard the horse panting softly, and saw the breath from its nostrils flickering upwards in the cold air; while the white-faced Crispin Sasserach was leaping about under the moon, whistling between his teeth, and calling out enthusiastically: "Martin! Mar-tin! Here he is!"

The sheer wall of forest echoed back the name. Indeed, the whole of the moonlight seemed to be filled with the name "Martin", and Mr. Bond had a fierce desire to see this Martin Sasserach whose sign was hanging high above the traveler's head. After repeated calls from Crispin, the landlord of 'The Headless Man' appeared, and Mr. Bond, expecting a very giant in physical stature, was shocked to see the small and bespectacled figure that had emerged from the house. Crispin Sasserach grew quick and calm in a moment. "Meet again," he whispered to Mr. Bond, shutting his eyes, and stretching his small mouth as though in ecstasy; then he gave the traveler a push towards the approaching Martin, and a moment later he was in his cart, and the horse was springing its way back to "The Rest of the Traveler."

Mr. Bond stood where he was, listening to the dying sound of the horse, and watching the landlord of "The Headless Man", and presently he was staring at two grey flickering eyes behind the landlord's glasses.

"Anyone arriving at my inn from my brother's is trebly welcome. He is welcome not only for Crispin's own sake and mine, but also for the sake of our brother Stephen." The voice was as quiet and as clear as the moonlight, and the speaker began to return to his inn with scarcely a pause between speech and movement. Mr. Bond examined curiously the strongly-lighted hall that in shape and size was the very double of Crispin's. Oil-lamps, gracefully columned, gleamed almost as brightly from their fluted silver surfaces as from their opal-lighted heads; and there was Martin stooping up the very stairs, it seemed, that Mr. Bond had walked at Crispin Sasserach's—a scanty man, his brother, throwing out monstrous shadows, turning once to peer back at his guest, and standing at last in a bright and airy bedroom, where, with courteous words from which his eyes, lost in thought and gently flickering, seemed to be far distant, he invited his guest to wash before dining.

Martin Sasserach fed Mr. Bond delicately on that evening of his arrival, presenting him with small, cold dishes of various kinds and always exquisitely cooked and garnished; and these, together with the almost crystalline cleanliness of the room and of the table, seemed appropriate to the chemist-like appearance of the host. A bottle of wine was opened for Mr. Bond, who, amongst his own people, was known to drink nothing headier than bottled cider. During dinner, the wine warmed up a brief moment of attention in Martin Sasserach. He peered with sudden interest at his guest. " 'The Headless Man?' There is, in fact, a story connected with that name. If you can call it a story." He smiled briefly, tapping his finger and a moment later was examining an ivory piece, elaborately carved, that held the bill of fare. "Lovely! Lovely! Isn't it? . . . In fact, there are many stories," he ended, as though the number of stories excused him from wasting his thought over the recital of merely one. Soon after dinner he retired, alluding distantly to work from which he never liked to be away long.

Mr. Bond went to bed early that night, suffering from dyspepsia, and glowering at the absence of home comforts in his bright and efficient bedroom.

The birds awakened him to a brisk, autumnal morning. Breathing heavily, he told himself that he was always very fond of birds and trees and flowers; and soon he was walking sleepily in Martin Sasserach's garden. The trimness of the beds began to please him. He followed the right-angled paths with dignified obesity, his very bones were proud to be alive.

A green gate at the garden-foot attracted Mr. Bond's attention; but, knowing that it would lead him on to the wild grass beyond, and thence to the forest, whose motionless crest could be seen all this while over the privet hedge, he chose to linger where he was, sniffing the clear scent of the flowers, and losing, with every breath and step, another whiff of Crispin's broth, to his intense delight.

Hunger drew him back into the house at last, and he began to pace the twilit rooms. Martin Sasserach, he saw, was very fond of ivory. He stooped and peered at the delicate things. Ivory objects of every description, perfectly carved: paper-knives, chess-men, salad-spoons; tiny busts and faces, often of grotesque appearance; and even delicate boxes, fretted from ivory.

The echo of his feet on the polished floors intensified the silence of "The Headless Man"; yet even this indoor hush was full of sound, when compared with the stillness of the scene beyond the uncurtained windows. The tufted grass was not yet lighted by the direct rays of the sun. The traveler stared towards the rowan trees that stood on the brink of the valley. Beyond them stretched a carpet of mist, raising the rest of the world to the height of the plateau; and Mr. Bond, recalling the house and town that he had left behind him, began to wonder whether he was glad or sorry that his adventures had brought him to this lost region. "Cold enough for my cape," he shivered, fetching it from the hall, and hurrying out of the inn; the desire had seized him to walk on the tufted grass, to foot it as far as the trees; and he had indeed gone some distance on his journey, wrapped in his thoughts and antique Inverness cape, when the note of a gong came up behind him, like a thread waving on the air.

"Hark at that," he whispered, staring hard at the ragged line of rowan trees on which his heart was set; then he shrugged his shoulders, and turned back to 'The Headless Man', where his host was standing lost in thought at the breakfast-table that still held the crumbs of the night before.

"Ah, yes. Yes. It's you. . . . You slept well?"

"Tolerably well," said Mr. Bond.

"We breakfast rather early here. It makes a longer day. Stennet will be back later. He's gone to my brother Crispin's."

"With news?" said Mr. Bond.

Martin Sasserach bowed courteously, though a trifle stiffly. He motioned his guest towards a chair at the table. Breakfast was cold and short and silent. Words were delicate things to rear in this crystalline atmosphere. Martin's skin sagged and was the color of old ivory. Now and then he looked up at his guest, his grey eyes focused beyond mere externals; and it seemed as though they lodged themselves in Mr. Bond's very bones. On one of these occasions the traveler made great play with his appetite. "It's all this upland air," he asserted, thumping his chest.

The sun began to rise above the plateau. Again the landlord vanished, murmuring his excuses; silence flooded "The Headless Man." The garden purred in the full blaze of the sun that now stood higher than the forest, and the graveled paths crunched slowly beneath Mr. Bond's feet. "News for Myrtle," he pondered, letting his thoughts stray back over his journey; and frequently he drifted through the house where all was still and spacious: dusty, museum-like rooms brimming with sunlight, while everywhere those ivory carvings caught his eye, possessing his sight as completely as the taste of Crispin's broth had lodged in his very lungs.

Lunch was yet another meal of cold food and silence, broken only by coffee that the landlord heated on a spirit stove at the end of the table, and by a question from the traveler, to which this thin-haired Martin, delicately flicking certain greyish dust off the front of his coat and sleeve, replied that he had been a collector of carvings for years past, and was continually adding to his collection. His voice drew out in length and seemed, in fact, to trail him from the sunlit dining-room, back to his everlasting work . . . and now the afternoon itself began to drag and presently to settle down in the sun as though the whole of time were dozing.

"Here's my indigestion back again," sighed Mr. Bond, mooning about. At home he would have rested in his bedroom, with its pink curtains and flowered wallpaper.

He crept into the garden, and eyed the back of the house. Which of those windows in the trimly-creepered stone lit up the landlord and his work? He listened for the whirring of a lathe, the scraping of a knife . . . and wondered, startled, why he had expected to hear such things. He felt the forest behind his back, and turned, and saw it looming above the privet hedge. Impulsively, he started to cross the sun-swept grass beyond the gate: but within a few yards of the forest his courage failed him again: he could not face the wall of trees: and with a cry he fled into the house, and seized his Inverness.

His eyes looked far beyond the rowans of the skyline as he

plodded over the tufted grass. Already he could see himself down there below, counties and counties away, on the valley level, in the house of his neighbors the Allcards, drinking their coffee or tea and telling them of his adventures and especially of *this* adventure. It was not often that a man of his age and secure position in the world went off alone, in search of joy or trouble. He scanned the distant line of rowan trees, and nodded, harking back: "As far as it has gone. I'll tell them this adventure, as far as it went." And he would say to them: "The things I might have seen, if I had stayed! Yes, Allcard, I was very glad to climb down into the valley that day, I can tell you! I don't mind admitting I was a bit frightened!"

The tippet of his cape caressed his shoulders, like the hand of a friend.

Mr. Bond was not yet half-way to the rowan trees when, looking back, he saw, against the darkness of the forest wall, a carriage rapidly approaching "The Headless Man." At once there flashed into his memory the eyes of the manservant Stennet who went between the Sasserach inns.

He knew that Stennet's eyes were on him now. The sound of the horses' feet was coming up to him like a soft ball bouncing over the grass. Mr. Bond shrugged his shoulders, and stroked his pendulous cheeks. Already he was on his way back to "The Headless Man," conscious that two flying horses could have overtaken him long before he had reached the rowans. "But why," he thought, holding himself with dignity, "should I imagine that these people are expecting me to run away? And why that sudden panic in the garden? It's all that deathly quietness of the morning getting on my nerves."

The carriage had disappeared some time before he reached the inn, over whose tiled and weather-stained roof the redness of the evening was beginning to settle. And now the traveler was conscious of a welcome that seemed to run out and meet him at the very door. He found a log fire crackling in the dining-room; and Mr. Bond, holding his hands to the blaze, felt suddenly at ease, and weary. He had intended to assert himself—to shout for Martin Sasserach—to demand that he be escorted down at once from the plateau . . . but now he wished for nothing better than to stand in front of the fire, waiting for Stennet to bring him tea.

A man began to sing in the heart of the house. Stennet? The fellow's eyes and hawk-like nose were suddenly visible in the fire. The singing voice grew louder . . . died at length discreetly into silence and the tread of footsteps in the hall . . . and again the traveler was listening to the flames as they roared in the chimney.

"Let me take your coat, sir," Stennet said.

Then Mr. Bond whipped round, his cheeks shaking with anger.

Why did they want to force this hospitality upon him, making him feel like a prisoner? He glared at the large-checked riding-breeches, at the muscular shoulders, at the face that seemed to have grown the sharper through swift driving. He almost shouted: "Where's that bowler hat?"

Fear? . . . Perhaps . . . But if fear had clutched him for a moment, it had left him now. He knew that the voice had pleased him, a voice of deference breaking into the cold and irreverent silence of "The Headless Man." The cape was already off his shoulders, hanging on Stennet's bent and respectful arm. And—God be praised!—the voice was announcing that tea would be ready soon. Mr. Bond's spirits leapt with the word. He and Stennet stood there, confidentially plotting. "China? Yes, sir. We have China," Stennet said.

"And buttered toast," said Mr. Bond, softly rubbing his chin. Some time after tea he was awakened from his doze by the hand of the manservant, who told him that a can of boiling water was waiting in his room.

Mr. Bond felt that dinner would be a rich meal that night, and it was. He blushed as the dishes were put before him. Hare soup! How did they know his favorite soup? Through entrée, remove, and roast, his hands, soft and pink from washing, were busier than they had been for days. The chicken was braised to a turn. Oh, what mushrooms *au gratin*! The partridge brought tears to his eyes. The Saxony pudding caused him to turn again to Martin, in Stennet's praise.

The landlord bowed with instant courtesy. "A game of chess?" he suggested, when dinner was over. "My last opponent was a man like yourself, a traveler making a tour of the inns. We started a game. He is gone from us now. Perhaps you will take his place?" smiled Martin Sasserach, his precise voice dropping and seeming to transmit its flow of action to the thin hand poised above the board. "My move," he whispered, playing at once; he had thought it out for a week. But although Mr. Bond tried to sink his thoughts into the problem so suddenly placed before him, he could not take them off his after-dinner dyspepsia, and with apologies and groans he scraped back his chair. "I'm sorry for that," smiled Martin, and his eyes flickered over the board. "I'm very sorry. Another night . . . undoubtedly . . . with your kind help . . . another night . . ."

The prospect of another day at "The Headless Man" was at

once disturbing and pleasant to Mr. Bond as he went wheezing up to bed.

"Ah, Stennet! Do *you* ever suffer from dyspepsia?" he asked mournfully, seeing the man at the head of the staircase. Stennet snapped his fingers, and was off downstairs in a moment; and a minute later he was standing at the traveler's door, with a bowl of Crispin's famous broth. "Oh, that!" cried Mr. Bond, staring down at the bowl. Then he remembered its fine effect on his indigestion at Crispin's; and when at last he pulled the sheets over his head, he fell asleep in comfort and did not wake until the morning.

At breakfast Martin Sasserach looked up from his plate.

"This afternoon," he murmured, "Stennet will be driving you to my brother Stephen's."

Mr. Bond opened his eyes. "Another inn? Another of you Sasserachs?"

"Crispin—Martin—Stephen. Just the three of us. A perfect number . . . if you come to think of it."

The traveler strode into the garden. Asters glowed in the lusterless light of the morning. By ten o'clock the sun was shining again, and by midday a summer heat lay on the plateau, penetrating even into Mr. Bond's room. The silence of the forest pulled him to the window, made him lift up his head and shut his eyes upon that monstrous mass of trees. Fear was trying to overpower him. He did not want to go to Stephen Sasserach's; but the hours were running past him quickly now, the stillness was gone from the inn.

At lunch, to which his host contributed a flow of gentle talk, the traveler felt rising within him an impatience to be off on the third stage of his journey, if such a stage must be. He jumped up from his chair without apology, and strode into the garden. The asters were now shining dimly in the strong sunlight. He opened the gate in the privet hedge, and walked on to the tufted grass that lay between it and the forest. As he did so, he heard the flap of a wing behind him and saw a pigeon flying from a window in the roof. The bird flew over his head and over the forest and out of sight; and for the first time he remembered seeing a pigeon taking a similar course when he was standing in the garden at Crispin's inn.

His thoughts were still following the pigeon over the boundless floor of tree-tops when he heard a voice calling to him in the silence. "Mr. Bond! Mr. Bond!" He walked at once to the gate and down the garden and into the house, put on his Inverness, and hitched his knapsack on to his shoulder; and in a short while he was perched beside Stennet in the flying buggy, staring at the ears of the two horses, and remember-

166

ing that Martin, at the last moment, instead of bidding his guest good-bye, had gone back to his work.

Though he never lost his fear of Stennet, Mr. Bond found Martin's man a good companion on a journey, always ready to speak when spoken to, and even able to arouse the traveler's curiosity, at times, in the monotonous landscape.

"See those rowans over there?" said Stennet, nodding to the left. "Those rowans belong to Mr. Martin. He owns them half-way back to Mr. Crispin's place, and half-way on to Mr. Stephen's. And so it is with Mr. Crispin and Mr. Stephen in their turn."

"And what about the forest?"

"Same again," said Stennet, waving his hand towards the right. "It's round, you know. And they each own a third, like a huge slice of cake."

He clicked his tongue, and the horses pricked up their ears, though on either side of the dashboard the performance was no more than a formality, so swiftly was the buggy moving. "Very much quicker than Crispin's cart!" gasped the passenger, feeling the wind against his face; yet, when the evening of the autumn day was closing in, he looked about him with surprise.

He saw the moon rise up above the valley.

Later still, he asked for information regarding the names of the three inns, and Stennet laughed.

"The gentlemen are mighty proud of them. I can tell you! Romantic and a bit fearsome, that's what I call them. Poetical, too. They don't say 'The Traveler's Rest,' but 'The Rest of the Traveler,' mind you. That's poetical. I don't think it was Mr. Crispin's idea. I think it was Mr. Martin's—or Mrs. Crispin's. They're the clever ones. 'The Headless Man' is merely grim—a grim turn of mind, Mr. Martin has—and it means, of course, no more than it says—a man without a head. And then again," continued Stennet, whistling to his horses, whose backs were gleaming in the moonlight, "the inn you're going to now—'The Traveler's Head'—well, inns are called 'The King's Head' sometimes, aren't they, in the King's honor? Mr. Stephen goes one better than that. He dedicates his inn to the traveler himself." By this time a spark of light had become visible in the distance, and Mr. Bond fixed his eyes upon it. Once, for a moment, the spark went out, and he imagined that Stephen's head had passed in front of the living-room lamp. At this picture, anger seized him, and he wondered, amazed, why he was submitting so tamely to the commands—he could call them no less—of these oddly hospitable brothers. Fanned by his rage, the spark grew steadily bigger and brighter, until at last it had achieved the shape and size of a glowing window through which a man's face was grinning into the moonshine.

"Look here, what's all this?" cried Mr. Bond, sliding to his feet.

" 'The Traveler's Head,' sir," answered Stennet, pointing aloft.

They both stared up at the sign above their heads; then Mr. Bond scanned the sprawling mass of the inn, and scowled at its surroundings. The night was still and vibrant, without sound; the endless forest stood like a wall of blue-white dust; and the traveler was about to raise his voice in wrath against the brothers Sasserach, when a commotion burst from the porch of the inn, and on to the moon-drenched grass there strode a tall and ungainly figure, swinging its arms, with a pack of creatures flopping and tumbling at its heels. "Here *is* Mr. Stephen," Stennet whispered, watching the approach; the landlord of "The Traveler's Head" was smiling pleasantly, baring his intensely white teeth, and when he had reached the traveler he touched his forehead with a gesture that was at once respectful and overbearing.

"Mr. Bond, sir?" Mr. Bond muttered and bowed, and stared down at the landlord's children—large-headed, large-bellied, primitive creatures flopping round their father and pulling the skirts of the Inverness cape.

Father and children gathered round the traveler, who, lost within this little crowd, soon found himself at the entrance of "The Traveler's Head," through which his new host urged him by the arm while two of the children pushed between them and ran ahead clumsily into the depths of the hall. The place was ill-lighted and ill-ventilated; and although Mr. Bond knew from experience exactly where the living-room would be situated, yet, after he had passed through its doorway, he found no further resemblance to those rooms in which he had spent two stages of a curious adventure. The oil-lamp, standing in the middle of the round center table, was without a shade; a moth was plunging audibly at the blackened chimney, hurling swift shadows everywhere over the ceiling and figured wallpaper; while, with the return of the children, a harmonium had started fitfully to grunt and blow.

"Let me take your cloak, your cape, Mr. Bond, sir," the landlord said, and spread it with surprising care on one of the vast sofas that looked the larger because of their broken springs and the stuffing that protruded through their soiled covers: but at once the children seized upon the cape, and would have torn it to pieces had not Mr. Bond snatched it from them—at this, they cowered away from the stranger, fixing him with their eyes.

Amidst this congestion of people and furniture, Stephen Sasserach smiled and moved continuously, a stooping giant whom none but Mr. Bond obeyed. Here was the type of man whose appearance the traveler likened to that of the old-time executioner, the axe-man of the Middle Ages—harsh, loyal, simple, excessively domesticated, with a bulging forehead and untidy eyebrows and arms muscled and ready for deeds. Stephen kept no order in his house. Noise was everywhere, yet little seemed to be done. The children called their father Steve, and put out their tongues at him. They themselves were unlovely things, and their inner natures seemed to ooze through their skins and form a surface from which the traveler recoiled. Three of their names were familiar to Mr. Bond. Here were Crispin and Martin and Stephen over again; while Dorcas and Lydia were sisters whose only virtue was their mutual devotion.

The food at "The Traveler's Head" was homely and palatable, and Stephen the father cooked it and served it liberally on chipped plates. He sat in his soiled blue shirt, his knotted arms looking richly sunburnt against the blue. He was never inarticulate, and this surprised Mr. Bond. On the contrary, he spoke rapidly and almost as if to himself, in a low rugged voice that was always a pleasure to hear. At moments he dropped into silence, his eyes shut, his eyebrows lowered, and his bulging forehead grew still more shiny with thought; on such occasions, Dorcas and Lydia would steal to the harmonium, while, backed by a wail from the instrument, Crispin the Younger and Martin the Younger would jump from the sofas on to the floor.

Rousing himself at last, Stephen the Elder thumped his fist on the table, and turned in his chair to shout at the children: "Get along with you, devils! Get out your board, and *practice*, you little devils!" Whereupon the children erected a huge board, punctured with holes; and each child began to hurl wooden balls through the holes and into pockets behind them with astonishing accuracy, except for Dorcas and Lydia. And presently their father reminded them: "The moon is shining!" At once the children scuttled out of the room, and Mr. Bond never saw them again.

The noise and the figured wallpaper, and the fat moth beating itself against the only source of light, had caused the traveler's head to grow heavy with sleep; and now it grew heavier still as he sat by the fire with Stephen after supper was over, listening to the talk of that strangely attractive man in the soiled blue shirt. "You fond of children, Mr. Bond, sir?" Mr. Bond nodded.

"Children and animals . . ." he murmured drowsily.

"One has to let them have their way," sighed Stephen Sasserach. The rugged voice came clearly and soothingly into Mr. Bond's ears, until at last it shot up, vigorously, and ordered the guest to bed. Mr. Bond pulled himself out of his chair, and smiled, and said good night, and the moth flew into his face. Where were the children, he wondered. Their voices could not be heard. Perhaps they had fallen asleep, suddenly, like animals. But Mr. Bond found it difficult to imagine those eyes in bed, asleep.

Lying, some minutes later, in his own massive bed in this third of the Sasserach inns, with an extinguished candle on his bedside table, and gazing towards the open window from which he had drawn apart one of the heavy embroidered curtains, Mr. Bond fancied that he could hear faint cries of triumph, and sounds of knocking, coming from the direction of the forest. Starting up into complete wakefulness, he went to the window, and stared at the forest beyond the tufted grass. The sounds, he fancied, putting his hand to his ear, were as those given forth by the children during their game— but louder, as though the game were bigger. Perhaps strange animals were uttering them. Whatever their origin, they were coming from the depth of trees whose stillness was deepened by the light of the moon.

"Oh, God!" thought Mr. Bond, "I'm sick to death of the moonlight!"—and with a sweep of the arm he closed the curtains, yet could not shut out the sounds of the forest, nor the sight of the frosted grass beneath the moon. Together, sound and sight filled him with foreboding, and his cheeks shook as he groped for the unlighted candle. He must fetch his Inverness from below, fetch it at once, and get away while there was time. He found his host still sitting by the lamp in the living-room. Stephen's fist, lying on the table, was closed; he opened it, and out flew the moth.

"He thinks he has got away," cried Stephen, looking up, and baring his teeth in a smile: "but he hasn't! He never will!"

"I've come for my Inverness," said Mr. Bond.

It was lying on one of the massive sofas. The fire was out, and the air chilly, and the depth of the room lay in darkness. An Idea crossed the mind of Mr. Bond. He said, lifting up the cape: "I thought I'd like it on my bed." And he shivered to show how cold he was. From one of the two folds the moth flew out, and whirled round the room like a mad thing.

"That's all right, Mr. Bond, sir. That's all right." The man had fallen into a mood of abstraction; his forehead shone in the rays of the lamp; and the traveler left the room, holding himself with dignity in his gay dressing-gown, the Inverness hanging on his arm.

He was about to climb the staircase when a voice spoke softly in his ear, and wished him good night.

Stennet! What was the man doing here? Mr. Bond lifted his candle and gazed in astonishment at the back of Martin's manservant. The figure passed into the shadows, and the soft and deliberate ticking of the grandfather clock in the hall deepened the silence and fear of the moments that followed.

Mr. Bond ran to his room, locked himself in, and began to dress. His dyspepsia had seized him again. If only he were back at Crispin's! He parted the curtains, and peeped at the night. The shadow of the inn lay on the yard and the tufted grass beyond, and one of the chimneys, immensely distorted, extended as far as the forest. The forest-wall itself was solid with moonlight; from behind it there came no longer the sounds of the knocking, and the silence set Mr. Bond trembling again.

"I shall escape at dawn," he whispered, "when the moon's gone down."

Feeling no longer sleepy, he took from his knapsack a volume of *Mungo Park*, and, fully dressed, settled himself in an easy chair, with the curtains drawn again across the window, and the candle burning close beside him. At intervals he looked up from his book, frowning, running his eyes over the group of three pagodas, in pale red, endlessly repeated on the wallpaper. The restful picture made him drowsy, and presently he slept and snored and the candle burned on.

At midnight he was awakened by crashing blows on his door; the very candle seemed to be jumping with fear, and Mr. Bond sprang up in alarm.

"Yes? Who's that?" he called out, feebly.

"What in the name of God is *that*?" he whispered, as the blows grew louder.

"What are they up to now?" he asked aloud, with rising terror.

A splinter flew into the room, and he knew in a flash that the end of his journey had come. Was it Stephen or Stennet, Stephen or Stennet behind the door? The candle flickered as he blundered to and fro. He had no time to think, no time to act. He stood and watched the corner of the axe-blade working in the crack in the panel. "Save me, save me," he whispered, wringing his hands. They fluttered towards his Inverness, and struggled to push themselves into the obstinate sleeves. "Oh, come on, come on," he whimpered, jerking his arms about, anger rising with terror. The whole room shuddered beneath the axe. He plunged at the candle and blew it out. In the darkness a ray of light shot through a crack in the door, and fell on the window curtain.

Mr. Bond remembered the creeper clinging beneath his window, and as soon as possible he was floundering, scrambling, slipping down to the house-shadowed garden below. Puffing out his cheeks, he hurried onward, while the thuds of the axe grew fainter in his ears. Brickbats lay in his path, a zinc tub wrenched at his cape and ripped it loudly, an iron hoop caught in his foot and he tottered forward with outstretched hands. And now, still running in the far-flung shadow of the house, he was on the tufted grass, whimpering a little, struggling against desire to look back over his shoulder, making for the forest that lay in the full beams of the moonlight. He tried to think, and could think of nothing but the size and safety of the shadow on which he was running. He reached the roof of the inn at last: plunged aside from his course of flight: and now he was running up the monstrous shadow of the chimney, thinking of nothing at all because the forest stood so near. Blindingly a moon-filled avenue stretched before him: the chimney entered the chasm, and stopped: and it was as though Mr. Bond were a puff of smoke blowing into the forest depths. His shadow, swinging its monstrously distorted garments, led him to an open space at the end of the avenue. The thick-set trees encircled it with silence deeper than any that Mr. Bond had known. Here, in this glade, hung silence within a silence. Yet, halting abruptly, and pressing the flat of his hands to his ribs in the pain of his sudden burst of breathing, Mr. Bond had no ears for the silence, nor eyes for anything beyond the scene that faced him in the center of the forest glade: a group of upright posts, or stakes, set in a concave semicircle, throwing long shadows, and bearing on each summit a human skull. " 'The Traveler's Head,' 'The Headless Man,' " he whispered, stricken with terror, whipping his back on the skulls: and there was Stephen Sasserach in silhouette, leaping up the avenue, brandishing his axe as though he were a demented woodcutter coming to cut down trees.

The traveler's mind continued to run swiftly through the names of the three inns. " 'The Traveler's Head,' " he thought, " 'The Headless Man,' 'The Rest of the Traveler.' " he remembered the carrier pigeons that had flown ahead of him from inn to inn; he remembered the dust on the front of Martin's coat . . .

He was staring at the figure in the soiled blue shirt. It had halted now, as still as a tree, on the verge of the moon-filled glade: but the whirling thoughts of Mr. Bond were on the verge of light more blinding than this; they stopped, appalled: and the traveler fled beyond the skulls, fruitlessly searching for cover in the farthest wall of trees.

Then Stephen sprang in his wake, flinging up a cry that went knocking against the tree-trunks.

The echoes were echoed by Mr. Bond, who, whipping round to face his enemy, was wriggling and jerking in his Inverness cape, slipping it off at last, and swinging it in his hand, for his blood was up. And now he was deep in mortal combat, wielding his Inverness as the gladiators used to wield their nets in the old arenas. Time and again the axe and the cape engaged each other; the one warding and hindering; the other catching and ripping, clumsily enough, as though in sport. Around the skulls the two men fought and panted, now in darkness, now in the full light pouring down the avenue. Their moon-cast shadows fought another fight together, wilder still than theirs. Then Stephen cried: "Enough of this!" and bared his teeth for the first time since the strife had started.

"B-but you're my friend!" bleated Mr. Bond; and he stared at the shining thread of the axe.

"The best you ever had, sir, Mr. Bond, sir!" answered Stephen Sasserach; and, stepping back, the landlord of "The Traveler's Head" cut off the traveler's head.

The thump of the head on the sticks and leaves and grass of the forest glade was the first sound in the new and peaceful life of Mr. Bond, and he did not hear it; but to the brothers Sasserach it was a promise of life itself, a signal that all was ready now for them to apply their respective talents busily and happily in the immediate future.

Stephen took the head of Mr. Bond, and with gentle though rather clumsy fingers pared it to a skull, grinning back at it with simple satisfaction when the deed was over and after that he set it up as a fine mark for his brood of primitives, the game's endeavor being to see who could throw the ball into the eye-sockets; and to his brother Martin, landlord of "The Headless Man," he sent the headless man, under the care of Stennet: and Martin, on a soft, autumnal day, reduced the headless body to a skeleton, with all its troubles gone, and through the days and nights he sat at work, with swift precision in his fingers, carving and turning, powdering his coat with dust, creating his figures and trinkets, his paper-knives and salad-spoons and fretted boxes and rare chess-men; and to his brother Crispin, landlord of "The Rest of the Traveler," Martin sent the rest of the traveler, the soft and yielding parts, the scraps, the odds and ends, the miscellaneous pieces, all the internal lumber that had gone to fill the skin of the man from the Midlands and to help to render him in middle years a prey to dyspepsia. Crispin received the parcel with a pursing of his small mouth, and a call to Myrtle in his clear falsetto: "Stennet's here!"

She answered from the kitchen. "Thank you, Cris!" Her hands were soft and swollen as she scoured the tureen. The back of the inn was full of reflected sunlight, and her dark hair shone.

"It's too late in the season now," she said, when tea-time came. "I don't suppose we'll have another one before the spring."

Yet she was wrong. That very evening, when the moon had risen from beyond the valley, Myrtle murmured: "There he comes," and continued to stir her ladle in the bowl.

Her husband strolled into the hall, and wound the clock.

He took the lamp from its bracket on the wall.

He went to the door, and flung it open to the moonlight, holding the lamp above his head.

"Come in, come in," he said, to the stranger standing there; "she is cooking a *lovely* broth tonight!"

THE ELEPHANT MAN

From The Elephant Man and other Reminiscences

Sir Frederick Treves Bart

IN THE Mile End Road, opposite to the London Hospital, there was (and possibly still is) a line of small shops. Among them was a vacant greengrocer's which was to let. The whole of the front of the shop, with the exception of the door, was hidden by a hanging sheet of canvas on which was the announcement that the Elephant Man was to be seen within and that the price of admission was twopence. Painted on the canvas in primitive colors was a life-size portrait of the Elephant Man. This very crude production depicted a frightful creature that could only have been possible in a nightmare. It was the figure of a man with the characteristics of an elephant. The transfiguration was not far advanced. There was still more of the man than of the beast. This fact—that it was still human—was the most repellent attribute of the creature. There was nothing about it of the pitiableness of the misshapen or the deformed, nothing of the grotesqueness of the freak, but merely the loathsome insinuation of a man being changed into an animal. Some palm trees in the background of the picture suggested a jungle and might have led the imaginative to assume that it was in this wild that the perverted object had roamed.

When I first became aware of this phenomenon the exhibition was closed, but a well-informed boy sought the proprietor in a public house and I was granted a private view on payment of a shilling. The shop was empty and grey with dust. Some old tins and a few shriveled potatoes occupied a shelf and some vague vegetable refuse the window. The light in the place was dim, being obscured by the painted placard outside. The far end of the shop—where I expect the late proprietor sat at a desk—was cut off by a curtain or rather by a red tablecloth suspended from a cord by a few rings. The room was cold and dank, for it was the month of November. The year, I might say, was 1884.

The showman pulled back the curtain and revealed a bent figure crouching on a stool and covered by a brown blanket. In front of it, on a tripod, was a large brick heated by a Bunsen burner. Over this the creature was huddled to warm itself. It never moved when the curtain was drawn back. Locked up in an empty shop and lit by the faint blue light of the gas jet, this hunched-up figure was the embodiment of loneliness. It might have been a captive in a cavern or a wizard watching for unholy manifestations in the ghostly flame. Outside the sun was shining and one could hear the footsteps of the passers-by, a tune whistled by a boy, and the companionable hum of traffic in the road.

The showman—speaking as if to a dog—called out harshly: "Stand up." The thing arose slowly and let the blanket that covered its head and back fall to the ground. There stood revealed the most disgusting specimen of humanity that I have ever seen. In the course of my profession I had come upon lamentable deformities of the face due to injury or disease, as well as mutilations and contortions of the body depending upon like causes; but at no time had I met with such a degraded or perverted version of a human being as this lone figure displayed. He was naked to the waist, his feet were bare, he wore a pair of threadbare trousers that had once belonged to some fat gentleman's dress suit.

From the intensified painting in the street I had imagined the Elephant Man to be of gigantic size. This, however, was a little man below the average height and made to look shorter by the bowing of his back. The most striking feature about him was his enormous and misshapen head. From the brow there projected a huge bony mass like a leaf, while from the back of the head hung a bag of spongy, fungous-looking skin, the surface of which was comparable to brown cauliflower. On the top of the skull were a few long lank hairs. The osseous growth on the forehead almost occluded one eye. The circumference of the head was no less than that of the man's waist. From the upper jaw there projected another mass of bone. It protruded from the mouth like a pink stump, turning the upper lip inside out and making of the mouth a mere slobbering aperture. This growth from the jaw had been so exaggerated in the painting as to appear to be a rudimentary trunk or tusk. The nose was merely a lump of flesh, only recognizable as a nose from its position. The face was no more capable of expression than a block of gnarled wood. The back was horrible, because from it hung, as far down as the middle of the thigh, huge, sack-like masses of flesh covered by the same loathsome cauliflower skin.

The right arm was of enormous size, and shapeless: It suggested the limb of the subject of elephantiasis. It was overgrown also with pendent masses of the same cauliflower-like skin. The hand was large and clumsy—a fin or paddle rather than a hand. There was no distinction between the

176

palm and the back. The thumb had the appearance of a radish, while the fingers might have been thick, tuberous roots. As a limb it was almost useless. The other arm was remarkable by contrast. It was not only normal but was, moreover, a delicately shaped limb covered with fine skin and provided with a beautiful hand which any woman might have envied. From the chest hung a bag of the same repulsive flesh. It was like a dewlap suspended from the neck of a lizard. The lower limbs had the characters of the deformed arm. They were unwieldy, dropsical looking, and grossly misshapen.

To add a further burden to his trouble the wretched man, when a boy, developed hip disease, which had left him permanently lame, so that he could only walk with a stick. He was thus denied all means of escape from his tormentors. As he told me later, he could never run away. One other feature must be mentioned to emphasize his isolation from his kind. Although he was already repellent enough, there arose from the fungous skin-growth with which he was almost covered a very sickening stench which was hard to tolerate. From the showman I learnt nothing about the Elephant Man, except that he was English, that his name was John Merrick, and that he was twenty-one years of age.

As at the time of my discovery of the Elephant Man I was the Lecturer on Anatomy at the Medical College opposite, I was anxious to examine him in detail and to prepare an account of his abnormalities. I therefore arranged with the showman that I should interview his strange exhibit in my room at the college. I became at once conscious of a difficulty. The Elephant Man could not show himself in the streets. He would have been mobbed by the crowd and seized by the police. He was, in fact, as secluded from the world as the Man with the Iron Mask. He had, however, a disguise, although it was almost as startling as he was himself. It consisted of a long black cloak which reached to the ground. Whence the cloak had been obtained I cannot imagine. I had only seen such a garment on the stage wrapped about the figure of a Venetian bravo. The recluse was provided with a pair of bag-like slippers in which to hide his deformed feet. On his head was a cap of a kind that never before was seen. It was black like the cloak, had a wide peak, and the general outline of a yachting cap. As the circumference of Merrick's head was that of a man's waist, the size of this headgear may be imagined. From the attachment of the peak, a grey flannel curtain hung in front of the face. In this mask was cut a wide horizontal slit through which the wearer could look out. This costume, worn by a bent man hobbling along with a stick, is probably the most remarkable and the most uncanny that has as yet been designed. I arranged that Merrick should cross the road in a cab, and to ensure his immediate admission to the college I gave him my card. This card was destined to play a critical part in Merrick's life.

I made a careful examination of my visitor, the result of which I embodied in a paper.* I made little of the man himself. He was shy, confused, not a little frightened, and evidently much cowed. Moreover, his speech was almost unintelligible. The great bony mass that projected from his mouth blurred his utterance and made the articulation of certain words impossible. He returned in a cab to the place of exhibition, and I assumed that I had seen the last of him, especially as I found next day that the show had been forbidden by the police and that the shop was empty.

I supposed that Merrick was imbecile and had been imbecile from birth. The fact that his face was incapable of expression, that his speech was a mere spluttering, and his attitude that of one whose mind was void of all emotions and concerns, gave grounds for this belief. The conviction was no doubt encouraged by the hope that his intellect was the blank I imagined it to be. That he could appreciate his position was unthinkable. Here was a man in the heyday of youth who was so vilely deformed that everyone he met confronted him with a look of horror and disgust. He was taken about the country to be exhibited as a monstrosity and an object of loathing. He was shunned like a leper, housed like a wild beast, and got his only view of the world from a peephole in a showman's cart. He was, moreover, lame, had but one available arm, and could hardly make his utterances understood. It was not until I came to know that Merrick was highly intelligent, that he possessed an acute sensibility and—worse than all—a romantic imagination, that I realized the overwhelming tragedy of his life.

The episode of the Elephant Man was, I imagined, closed; but I was fated to meet him again—two years later—under more dramatic conditions. In England the showman and Merrick had been moved on from place to place by the police, who considered the exhibition degrading and among the things that could not be allowed. It was hoped that in the uncritical retreats of Mile End a more abiding peace would be found. But it was not to be. The official mind there, as elsewhere, very properly decreed that the public exposure of Merrick and his deformities transgressed the limits of decency. The show must close.

* British Medical Journal, December 1886, and April 1890.

The showman, in despair, fled with his charge to the Continent. Whither he roamed at first I do not know; but he came finally to Brussels. His reception was discouraging. Brussels was firm; the exhibition was banned; it was brutal, indecent, and immoral, and could not be permitted within the confines of Belgium. Merrick was thus no longer of value. He was no longer a source of profitable entertainment. He was a burden. He must be got rid of. The elimination of Merrick was a simple matter. He could offer no resistance. He was as docile as a sick sheep. The impresario, having robbed Merrick of his paltry savings, gave him a ticket to London, saw him into the train and no doubt in parting condemned him to perdition.

His destination was Liverpool Street. The journey may be imagined. Merrick was in his alarming outdoor garb. He would be harried by an eager mob as he hobbled along the quay. They would run ahead to get a look at him. They would lift the hem of his cloak to peep at his body. He would try to hide in the train or in some dark corner of the boat, but never could he be free from that ring of curious eyes or from those whispers of fright and aversion. He had but a few shillings in his pocket and nothing either to eat or drink on the way. A panic-dazed dog with a label on his collar would have received some sympathy and possibly some kindness. Merrick received none.

What was he to do when he reached London? He had not a friend in the world. He knew no more of London than he knew of Pekin. How could he find a lodging, or what lodging-house keeper would dream of taking him in? All he wanted was to hide. What most he dreaded were the open street and the gaze of his fellow-men. If even he crept into a cellar the horrid eyes and the still more dreaded whispers would follow him to its depths. Was there ever such a homecoming!

At Liverpool Street he was rescued from the crowd by the police and taken into the third-class waiting-room. Here he sank on the floor in the darkest corner. The police were at a loss what to do with him. They had dealt with strange and moldy tramps, but never with such an object as this. He could not explain himself. His speech was so maimed that he might as well have spoken in Arabic. He had, however, something with him which he produced with a ray of hope. It was my card.

The card simplified matters. It made it evident that this curious creature had an acquaintance and that the individual must be sent for. A messenger was dispatched to the London Hospital, which is comparatively near at hand. Fortunately I was in the building and returned at once with the messenger to the station. In the waiting-room I had some difficulty in making a way through the crowd, but there, on the floor in the corner, was Merrick. He looked a mere heap. It seemed as if he had been thrown there like a bundle. He was so huddled up and so helpless looking that he might have had both his arms and his legs broken. He seemed pleased to see me, but he was nearly done. The journey and want of food had reduced him to the last stage of exhaustion. The police kindly helped him into a cab, and I drove him at once to the hospital. He appeared to be content, for he fell asleep almost as soon as he was seated and slept to the journey's end. He never said a word, but seemed to be satisfied that all was well.

In the attics of the hospital was an isolation ward with a single bed. It was used for emergency purposes—for a case of delirium tremens, for a man who had become suddenly insane, or for a patient with an undetermined fever. Here the Elephant Man was deposited on a bed, was made comfortable, and was supplied with food. I had been guilty of an irregularity in admitting such a case, for the hospital was neither a refuge nor a home for incurables. Chronic cases were not accepted but only those requiring active treatment, and Merrick was not in need of such treatment. I applied to the sympathetic chairman of the committee, Mr. Carr Gomm, who not only was good enough to approve my action, but who agreed with me that Merrick must not again be turned out into the world.

Mr. Carr Gomm wrote a letter to *The Times* detailing the circumstances of the refugee and asking for money for his support. So generous is the English public that in a few days—I think in a week—enough money was forthcoming to maintain Merrick for life without any charge upon the hospital funds. There chanced to be two empty rooms at the back of the hospital which were little used. They were on the ground floor, were out of the way, and opened upon a large courtyard called Bedstead Square, because here the iron beds were marshalled for cleaning and painting. The front room was converted into a bed-sitting room and the smaller chamber into a bathroom. The condition of Merrick's skin rendered a bath at least once a day a necessity, and I might here mention that with the use of the bath the unpleasant odor to which I have referred ceased to be noticeable. Merrick took up his abode in the hospital in December 1886.

Merrick had now something he had never dreamed of, never supposed to be possible—a home of his own for life. I at once began to make myself acquainted with him and to endeavor to understand his mentality. It was a study of much interest. I very soon learnt his speech so that I could talk freely with him. This afforded him great satisfaction, for, curiously enough, he had a passion for conversation, yet all his life had had no one to talk to. I—having then much leisure—saw him almost every day, and made a point of spending some two hours with him every Sunday morning when he would chatter almost without ceasing. It was unreasonable to expect one nurse to attend him continuously, but there was no lack of temporary volunteers. As they did not all acquire his speech it came about that I had occasionally to act as an interpreter.

I found Merrick, as I have said, remarkably intelligent. He had learnt to read and had become a most voracious reader. I think he had been taught when he was in hospital with his diseased hip. His range of books was limited. The Bible and Prayer Book he knew intimately, but he had subsisted for the most part upon newspapers, or rather upon such fragments of old journals as he had chanced to pick up. He had read a few stories and some elementary lesson books, but the delight of his life was a romance, especially a love romance. These tales were very real to him, as real as any narrative in the Bible, so that he would tell them to me as incidents in the lives of people who had lived. In his outlook upon the world he was a child, yet a child with some of the tempestuous feelings of a man. He was an elemental being, so primitive that he might have spent the twenty-three years of his life immured in a cave.

Of his early days I could learn but little. He was very loath to talk about the past. It was a nightmare, the shudder of which was still upon him. He was born, he believed, in or about Leicester. Of his father he knew absolutely nothing. Of his mother he had some memory. It was very faint and had, I think, been elaborated in his mind into something definite. Mothers figured in the tales he had read, and he wanted his mother to be one of those comfortable lullaby-singing persons who are so lovable. In his subconscious mind there was apparently a germ of recollection in which someone figured who had been kind to him. He clung to this conception and made it more real by invention, for since the day when he could toddle no one had been kind to him. As an infant he must have been repellent, although his deformities did not become gross until he had attained his full stature.

It was a favorite belief of his that his mother was beautiful. The fiction was, I am aware, one of his own making, but it was a great joy to him. His mother, lovely as she may have been, basely deserted him when he was very small, so small that his earliest clear memories were of the workhouse to which he had been taken. Worthless and inhuman as this mother was, he spoke of her with pride and even with reverence. Once, when referring to his own appearance, he said: "It *is* very strange, for, you see, Mother was so beautiful."

The rest of Merrick's life up to the time I met him at Liverpool Street Station was one dull record of degradation and squalor. He was dragged from town to town and from fair to fair as if he were a strange beast in a cage. A dozen times a day he would have to expose his nakedness and his piteous deformities before a gaping crowd who greeted him with such mutterings as 'Oh! what a horror! What a beast!' He had had no childhood. He had had no boyhood. He had never experienced pleasure. He knew nothing of the joy of living nor of the fun of things. His sole idea of happiness was to creep in to the dark and hide. Shut up alone in a booth, awaiting the next exhibition, how mocking must have sounded the laughter and merriment of the boys and girls outside who were enjoying the "fun of the fair"! He had no past to look back upon and no future to look forward to. At the age of twenty he was a creature without hope. There was nothing in front of him but a vista of caravans creeping along a road, of rows of glaring show tents and of circles of staring eyes with, at the end, the spectacle of a broken man in a poor law infirmary.

Those who are interested in the evolution of character might speculate as to the effect of this brutish life upon a sensitive and intelligent man. It would be reasonable to surmise that he would become a spiteful and malignant misanthrope, swollen with venom and filled with hatred of his fellow-men, or, on the other hand, that he would degenerate into a despairing melancholic on the verge of idiocy. Merrick, however, was no such being. He had passed through the fire and had come out unscathed. His troubles had ennobled him. He showed himself to be a gentle, affectionate, and lovable creature, as amiable as a happy woman, free from any trace of cynicism or resentment, without a grievance and without an unkind word for anyone. I have never heard him complain. I have never heard him deplore his ruined life or resent the treatment he had received at the hands of callous keepers. His journey through life had been indeed along a *via dolorosa*, the road had been uphill all the way, and now, when the night was at its blackest and the way most steep, he had suddenly found himself, as it were, in a friendly inn, bright with light and warm with welcome. His gratitude to those about him was pathetic in its sincerity and eloquent in the childlike simplicity with which it was expressed.

As I learnt more of this primitive creature I found that there were two anxieties which were prominent in his mind and which he revealed to me with diffidence. He was in the occupation of the rooms assigned to him and had been assured that he would be cared for to the end of his days. This, however, he found hard to realize, for he often asked me timidly to what place he would next be moved. To understand his attitude it is necessary to remember that he had been moving on and moving on all his life. He knew no other state of existence. To him it was normal. He had passed from the workhouse to the hospital, from the hospital back to the workhouse, then from this town to that town, or from one showman's caravan to another. He had never known a home nor any semblance of one. He had no possessions. His sole belongings, besides his clothes and some books, were the monstrous cap and the cloak. He was a wanderer, a pariah and an outcast. That his quarters at the hospital were his for life he could not understand. He could not rid his mind of the anxiety which had pursued him for so many years—where am I to be taken next?

Another trouble was his dread of his fellow-men, his fear of people's eyes, the dread of being always stared at, the lash of the cruel mutterings of the crowd. In his home in Bedstead Square he was secluded; but now and then a thoughtless porter or a wardmaid would open his door to let curious friends have a peep at the Elephant Man. It therefore seemed to him as if the gaze of the world followed him still.

Influenced by these two obsessions he became, during his first few weeks at the hospital, curiously uneasy. At last, with much hesitation, he said to me one day: "When I am next moved can I go to a blind asylum or to a lighthouse?" He had read about blind asylums in the newspapers and was attracted by the thought of being among people who could not see. The lighthouse had another charm. It meant seclusion from the curious. There at least no one could open a door and peep in at him. There he would forget that he had once been the Elephant Man. There he would escape the vampire showman. He had never seen a lighthouse, but he had come upon a picture of the Eddystone, and it appeared to him that this lonely column of stone in the waste of the sea was such a home as he had longed for.

I had no great difficulty in ridding Merrick's mind of these ideas. I wanted him to get accustomed to his fellow-men, to become a human being himself, and to be admitted to the communion of his kind. He appeared day by day less frightened, less haunted looking, less anxious to hide, less alarmed when he saw his door being opened. He got to know most of the people about the place, to be accustomed to their comings and goings, and to realize that they took no more than a friendly notice of him. He could only go out after dark, and on fine nights ventured to take a walk in Bedstead Square clad in his black cloak and his cap. His greatest adventure was on one moonless evening when he walked alone as far as the hospital garden and back again.

To secure Merrick's recovery and to bring him, as it were, to life once more, it was necessary that he should make the acquaintance of men and women who would treat him as a normal and intelligent young man and not as a monster of deformity. Women I felt to be more important than men in bringing about his transformation. Women were the more frightened of him, the more disgusted at his appearance, and the more apt to give way to irrepressible expressions of aversion when they came into his presence. Moreover, Merrick had an admiration of women of such a kind that it attained almost to adoration. This was not the outcome of his personal experience. They were not real women, but the products of his imagination. Among them was the beautiful mother surrounded, at a respectful distance, by heroines from the many romances he had read.

His first entry to the hospital was attended by a regrettable incident. He had been placed on the bed in the little attic, and a nurse had been instructed to bring him some food. Unfortunately, she had not been fully informed of Merrick's unusual appearance. As she entered the room she saw on the bed, propped up by white pillows, a monstrous figure as hideous as an Indian idol. She at once dropped the tray she was carrying and fled, with a shriek, through the door. Merrick was too weak to notice much, but the experience, I am afraid, was not new to him.

He was looked after by volunteer nurses whose ministrations were somewhat formal and constrained. Merrick, no doubt, was conscious that their service was purely official, that they were merely doing what they were told to do, and that they were acting rather as automata than as women. They did not help him to feel that he was of their kind. On the contrary, they, without knowing it, made him aware that the gulf of separation was immeasurable.

Feeling this, I asked a friend of mine, a young and pretty widow, if she thought she could enter Merrick's room with a smile, wish him good morning, and shake him by the hand. She said she could, and she did. The effect upon poor Merrick was not quite what I had expected. As he let go her

184

hand he bent his head on his knees and sobbed until I thought he would never cease. The interview was over. He told me afterwards that this was the first woman who had ever smiled at him, and the first woman, in the whole of his life, who had shaken hands with him. From this day the transformation of Merrick commenced and he began to change, little by little, from a hunted thing into a man. It was a wonderful change to witness and one that never ceased to fascinate me.

Merrick's case attracted much attention in the papers, with the result that he had a constant succession of visitors. Everybody wanted to see him. He must have been visited by almost every lady of note in the social world. They were all good enough to welcome him with a smile and to shake hands with him. The Merrick whom I had found shivering behind a rag of a curtain in an empty shop was now conversant with duchesses and countesses and other ladies of high degree. They brought him presents, made his room bright with ornaments and pictures and, what pleased him more than all, supplied him with books. He soon had a large library, and most of his day was spent in reading. He was not the least spoiled; not the least puffed up; he never asked for anything; never presumed upon the kindness meted out to him, and was always humbly and profoundly grateful. Above all, he lost his shyness. He liked to see his door pushed open and people to look in. He became acquainted with most of the frequenters of Bedstead Square, would chat with them at his window, and show them some of his choicest presents. He improved in his speech, although to the end his utterances were not easy for strangers to understand. He was beginning, moreover, to be less conscious of his unsightliness, a little disposed to think it was, after all, not so very extreme. Possibly this was aided by the circumstance that I would not allow a mirror of any kind in his room.

The height of his social development was reached on an eventful day when Queen Alexandra—then Princess of Wales—came to the hospital to pay him a special visit. With that kindness which has marked every act of her life, the Queen entered Merrick's room smiling and shook him warmly by the hand. Merrick was transported with delight. This was beyond even his most extravagant dream. The Queen has made many people happy, but I think no gracious act of hers has ever caused such happiness as she brought into Merrick's room when she sat by his chair and talked to him as to a person she was glad to see.

Merrick, I may say, was now one of the most contented creatures I have chanced to meet. More than once he said to me: "I am happy every hour of the day." This was good to think upon when I recalled the half-dead heap of miserable humanity I had seen in the corner of the waiting-room at Liverpool Street. Most men of Merrick's age would have expressed their joy and sense of contentment by singing or whistling when they were alone. Unfortunately, poor Merrick's mouth was so deformed that he could neither whistle nor sing. He was satisfied to express himself by beating time upon the pillow to some tune that was ringing in his head. I have many times found him so occupied when I have entered his room unexpectedly. One thing that always struck me as sad about Merrick was the fact that he could not smile. Whatever his delight might be, his face remained expressionless. He could weep but he could not smile.

The Queen paid Merrick many visits and sent him every year a Christmas card with a message in her own handwriting. On one occasion she sent him a signed photograph of herself. Merrick, quite overcome, regarded it as a sacred object and would hardly allow me to touch it. He cried over it, and after it was framed, had it put up in his room as a kind of ikon. I told him that he must write to Her Royal Highness to thank her for her goodness. This he was pleased to do, as he was very fond of writing letters, never before in his life having had anyone to write to. I allowed the letter to be dispatched unedited. It began, "My dear Princess," and ended, "Yours very sincerely." Unorthodox as it was, it was expressed in terms any courtier would have envied.

Other ladies followed the Queen's gracious example and sent their photographs to this delighted creature who had been all his life despised and rejected of men. His mantel-piece and table became so covered with photographs of handsome ladies, with dainty knicknacks and pretty trifles, that they may almost have befitted the apartment of an Adonis-like actor or of a famous tenor.

Through all these bewildering incidents, and through the glamor of this great change, Merrick still remained in many ways a mere child. He had all the invention of an imaginative boy or girl, the same love of "make-believe," the same instinct of "dressing up," and of personating heroic and impressive characters. This attitude of mind was illustrated by the following incident. Benevolent visitors had given me, from time to time, sums of money to be expended for the comfort of the *ci-devant* Elephant Man. When one Christmas was approaching I asked Merrick what he would like me to purchase as a Christmas present. He rather startled me by saying shyly that he would like a dressing-bag with silver fittings. He had seen a picture of such an article in an advertisement which he had furtively preserved.

The association of a silver-fitted dressing-bag with the poor wretch wrapped up in a dirty blanket in an empty shop was hard to comprehend. I fathomed the mystery in time, for Merrick made little secret of the fancies that haunted his boyish brain. Just as a small girl with a tinsel coronet and a window curtain for a train will realize the conception of a countess on her way to court, so Merrick loved to imagine himself a dandy and a young man about town. Mentally, no doubt, he had frequently "dressed up" for the part. He could "make-believe" with great effect, but he wanted something to render his fancied character more realistic. Hence the jaunty bag which was to assume the function of the toy coronet and the window curtain that could transform a mite with a pigtail into a countess.

As a theatrical "property" the dressing-bag was ingenious, since there was little else to give substance to the transformation. Merrick could not wear the silk hat of the dandy, nor, indeed, any kind of hat. He could not adapt his body to the trimly cut coat. His deformity was such that he could wear neither collar nor tie, while in association with his bulbous feet, the young blood's patent-leather shoe was unthinkable. What was there left to make up the character? A lady had given him a ring to wear on his undeformed hand, and a noble lord had presented him with a very stylish walking-stick. But these things, helpful as they were, were hardly sufficing.

The dressing-bag, however, was distinctive, was explanatory, and entirely characteristic. So the bag was obtained, and Merrick the Elephant Man became, in the seclusion of his chamber, the Piccadilly exquisite, the young spark, the gallant, the "nut." When I purchased the article I realized that, as Merrick could never travel, he could hardly want a dressing-bag. He could not use the silver-backed brushes and the comb because he had no hair to brush. The ivory-handled razors were useless because he could not shave. The deformity of his mouth rendered an ordinary toothbrush of no avail, and as his monstrous lips could not hold a cigarette, the cigarette-case was a mockery. The silver shoe-horn would be of no service in the putting on of his ungainly slippers, while the hat-brush was quite unsuited to the peaked cap with its visor.

Still, the bag was an emblem of the real swell and of the knockabout Don Juan of whom he had read. So every day Merrick laid out upon his table, with proud precision, the silver brushes, the razors, the shoe-horn, and the silver cigarette-case, which I had taken care to fill with cigarettes. The contemplation of these gave him great pleasure, and such is the power of self-deception that they convinced him he was the "real thing."

I think there was just one shadow in Merrick's life. As I have already said, he had a lively imagination; he was romantic; he cherished an emotional regard for women, and his favorite pursuit was the reading of love stories. He fell in love—in a humble and devotional way—with, I think, every attractive lady he saw. He, no doubt, pictured himself the hero of many a passionate incident. His bodily deformity had left unmarred the instincts and feelings of his years. He was amorous. He would like to have been a lover, to have walked with the beloved object in the languorous shades of some beautiful garden, and to have poured into her ear all the glowing utterances that he had rehearsed in his heart. And yet—the pity of it!—imagine the feelings of such a youth when he saw nothing but a look of horror creep over the face of every girl whose eyes met his. I fancy when he talked of life among the blind there was a half-formed idea in his mind that he might be able to win the affection of a woman if only she were without eyes to see.

As Merrick developed he began to display certain modest ambitions in the direction of improving his mind and enlarging his knowledge of the world. He was as curious as a child and as eager to learn. There were so many things he wanted to know and to see. In the first place, he was anxious to view the interior of what he called "a real house," such a house as figured in many of the tales he knew, a house with a hall, a drawing-room where guests were received, and a dining-room with plate on the sideboard and with easy chairs into which the hero could "fling himself." The workhouse, the common lodging-house, and a variety of mean garrets were all the residences he knew. To satisfy this wish I drove him up to my small house in Wimpole Street. He was absurdly interested, and examined everything in detail and with untiring curiosity. I could not show him the pampered menials and the powdered footmen of whom he had read, nor could I produce the white marble staircase of the mansion of romance nor the gilded mirrors and the brocaded divans which belong to that style of residence. I explained that the house was a modest dwelling of the Jane Austen type, and as he had read *Emma* he was content.

A more burning ambition of his was to go to the theatre. It was a project very difficult to satisfy. A popular panto-mime was then in progress at Drury Lane Theatre, but the problem was how so conspicuous a being as the Elephant

Man could be got there, and how he was to see the performance without attracting the notice of the audience and causing a panic or, at least, an unpleasant diversion. The whole matter was most ingeniously carried through by that kindest of women and most able of actresses—Mrs. Kendal. She made the necessary arrangements with the lessee of the theatre. A box was obtained. Merrick was brought up in a carriage with drawn blinds and was allowed to make use of the royal entrance so as to reach the box by a private stair. I had begged three of the hospital sisters to don evening dress and to sit in the front row in order to 'dress' the box, on the one hand, and to form a screen for Merrick on the other. Merrick and I occupied the back of the box, which was kept in shadow. All went well, and no one saw a figure, more monstrous than any on the stage, mount the staircase or cross the corridor.

One has often witnessed the unconstrained delight of a child at its first pantomime, but Merrick's rapture was much more intense as well as much more solemn. Here was a being with the brain of a man, the fancies of a youth, and the imagination of a child. His attitude was not so much that of delight as of wonder and amazement. He was awed. He was enthralled. The spectacle left him speechless, so that if he were spoken to he took no heed. He often seemed to be panting for breath. I could not help comparing him with a man of his own age in the stalls. This satiated individual was bored to distraction, would look wearily at the stage from time to time, and then yawn as if he had not slept for nights; while at the same time Merrick was thrilled by a vision that was almost beyond his comprehension. Merrick talked of this pantomime for weeks and weeks. To him, as to a child with the faculty of make-believe, everything was real; the palace was the home of kings, the princess was of royal blood, the fairies were as undoubted as the children in the street, while the dishes at the banquet were of unquestionable gold. He did not like to discuss it as a play but rather as a vision of some actual world. When this mood possessed him, he would say: "I wonder what the prince did after we left," or "Do you think that poor man is still in the dungeon?" and so on and so on.

The splendor and display impressed him, but, I think, the ladies of the ballet took a still greater hold upon his fancy. He did not like the ogres and the giants, while the funny men impressed him as irreverent. Having no experience as a boy of romping and ragging, of practical jokes or of "larks," he had little sympathy with the doings of the clown, but, I think (moved by some mischievous instinct in his subconscious mind), he was pleased when the policeman was smacked in the face, knocked down, and generally rendered undignified.

Later on another longing stirred the depth of Merrick's mind. It was a desire to see the country, a desire to live in some green secluded spot and there learn something about flowers and the ways of animals and birds. The country as viewed from a wagon on a dusty high road was all the country he knew. He had never wandered among the fields nor followed the windings of a wood. He had never climbed to the brow of a breezy down. He had never gathered flowers in a meadow. Since so much of his reading dealt with country life he was possessed by the wish to see the wonders of that life himself.

This involved a difficulty greater than that presented by a visit to the theatre. The project was, however, made possible on this occasion also by the kindness and generosity of a lady—Lady Knightley—who offered Merrick a holiday home in a cottage on her estate. Merrick was conveyed to the railway station in the usual way, but as he could hardly venture to appear on the platform the railway authorities were good enough to run a second-class carriage into a distant siding. To this point Merrick was driven and was placed in the carriage unobserved. The carriage, with the curtains drawn, was then attached to the mainline train.

He duly arrived at the cottage, but the housewife (like the nurse at the hospital) had not been made clearly aware of the unfortunate man's appearance. Thus it happened that when Merrick presented himself, his hostess, throwing her apron over her head, fled, gasping, to the fields. She affirmed that such a guest was beyond her powers of endurance, for, when she saw him, she was "that took" as to be in danger of being permanently "all of a tremble."

Merrick was then conveyed to a gamekeeper's cottage which was hidden from view and was close to the margin of a wood. The man and his wife were able to tolerate his presence. They treated him with the greatest kindness, and with them he spent the one supreme holiday of his life. He could roam where he pleased. He met no one on his wanderings, for the wood was preserved and denied to all but the gamekeeper and the forester.

There is no doubt that Merrick passed in this retreat the happiest time he had as yet experienced. He was alone in a land of wonders. The breath of the country passed over him like a healing wind. Into the silence of the wood the fearsome voice of the showman could never penetrate. No cruel eyes could peep at him through the friendly undergrowth. It seemed as if in this place of peace all stain had been wiped away from his sullied past. The Merrick who had once crouched terrified in the filthy shadows of a Mile End shop was now sitting in the sun, in a clearing among the trees, arranging a bunch of violets he had gathered.

His letters to me were the letters of a delighted and enthusiastic child. He gave an account of his trivial adventures, of the amazing things he had seen, and of the beautiful sounds he had heard. He had met with strange birds, had startled a hare from her form, had made friends with a fierce dog, and had watched the trout darting in a stream. He sent me some of the wild flowers he had picked. They were of the commonest and most familiar kind, but they were evidently regarded by him as rare and precious specimens.

He came back to London, to his quarters in Bedstead Square, much improved in health, pleased to be "home" again, and to be once more among his books, his treasures, and his many friends.

Some six months after Merrick's return from the country he was found dead in bed. This was in April 1890. He was lying on his back as if asleep, and had evidently died suddenly and without a struggle, since not even the coverlet of the bed was disturbed. The method of his death was peculiar. So large and so heavy was his head that he could not sleep lying down. When he assumed the recumbent position the massive skull was inclined to drop backward, with the result that he experienced no little distress. The attitude he was compelled to assume when he slept was very strange. He sat up in bed with his back supported by pillows, his knees were drawn up, and his arms clasped round his legs, while his head rested on the points of his bent knees.

He often said to me that he wished he could lie down to sleep "Like other people." I think on this last night he must, with some determination, have made the experiment. The pillow was soft, and the head, when placed on it, must have fallen backwards and caused a dislocation of the neck. Thus it came about that his death was due to the desire that had dominated his life—the pathetic but hopeless desire to be "like other people."

As a specimen of humanity, Merrick was ignoble and repulsive; but the spirit of Merrick, if it could be seen in the form of the living, would assume the figure of an upstanding and heroic man, smooth browed and clean of limb, and with eyes that flashed undaunted courage.

His tortured journey had come to an end. All the way he, like another, had borne on his back a burden almost too grievous to bear. He had been plunged into the Slough of

Despond, but with manly steps had gained the farther shore. He had been made "a spectacle to all men" in the heartless streets of Vanity Fair. He had been ill-treated and reviled and bespattered with the mud of Disdain. He had escaped the clutches of the Giant Despair, and at last had reached the "Place of Deliverance," where "his burden loosed from off his shoulders and fell from off his back, so that he saw it no more."